MUST LOVE DOGS: HEARTS & BARKS

Book 7 of the Must Love Dogs series

CLAIRE COOK

MARSHBURY
BEACH
BOOKS

Books by Claire Cook

The Wildwater Walking Club (#1)

The Wildwater Walking Club: Back on Track (#2)

Shine On: How to Grow Awesome Instead of Old

Never Too Late: Your Roadmap to Reinvention

Must Love Dogs Boxed Set Books 1-3

Must Love Dogs (#1)

Must Love Dogs: New Leash on Life (#2)

Must Love Dogs: Fetch You Later (#3)

Must Love Dogs: Bark & Roll Forever (#4)

Must Love Dogs: Who Let the Cats In? (#5)

Must Love Dogs: A Howliday Tail (#6)

Must Love Dogs: Hearts & Barks (#7)

Best Staged Plans

Seven Year Switch

Summer Blowout

Life's a Beach

Multiple Choice

Time Flies

Wallflower in Bloom

Ready to Fall

Praise for Must Love Dogs

"Whether you are a long-time fan or a new reader, jump right in to Claire Cook's newest *Must Love Dogs* adventures. Your spirits will be lifted, and you'll be charmed by the witty repartee, the twinkle in the author's eye, a beautifully structured plot, and a wonderfully resilient main character to cheer for."—*Pamela Kramer*

"*Must Love Dogs* has already been a major motion picture, and now *New York Times* bestselling author Claire Cook's hilarious and heartwarming series is begging to hit the screen again as a miniseries or a sitcom."
—*Nancy Carty Lepri, New York Journal of Books*

"These characters are so engaging I would probably enjoy reading about them sitting around discussing dish soap, but fortunately, the plot here is fresh, heartfelt, and always moving forward—not to mention laugh-out-loud funny."
—*Stephanie Burns, Book Perfume*

"Funny and pitch perfect."—*Chicago Tribune*

"Wildly witty."—*USA Today*

"Cook dishes up plenty of charm."—*San Francisco Chronicle*

"A HOOT"—*The Boston Globe*

MUST LOVE DOGS: HEARTS & BARKS

Marshbury Beach Books
Cover Photo: cynoclub
Must Love Dogs: Hearts & Barks (#7)/ Claire Cook
ISBN paper: 978-1-942671-25-1
ISBN ebook: 978-1-942671-26-8

Chapter One

Valentine's Day was in the air. Given my track record in the hearts and flowers department, there was a slight chance that this could turn out to be a problem. Just a hunch.

John and I kissed each other good morning, the five Fancy Feast paté-filled cat bowls I cradled in my arms pressed between us. He tasted like toothpaste and coffee, but in a good way. I lingered, taking in the woodsy smell of his soap.

When I juggled the cat bowls to rest my hand on John's forearm, I managed to dunk my fingers into one of the two canned Blue Buffalo Wilderness-filled dog dishes he was holding.

"Eww," I said.

"Not you," I added. I was considerate like that. I high-tailed it over to the cat-feeding station in one corner of the kitchen. Pebbles and her four kittens followed me single-file like I was the Pied Piper.

Diagonally across the kitchen in the dog-feeding station, John put the two upscale dog dishes down on the cracked linoleum floor next to the water bowl. Horatio and Scruffy Dog sat. They waited until John clapped his hands, then both dogs dug in.

The cats were already chowing down, since cats basically call the shots. John had accidentally done a little bit of clicker training with them while he was working with Horatio, but if we were going to take it up a notch, my vote would be to try to get the cats to use the toilet. Cleaning litterboxes for five cats was almost as much work as being a preschool teacher. And sometimes not all that different.

"If we make reservations today," John was saying, "we've still got time to plan a quick Valentine's Day elopement." John's Heath Bar eyes, circles of toffee ringed in dark chocolate, held my ordinary hazel eyes. I felt that same little jolt I always did. Well, almost always.

"How about Tulum, Mexico?" John continued. "No stress, no pressure, entirely laid back. If we're feeling adventurous, we could get married on horseback."

John ran the accounting department at a digital game company called Necrogamiac. We'd recently sold my tiny ranchburger, rented out John's Boston condo through a short-term executive rental company, and bought and begun to renovate the 1890 Victorian I'd grown up in. John's boss had agreed to let him work remote most days, so he wouldn't have to deal with the ridiculous commute into Boston.

"Or even on his and her turquoise beach cruiser bicycles," John said.

There should be a rule that people who work remotely shouldn't start conversations like this on work mornings with people who don't. That little love jolt I'd felt had been completely replaced by a hot streak of pressure shooting upward from the pit of my stomach, like mercury in an old thermometer. Maybe people shouldn't start conversations like this at all.

"Turquoise?" I said. "Matching?"

John shrugged. "Unless you'd prefer separate colors. Or in the interests of simplicity, getting married barefoot on the beach could work."

"You *hate* to go barefoot." I gave the ancient kitchen clock a quick glance. "The soles of those Midwestern feet of yours are landlubber soft. Unlike mine, which were scorched from Memorial Day until Labor Day by the hot sand of the Marshbury beaches throughout my formative years."

John gave me his *you're missing the point* look.

I couldn't seem to stop myself. "You know, Gandhi walked barefoot most of the time, which produced an impressive set of calluses on *his* feet. He also ate very little, which made him frail. And because of his diet, he suffered from bad breath. This made him—wait for it—a super calloused fragile mystic hexed by halitosis."

John was still giving me that look. Out of the corner of my eye, I saw Polly putting on her coat as she walked by in the wide center hallway without glancing in our direction.

"Get it?" I said to John as the front door creaked open. "It's a pun on *supercalifragilisticexpialidocious,* one of my favorite words in the whole wide world. I'm still not over the fact that I wasn't old enough to get in to see the original *Mary Poppins* at the Marshbury Playhouse for free by saying the word correctly when the movie was first released." I gulped down some air. "Basically, because I wasn't quite born yet. But still—"

"Besides," I said, interrupting myself, because somebody had to, "eloping on Valentine's Day is the ultimate cliché."

John slid his glasses up the bridge of his nose and closer to his eyes, perhaps the better to see me. "*Or* the ultimate romantic adventure."

I chugged some coffee, made a mental note to cut back on my morning caffeine and leave the stale puns to John, who was better at them. I looked at the kitchen clock again. Wondered if I had time to point out a few of our many and myriad elopement obstacles before I was late for work.

For starters, John and his dog Horatio had been a package deal. Right after we'd decided to buy my family house, a feral cat we named Pebbles had given birth to four kittens under the front porch, and we'd kept them all. Scruffy Dog was our most recent canine addition—she'd been a stray, and she and Horatio had fallen madly in love at the beach. It took John a while to come around, but eventually he did the right thing and Scruffy Dog became part of our pack.

It wasn't easy to find someone to keep an eye on seven pets, plus my father, who'd come with the Hurlihy family house and was even more work than all the animals put together. My pregnant and single assistant teacher Polly had moved in with us, too, after being traumatized when a nor'easter rolled through her waterfront winter rental on the other side of Marshbury. And last time I checked, my brother Johnny was still separated from his wife and living out back in my father's friend Ernie's canned ham trailer.

Both my father and brother appeared to be madly in love with Polly, so even if she was willing to take care of the animals, who would protect Polly?

As if that wasn't enough, John and I had put trying to have our own baby on the backburner until we finished renovating our new old house. My father had moved into his fancy man cave which took over the old garage as well as the former secret room above it. John and I were settled into our new private sanctuary on the second floor of the main house, and we even had a locked door that protected us from the shared space below. We were waiting for a frost-free stretch so my sister Christine's husband Joe could break ground on the new garage addition with a second private entrance for us.

A thaw in February in Marshbury, Massachusetts seemed about as likely as John letting go of his ridiculous wedding fantasies. I mean, what part of *I don't want to get married and risk screwing up our lives* did he not understand?

Life was just too damn complicated.

John and I stared each other down.

"And now," I said. "I'm officially late for school."

Twelve minutes later, I hit my blinker. If my commute to Bayberry Preschool was a minute or two longer, the heat on my trusty old Honda Civic probably would have kicked in. I shivered as I hung a right off the main road, peered through the porthole I'd managed to scrape in the February frost, gazed up at the gray bruise of a sky.

The trees flanking the long uphill drive bowed under the weight of the heavy wet snow. "I feel ya," I said. "February is no picnic for teachers either."

"Love Stinks" was playing on the Marshbury classic rock radio station. Of course it was. I sang along with J. Geils at the top of my lungs, really belted out the part about how till the day that you die, love is going to make you cry.

I passed a totem pole made of brightly colored clay fish that now looked like they were dotted with huge fluffy white cotton balls. A row of painted plywood cutouts of teddy bears appeared to be wearing snow helmets.

Fortunately, the pavement had been well-sanded to protect our precious students and their designated drivers from any potential black ice lurking beneath. I managed to whip into one of the last remaining parking spaces in the upper level parking lot without taking out one of my colleagues' cars.

I stayed put until the song was finished. You can never be too careful, so I liked to make sure I turned off my radio on a positive note. When the Turtles started singing, "Happy Together," I breathed a sigh of relief. If fortune telling by radio wasn't a thing, it should be.

"I'm not really late-late," I said as I climbed out of my car. "More like fashionably late-ish." I threw my teacher bag over my shoulder, skated across the parking lot in my purple UGG knock-offs.

Even in winter, Bayberry Preschool was that perfect combination of artsy fartsy and impeccably groomed landscaping that kept the students happy while allowing their parents to justify the exorbitant tuition they paid. Snow-covered boxwood sheared in the shape of ducks edged the walkway to the Cape Cod-shingled building. Someone had whimsically tied camel-and-red plaid scarves, possibly real Burberry, around their topiary necks and rested child-sized metal snow shovels with red handles against their topiary bodies.

"You quack me up," I said as I boot-shuffled past the ducks. My breath fogged out in front of me, creating a flimsy pocket of warmth.

Any day now, my bitch of a boss Kate Stone would hire a chainsaw-wielding ice sculptor, like she did every year, to turn a massive block of ice into a perky penguin or polar bear, while our students looked on. The kids would be moderately impressed by the ice sculpture. Mostly they'd beg for a turn with the chainsaw.

Polly was standing in the hallway, staring at our closed classroom door. A fringed burgundy blanket-like poncho skimmed her seven-month baby bump. Her black maternity leggings were tucked into cozy gray slip-on shearling ankle boots with buttons on the sides. Strands of silver sparkled like tinsel in her auburn hair, and her freckles popped against her pink cheeks. She looked like a ripe pomegranate, only cuter.

If I ever managed to get pregnant, I'd probably end up looking slightly cuter than a sumo wrestler. A flash of envy came out of nowhere and caught me by surprise. I liked Polly. I was happy for her. But I wanted what Polly had. To be pregnant, even pseudo-sumo wrestler pregnant. Unfortunately, my biological clock was barely ticking anymore, so it probably wasn't going to happen.

I slid out of my long black puffy down-filled coat, which John had recently found for me in one of the boxes I'd been getting around to unpacking.

"You beat me," I said. "Imagine that."

Polly ignored my feeble attempt at late-to-work humor and kept staring. A tiny pink candy conversation heart was attached to the door with clear plastic tape at grown-up eye level. I squinted, pulled my reading glasses out of my bag so I could actually read it:

CRAZY 4 U

"Ooh," I said. "Looks like you've got a secret admirer, as opposed to your usual bevy of not-so-secret ones."

Polly's cheeks went from pink to pinker. It was kind of heartening the way available and unavailable men flocked around Polly like so many knights in shining armor. Maybe that thing about men needing to feel needed, to have a purpose, was actually true. I wondered if John would dust off his coat of armor if I ever got pregnant. He was just dorky enough to literally have a coat of armor. In high school, I probably wouldn't have given him a second look, but I'd matured enough to think that John's residual dorkiness was a part of his charm.

A picture of John parading around our new master suite in his shining armor and nothing else popped into my head. I wasn't much of an armor expert, but in my version the suit of metal was open in the back like a hospital johnny. I had to admit John looked pretty fetching from that angle.

I shook my head to dislodge the image, checked the time on my big analog teacher's watch. Then I slid out of my faux UGGs so I wouldn't track slush into our classroom while I hunted down my teacher slippers.

The outside doors opened, and the first of the students blew in with a cold blast of air.

Polly ripped the tiny heart off the door.

"Good reflexes," I said. "If anybody sees that, we could be brought up on Valentine's Day candy charges."

"I have to get up every hour to pee anyway, so if one of us

has to go to prison, I'll go." Polly held up the miniscule pink heart. "Shall I put this in the teachers' room with the rest of the contraband?"

"No way." I held out my hand. Polly gave me the heart.

I tossed it up in the air. We both opened our mouths. Polly caught it, possibly because she was eating for two now.

Four-year-old Juliette kicked a Gucci Kids boot toward her cubby. "Is that *candy*?"

Polly giggled. She started to choke, which made her giggle harder.

"It's just a vitamin, honey," I said to Juliette while I thumped Polly on the back.

Chapter Two

The Valentine's Day celebration rules at Bayberry Preschool had morphed considerably over the years.

Early on, students were given class lists to take home in their backpacks, along with instructions to make one valentine for each classmate. The idea was for the children and their parents to collaborate on charming, homemade valentines, heavy on the lace paper doilies. The kids would write their classmates' names in shaky block letters, or if they weren't there yet, they'd have a pre-writing experience while they watched their parents do the lettering.

The parents appeared to, as they say, miss the memo, and every year the valentines the kids brought in got more ostentatious. Professionally designed. Printed on extravagant mulberry silk paper. Laden with custom monogrammed chocolate or heart-shaped stick-on tattoos. Pop-up card Cupids extending semi-precious jewels to preschool recipients, each Valentine probably costing about the same amount as a Bayberry teacher's twice monthly paycheck. Or at least close to that.

Teachers were eventually drafted by our fearless leader to form a Valentine's Day Celebration Committee. After much deliberation, the committee decided that henceforth all valentines would be made under teacher supervision in the classroom. Parents could contribute by helping us collect shoeboxes, like so many miniature dumpsters, to create heart-covered mailboxes so the students could collect their class-made valentines.

We pictured the parents rooting around in basements and attics and closets for tattered cardboard, but it turned into a shoebox competition of Olympic scale. Manolo Blahnik. Jimmy Choo. Christian Louboutin. And lots of other shoes I was pretty sure I'd never seen at Target. Eventually, we ditched the shoebox mailboxes.

A new Valentine's Day Celebration Committee was formed. As some educator or another had once said, persistence is the key to success. Or maybe it was perspiration.

Just yesterday another Valentine's Day letter had gone home in the kids' backpacks:

Dear Bayberry Parents,

Valentine's Day will soon be upon us. We fully comprehend that this is one of our students' favorite holidays. Rest assured that your child's teachers will take complete advantage of the many wonderful opportunities the holiday provides for healthy, safe, and age-appropriate learning and celebration.

We also recognize that Valentine's Day can trigger bullying, hurt feelings and popularity contests, even at this tender age. While an "everyone gets a card" approach might at first glance appear to be the solution, Bayberry Preschool firmly believes that affection is a choice. Children have the right to assert healthy boundaries and need to know that they always have the power to say yes or no to offering or receiving expressions of affection.

Please do your part by adhering to the following ironclad, nonnegotiable rules:

While Bayberry Preschool recognizes the significance of Valentine's Day and its customs such as sending flowers, gifts and cards, please confine these activities to your home.

DO NOT send valentines to school. DO NOT send balloons. DO NOT send toys or live animals/pets. No deliveries for your child, including those sent by messengers in costume, uniform, or Cupid disguise, will be accepted. The office will be unable to sign for any such gifts. If they are left on school property, they will be immediately confiscated and delivered to another preschool.

Absolutely DO NOT send candy or treats to school on Valentine's Day or any other day, in part because of the dramatic increase in peanut allergies, childhood obesity, and gluten/lectin/dairy/eggs/etcetera sensitivity. Additionally, our professional experience is that Bayberry parents are better able to deal with the repercussions of their offspring's sugar highs in the safety of their own homes.

But of course, dearest parents, Valentine's Day would not be the same without your much-valued participation. We are thinking globally this year. We invite our Bayberrian families to participate by asking your friends and extended families to snail mail postcards (addressed to Bayberry Preschool) from all over the world. In exchanging potential hurt feelings for a positive learning experience, our goal is to receive postcards from each of the 50 states, as well as from a multitude of other countries. We'll coordinate a display in our Arts Barn, and all classrooms will make viewing the display a part of their educational and age-appropriate Valentine's celebration.

Thanks in advance for your unwavering (compulsory) support,

Kate Stone, Principal

Once the students had arrived, Polly and I herded them over to sit on the circle. The circle is the heart of the classroom, an implied group hug. It provides togetherness. It brings order and a sense of security, limits as well as predictability. It becomes a theater-in-the-round for singing, sharing, stories, games, activities.

We'd tweaked our fluorescent-tape circle for Valentine's Day by covering the multicolored circles that marked individual spaces with red heart-shaped stickers. It was a bold move, but I figured we'd be safe from the Valentine's Day police as long as one of our kids didn't choke while trying to lick a heart sticker off the circle.

"Let's all sit crisscross applesauce," Polly and I sang.

The kids aimed their preschool butts at the hearts. Eventually they came in for a landing and crossed their legs in front of them. All but Josiah, who tried to slip into a W-sitting position with both knees bent and his feet tucked out behind him. As any good preschool teacher knows, W-sitting keeps kids from developing strong trunk muscles, so I casually helped Josiah rearrange his legs in front of him without calling attention to it.

Depp turned to face Celine. "You're the pie in the sky, baby," he said. Since Depp called all the kids *baby*, including the boys, there didn't seem to be any gender bias, so we usually let it go.

He held out two closed fists in her direction. "Hearts or farts," Depp said.

Celine tapped Depp's right fist.

Depp let out an impressively loud fart.

"Disgusting," Celine said. She pinched her nose between thumb and forefinger, exhibiting excellent small motor control, and added, "tootsie pants."

"My turn," Pandora said from Depp's other side. "Tootsie pants."

The day had barely started, and we were already heading into dangerous territory. A game like hearts or farts could spread like wildfire and reappear at the dinner table, resulting in more parental phone calls than I had any intention of dealing with on my off time. And who even wanted to think about how *tootsie pants* could be misinterpreted.

As every preschool teacher knows, when they go low, we change the subject.

I jumped to my feet, ready to redirect. "Hearts or parts," I sang. Too late, I realized I should have gone with *smarts* instead of *parts*.

Sure enough, Harper jumped right in. "My daddy has a huge peanuts."

Gulliver held his arms wide like he was telling a fish story. "When I grow up, my peanuts is gonna be *this* big."

Pandora rolled her eyes. "As if."

"My mom sleeps naked!" Millicent said.

"My brother eats drugs!" Violet said. "He's groundered. For life."

Pandora flipped her hair. "These kids are driving me crazy."

"Does your baby sleep naked?" Harper asked Polly.

The circle went totally quiet. Polly looked at me. I shrugged. A couple of the kids shrugged, too, like so many preschool parrots.

"I don't know yet," Polly said. "I guess we'll have to wait until my baby's born to find out."

"The wheels on the bus go mush and mush," I sang by way of redirection as I circled my arms. "All through the slush."

Once we got the kids settled in with individual work—letter tracing, wooden puzzles, heart-shaped button counting—Polly and I had time to do a little bit of teacher-whispering.

"I wonder if that conversation heart on the door was from *Ethan*," I whispered.

Polly shook her head and blushed at the same time. Ethan was our co-teacher. He was also the resident school hunk, not that there was all that much competition in the preschool hunk department. Ethan had the lean torso and sun-streaked hair of a surfer, and he walked with a limp he'd acquired when he totaled his car after his life as an indie filmmaker imploded. Kate Stone was his godmother, and she was the only one who'd been willing to give him a chance. He and Polly were close in a way that didn't really have a category, since Ethan was trying to put the pieces back together with his ex, a relationship that had imploded along with the rest of his life.

I watched Griffin push himself away from the button-counting activity. He crossed the room, climbed into our reading boat, grabbed a book and a pillow. He sat there for a moment, his eyes filling with tears and his lower lip quivering. "I can't swim!" he yelled. Then he flopped back and fell immediately to sleep.

The reading boat was the pride and joy of our classroom. Polly had surprised me with it right after I'd hired her. Ethan had recently been hired at Bayberry, too, and she'd asked him if he had any idea where she could find a boat. He just happened to have a non-seaworthy one in his storage unit from his film-making days.

The two of them had put their heads and creativity together. As a result, an entire small fiberglass boat was now tucked into the far corner of the room. Nautical-striped pillows cushioned the bottom. The stern was fitted out with a low bookshelf, a smaller bookshelf tucked into the bow. READ READ READ YOUR BOOKS GENTLY

THROUGH YOUR LIFE was stenciled in big block letters on one side of the boat. The other side said MERRILY MERRILY MERRILY MERRILY READING IS A DREAM.

The reading boat was by far the coolest thing in the room.

I walked over and counted the heart-shaped buttons to make sure Griffin hadn't swallowed any. He was one of our more orally fixated kids. He also wasn't quite as toilet trained as his parents had led us to believe he was. Other than that, he was a model student.

Polly sidled up to me. "Maybe *you're* the one with a secret admirer," she whispered. "Maybe the candy heart was from that wasband of yours."

Back when I was married to my former husband Kevin, he was never quite ready to have kids. I was almost ready, then ready, then more than ready. Just when I was verging on too late, Kevin left me for someone named Nikki, chatty as hell and ten years younger than me. And already pregnant with the kids he hadn't wanted with me. Twins, no less.

Like that wasn't enough, Kevin and Nikki had not only enrolled their offspring, one narcissistically named after each of them, at Bayberry, but they'd requested me as the teacher. I'd managed to nix the classroom placement, but my replacement's kids were still in the school. And, my life being my life, Nikki was pregnant again.

"Wasband," I repeated to Polly. "*Wasband* is too good for him. Maybe I could start referring to him as *my ex-baggage*. Or even *my ex-hole*."

"*HATT* has a nice ring to it," Polly said. "It's short for *husband at the time*."

"Sure," I said. "As long I can call him an ass-hatt."

Polly grinned. "Good one. But maybe it wasn't your whatchamacallit after all. Maybe John drove over and taped the heart on the door to remind you he's crazy about you."

"Right," I whispered. "If John wanted to express his craziness, he would have invited me to elope with him to Mexico on Valentine's Day."

Polly eyes lit up. "Really? I hope you said yes. Don't worry, I'll take care of all the animals for you."

I blew out a waft of air. "Don't be ridiculous. You can't change kitty litter—you're pregnant. And I have enough guilt from growing up Catholic without adding being responsible for your toxoplasmosis to my sin list. I mean, if I ever make it to Confession again, I'll be kneeling in that dark little cubicle for weeks as it is."

Polly smiled. "I can get your dad to change the kitty litter."

"Ha, that's really funny. My father had six kids without changing a single diaper—even you couldn't get him to scoop litter."

Polly shrugged. "Stranger things have happened."

"In my family," I teacher-whispered, "stranger things are always happening."

Chapter Three

Lorna, one of my favorite teachers and partners in crime, was mumbling to herself and shaking her head when I walked into the teachers' room for lunch. She was also glaring at a copy of this year's Valentine's Day letter tacked to the bulletin board that hung over the teachers' mailboxes. A towering pile of confiscated high-end candy had already taken up residency on the shelves next to the mailboxes.

"Let it go," I said. "Before we know it, it'll be St. Patrick's Day and we'll just have to worry about asking the kids to show us their IDs before we pour them a green beer."

I thought it was a fairly decent line for a school day, but Lorna didn't even bother to snort. "Postcards. Freakin' postcards? There's no way in hell any committee came up with that one. It's got our bitch of a boss's signature all over it. I wish we could vote her off the island."

"We'll try to get it in our next contract," I said.

Lorna blew out a long gusty breath. "That'll happen a week from never. And, I mean, where do you even find postcards anymore—they're practically *obsolete*."

"Don't worry about it," I said. "We can reach out to everyone we know who's away at a meditation retreat or a rehab facility. If they're not allowed to have digital devices, it only stands to reason they have postcards."

"Watch it," Ethan said as he walked in. A shard of winter sunlight pierced the window and caught the blond streaks in his surfer boy hair. "Some of us who've actually been to rehab might be sensitive."

"Sorry," I said. "But if you have any leftover postcards, I hope you'll share."

Lorna let out a long-suffering sigh. "What a freakin' shit show."

"Relax, honey. In the scheme of things, it's only a little bit of poo-poo." Gloria, another favorite teacher, patted Lorna on the shoulder on her way to the coffee. A ray of sunlight completely disappeared into her Brillo pad hair.

"Exactly," I said. "It's pure busywork. You know, keep the parents occupied so they don't have time to storm the office with Valentine's Day complaints."

"Even if we actually get enough of them," Lorna said, "who has time to tack all those damn postcards on some ridiculous display and parade the kids around to look at them? As if preschoolers might be interested in *postcards*. And it's not like valentines and postcards are exactly synonymous anyway. I mean, be still my heart, Happy Postcard Day."

I found a coffee mug in the cupboard, rinsed it out in case the teacher who'd washed it last was a slacker. I spun the carousel, closed my eyes, grabbed a coffee pod.

Lorna gulped down some of her own coffee. "*Bayberrian*," she mumbled. "Where the hell did *that* come from? I've never once heard the term *Bayberrian*, and I've been working here for centuries."

I shrugged. "I think it's got a nice ring to it. I like that it just hints at *barbarian* without being too in-your-face about it. You know, like an insult that slides just under the radar. Not that I want to give Birkenstock Boss too much credit or anything." If I was going to upgrade the way I referred to my wasband, I might as well come up with some new names for our bitch of a boss, too. The Great Mighty Poo-Poo?

We all looked over our shoulders to make sure Kate Stone wasn't sneaking up on us.

I found my lunch in the teachers' fridge, thought about microwaving last night's casserole vs. eating it cold, decided microwaving was too much work. Took a bite of a cold block of something vaguely turkey-ish and no more identifiable than it had been last night.

Lorna moved a heart-shaped Godiva box to the center of the long table. She did a soundless eeny-meeny-miny-moe, then pinched the bottom of a chocolate.

"Crap-o-rama," she said as she put the injured chocolate back in the box. "I was sure it was a cappuccino truffle. I hate cherry cordials."

Lorna pinched four more chocolates, popped a fifth in her mouth, chewed. Made a face. "Why the hell do they mix perfectly good dark chocolate with raspberry ganache? If I wanted fruit, I'd cut to the chase and eat a damn apple."

I ditched my leftover casserole and reached for a chocolate. Turned it over to make sure it hadn't already been pinched, popped it into my mouth. Sighed.

Lorna narrowed her eyes at me. "That better not be a cappuccino truffle."

As if I were one of my own students, I stuck out my tongue to show her.

"Congratulations," Lorna said. "The person who gets the cappuccino truffle has to write a little ditty about the postcards. We'll email it to the teacher list and ask everyone to email it to their contact lists and post it on Facebook, along with the school's address. That way if the parents don't come through with enough exotic postcards, we'll still be able to hang on to our pathetic, soul-crushing jobs."

You can't fight Lorna, so I licked the rest of the chocolate off my fingers and wrote the damn ditty.

Been to Tulum
Or Timbuktu?
Send us a postcard
Why don't you.

⊏══⊐

"What fresh hell is this?" I whispered to Polly in my best Dorothy Parker imitation as we walked into our afterschool teachers' meeting. Kate Stone took inordinate pleasure in torturing her employees with new experiences. That these experiences were supposed to be for our own personal growth only made it worse. It seemed to me that if we wanted to grow, we should be able to choose how and why, and then do it on our own time. I mean, not that I had anything against personal growth or anything. At least in theory.

Multicolored yoga mats were spaced evenly across the wooden floor of the fancy new Arts Barn the teachers still called the all-purpose room, a legacy of the lesser room it had replaced. Batik Boss was up front, seated cross-legged on a cranberry mat that exactly matched one of the batik tunics she'd been rotating for most of my career. She was wearing black yoga pants under the tunic, and she'd placed her metallic ocean blue Birkenstocks beside her mat.

Polly and I stopped next to two side-by-side mats at the back of the room, one teal, the other bright orange.

"I think I can still get down there," Polly whispered, "but you might have to call in a crane to lift me back up again. It's like my belly has its own zip code now."

"No problem," I whispered back. "If we can't find a crane, you can just stay down there and nap till the baby is born."

"Don't tempt me." Polly hovered over the orange mat, one knee on either side of her baby bump. She put her hands down, lowered herself carefully. I made a mental note to casually suggest we might want to start bringing one of the kiddie chairs over for her at circle time.

"You okay?" I whispered.

"I'm down, dog," Polly whispered back.

"Impressive," I whispered. "You can sit and make yoga jokes at the same time."

"That's my jam," Polly whispered.

I put my teacher bag down, tripped on the corner of the teal mat, took some quick steps to keep from falling, sat down with a hard thud.

Everybody turned around. Lorna gave me a thumbs up.

Kate Stone tapped a handheld chime with a brass mallet. The sound it made was resonant, ethereal.

"Let go of the day," our boss said in as soothing a voice as she could muster given her grating personality. She rearranged her expression into resting bitch face. There was a reason *bitch of a boss* was the nickname that stuck.

She hit the chimes again. "Let go of all the stress and the negative vibrations. Let go of the small, petty issues . . ."

"The runny noses," one of the teachers said. "The runaway students."

"The runaway teachers," somebody else said.

Even our bitch of a boss laughed.

Kate Stone put the chime and the mallet down beside her. She crossed her legs, touched her thumbs and index fingers together. We followed her, teacher see teacher do.

"Close your eyes," she said slowly. "Breathe in through your nose. Breathe out through your mouth. Now go to your happy place."

I didn't have to be asked twice. I pictured myself walking the beach on a warm breezy day. The splash of the waves, the sun on my face, the sand between my toes, a whole summer off.

The door behind me opened. A distinctly un-summerlike gust of frigid air blew in.

I turned. My father and the three Bark 'n' Roll Forever women he worked for strolled in wearing matching T-shirts under their winter coats. VINCENT VAN GOAT YOGA the T-shirts said in swoopy yellow and orange letters over a vaguely Starry Starry Night scene. Attached to the leashes they held were not the dogs I'd come to expect from them, but an assortment of miniature goats.

"Aww," the roomful of teachers said in unison as my father and company took off their jackets and unleashed the goats.

Back in the day, the school had purchased its own sheep and goats and there'd been vague plans of preschool yarn-spinning and knitting, even cheese-making. Coyotes put a tragic end to that dream, and the school went back to housing the occasional classroom guinea pig. Goat yoga was a new wrinkle, and I was pretty sure this was the closest our fancy Arts Barn had come to living up to the second half of its name.

My father looked past me to wink at Polly as he dropped a partial bale of hay to the floor. He puffed out his chest and ambled over to join us. Betty Ann, the leader of the Bark 'n' Roll pack, hooked her arm through my father's and expertly circled him away from Polly.

Betty Ann smiled at me as they passed.

"Expanding the biz?" I asked her as one of the goats galloped by.

"Just moonlighting for some friends," Betty Ann said. "They can't keep up with the demand."

I could see why. The tiny goats were adorable. They had great names, too—Butthead and Scapegoat and Buttinsky. And Buttah, which was pronounced with an obligatory Boston accent. We learned that they were Nigerian goats, which are smart and gentle and the smallest breed of dairy goat. We learned that all female goats are nanny goats and all male goats are billy goats, and collectively they're called kids. Beards didn't seem to be a gender-based thing. A black and white beauty named Nellybelle had blue eyes and a round swell of a belly, plus long braided and beaded chin hair.

We learned that goats remain fertile until death.

"Just shoot me now," Polly said as she cradled her baby bump. Everybody cracked up.

The three Bark 'n' Roll women took over and led us through a series of cat stretches and downward dogs. They were amazingly flexible. Their hair was long and flowy, and it ranged in color from salt and pepper to sterling silver to snow white. I could just make out the tattooed block letters on the inside of Betty Ann's wrist: ROCK ON. As always, I hoped I'd be half as cool as they were when I got to be their age.

It was like a yoga class crossed with a petting zoo. The smell of hay filled the room. The goats wandered around, doing what I could only assume was goat yoga, which basically consisted of chewing on the yoga mats and sniffing the teachers.

My father brushed an errant hunk of thick white hair out of his eyes as he walked around the room with a roll of paper towels. I was about to be impressed that he'd learned a new skill when he winked at June, my former teacher assistant, and handed the paper towels over to her. She flipped her long blond hair and smiled at him.

"I wish we could get the three-year-olds who aren't quite toilet trained to poop like this," June said as she scooped up some cute little pellets from her mat.

"No problem," Lorna said. "We'll just start putting out hay bales for snack tomorrow."

As soon as we all segued into a child's pose, a goat walked up and stood on my back.

"Get a picture," I hissed at Polly.

She fumbled in my teacher bag for my phone while the goat chomped on the ends of my hair.

All semblance of human yoga ended as everybody reached for their phones. Even our bitch of a boss took a selfie with a goat that was chewing on one of her Birkenstocks. When one of the goats nibbled at Ethan's fly, just about everybody got a picture of that.

My father grabbed the hooves of a goat who made the mistake of jumping up on him. "I want to dance with somebody," my father sang, "with some baaa baaa baaa body who loves me."

He was making googly eyes at Polly while he sang, but before I had to head him off at the pass, Betty Ann cut in on the goat and danced my father away from her.

The Bark 'n' Roll Forever women circled around, taking photos and videos for the teachers. My dad flirted. The goats mingled and pooped, pooped and mingled.

Out of the corner of my eye I noticed Nellybelle pawing the floor. She walked over to the back corner of the room, got down on the floor, pushed herself up again, pawed the floor some more.

"Yikes," I said. "Somebody do something."

We all gathered around Nellybelle.

The first thing we saw was the amniotic sac.

Polly's freckles popped as the color drained out of her face. Nellybelle's water broke.

"Avert your eyes, darlin'," my father said to Polly. He draped an arm across her shoulders. Polly buried her head in her hands.

Two small hooves appeared next, and then a little nose tucked between the front legs. The head and shoulders followed, and then the rest of the body slipped right out.

"They're easy birthers," Betty Ann said.

"No shit," one of the teachers said. "I would have killed for a labor like that."

Ethan's face had lost its surfer boy tan. "We don't have to do goat yoga with the kids, do we?" he whispered.

"Don't worry, honey," Gloria whispered back. "My best

guess is that goat yoga in the classroom is being definitively ruled out as we speak."

The baby had Nellybelle's blue eyes. It took a while to reach agreement in a roomful of teachers, but eventually we named her FlufferButter.

Everybody oohed and aahed and cleaned things up with multiple rolls of paper towels. Nellybelle wandered off for a quick bite of hay. When she came back about two minutes later, her baby was already up on its feet, wobbly but standing. FlufferButter started nursing like a pro.

Polly finally opened her eyes and smiled.

I did my best to smile, too, but I was really thinking about how much it sucked that even yoga goats got pregnant and had babies like it was no big deal at all.

Chapter Four

Horatio and Scruffy Dog barked their hellos. Pebbles crossed back and forth in front of me, rubbing up against my shins to mark me as her territory. The four kittens imitated their mom. Squiggy miscalculated and toppled over, causing a major kitty pileup.

I let my teacher bag drop to the kitchen floor and slid out of my puffy down coat so I could pet everybody.

John looked up from his computer.

"Hey," I said. "Sorry we got off to a bad start this morning."

"If you don't want to elope with me," he said, "I'd appreciate you not making fun of the proposed destination in a group email."

"What?" I said.

John looked down at his computer. "Been to Tulum/Or Timbuktu?/Send us a postcard/Why don't you."

"Oh, that. It had nothing to do with us. We need postcards at school for this stupid project, and I got the cappuccino truffle chocolate, so I had to write a little ditty, and Timbuktu had a nice ring to it. Plus it gave me a rhyme, so then I just needed a little bit of alliteration."

John didn't say anything.

I took a deep breath. "Where is Timbuktu anyway? I always forget. I know, pretty geographically impaired for a teacher, right? But in my defense, when I went to high school, the smart kids got to skip geography and go right to social studies. Not a brilliant curriculum move, hindsight 20/20, but I guess who knew the global thing would happen. Oh, wait, now I remember, Timbuktu is in Mali. West Africa. How was your day?"

John looked at me. I looked at John.

"Okay, then," I said. "So tonight is St. Brigid's Day Eve. My father and Polly should be back with the marsh grass any minute."

John still didn't say anything.

I opened the freezer, scanning the casserole options like a 3-D menu.

A steady stream of women had been showing up at the door with casseroles for my father since my mother's wake, which was more years ago than I wanted to think about. Sometimes my dad smiled his sad widower smile and said thank you. Most of the time he dated the casserole-carrying women, which led to even more casseroles. All by way of saying the freezer had become my 24-hour grocery store. Before John and I bought the house and moved in, I used to have to drive across town to grab dinner. Now I just strolled across the kitchen.

I squinted at the labels. "What do you think? Will Dot's Crunchy Classic Chicken Casserole and Maureen's Creamy Country Chicken Casserole be enough to feed everyone?"

John groaned.

"Fine," I said. I popped them in the oven. Managed to squeeze in Franny's Famous Fajita Chicken Casserole just to be sure.

I bent over, started scooping up kittens.

"I'll be in my father's man cave celebrating St. Brigid's Day Eve," I said. "You're coming, right?"

John looked down at his computer screen. "I think I'll pass."

I glared at the top of his head. "I put the casseroles on low. I'll be back for them before the smoke alarm goes off."

"Great," John said. "I'll be at the grocery store, looking for something green to eat. Besides marsh grass."

When our mother was still alive, she'd made St. Brigid's Day magical. I could still see all six of us kids curled up in our pajamas and robes and slippers, a hodgepodge of relatively new Christmas presents and the hand-me-downs that traveled through the family from oldest to youngest. Our mother would be dressed for our father in flats and a belted shirtdress, her lips freshly painted in Elizabeth Arden Brilliance. She owned the matching nail lacquer, too, but saved that for bigger holidays.

Holiday or no holiday, my sisters and I wore pale frosted nails to match the Yardley Slickers on our lips. I could still remember the full-page magazine ad I'd torn out and taped to my bedroom wall: *Candy's Dandy but Slicker's Quicker. Only Slickers Do It. Make You Soft, Wild, Whatever You Want To Be.* Even way back then, it seemed to straddle the line between innocently seductive and vaguely pornographic. And all these years later, I had to admit that I still didn't know exactly what I wanted to be.

Back then, our dad would come in, dressed like a boss in a suit and tie and the brogue oxfords we all took turns polishing with a tin of Kiwi shoe polish and a hand-me-down cloth diaper. He'd kiss our mom and then dip her like they'd just finished a dance. When he pulled her back up, she'd rub away the slash of red on his lips with the tip of her finger. Then she'd plant a big fat lip print on his cheek, and they'd both laugh like crazy.

We'd look on, half thrilled by the glamour, half completely grossed out that our parents still made out. Our dad would jingle the change in his pockets, and then he'd wriggle in between us on the couch. This always relocated a few of the six kids to the arms of the couch or to laps or to the floor. We were like a living embodiment of that old "Ten in the Bed" chant, so packed together that whenever anybody rolled over, one fell out.

Our mom would pull out a beautifully arranged basket of marsh grass and a pile of freshly ironed lavender-scented lace-edged handkerchiefs from one of her secret hiding places. She'd plug in our fondue pot in the kitchen, which would tease us with the sophisticated smell of glorified melted Velveeta cheese and crusty stale bread cubes while we slaved away making our crosses. When our mother came back to the living room, she'd stop to give us all one of her dazzling, perfectly crooked smiles.

"Is that Marjorie Hurlihy, the loveliest lovely, brilliantly brilliant, most perfect wife I've had all year?" our father would roar as our mother came over to join us on the sofa and the kids rearranged themselves again to make room for her.

"She's the only wife you've had all year!" we'd yell. We knew the routine by heart.

⸺

Now that our mother was gone, we just muddled through St. Brigid's Day preparations as best we could to pass it along to the next generation, hanging on to the tradition as if it would help us hang onto a piece of our mom.

We were waiting for Carol to make her entrance. Carol's two-year-old daughter Maeve and Christine's two-year-old daughter Sydney had taken off their shoes and were trampoline-jumping on my father's round bed. The multicolored LED lights that encircled the bed flashed their accompaniment.

Michael's daughters Annie and Lainie, who I was pretty sure were still nine and ten, were holding Horatio and Scruffy Dog's front paws and dancing around the bed with them. Carol's seventeen-year-old daughter Siobhan was off in a corner texting and looking bored. My nephews Trevor, Ian and Sean, whose ages I could never keep straight but were roughly between four and ten or eleven, were sitting on the floor in front of my father's monster TV taking turns playing a video game.

Mother Teresa, my brother Michael's St. Bernard, whined her displeasure at not having a dance partner. Sean handed the game controller over to Trevor. Sean did his best to dance with Mother Teresa, even though fully extended she was about a head taller than he was.

Pebbles and her kittens were hiding under the bed. I considered joining them, ruled it out because if I had to be here, I figured I should at least stay visible enough to get credit for it.

"It's so not fair," Christine said, "that Carol always gets to do this part just because she's the oldest girl."

"'Tis a sacred religious tradition born of the old sod," my father said. "We'll be kneeling down before the priest at Confession if we bend the rules." My father had never been to Ireland, and he only went to church for weddings and funerals, but in his mind that didn't tarnish either his Irishness or his devout lapsed Catholicism.

"Actually," I said, "I think St. Brigid started out as a pagan goddess."

"Bite your tongue," my father said.

"Love me a good pagan goddess," my niece Siobhan said without glancing up from her phone.

"Well, I guess I could look on the bright side," Christine

said. "As the first-born daughter, Carol has way more wrinkles than I do."

"I heard that," Carol said from the other side of the door.

"Hurry up, hurry up," Maeve and Sydney chanted as they jumped on the bed. The dancing dogs barked in accompaniment.

We heard a knock on the door. Carol's voice called out, "Go on your knees, open your eyes, and let Brigid in."

"Greetings, greetings to the noblewoman," we all roared in unison, although in our defense none of us knelt. There might also have been an eye roll or two involved.

Carol flung the door open. "Okay, where's that marsh grass? I've got more important things to do than stay here all night making crosses. There are too many freakin' holidays in this freakin' frackin' frockin' family."

"Ye gads and little fishes," my father said. "We'll have none of that talk under my roof. Never forget for a minute that not one of you is too old to have your mouth washed out with a fresh bar of Irish Spring."

"See," Christine said, "I'd make a way better Brigid. I'm totes avail to do it next year, by the way."

"You're too old to be totes avail," Michael said.

"Yeah," Johnny said. "You can only have an empty slot on your dance card."

Christine covertly scratched her chin with her middle finger, first at one brother, then at the other. Michael scratched back, but Johnny was too busy staring at Polly to notice.

Saint Brigid of Kildare is Ireland's most important female saint. She travels the countryside on the night before the first day of spring, blessing homes as she goes, accompanied by a white cow with red ears. St. Brigid's Day is the first of February, which in Ireland marks the start of spring. In Marshbury, Massachusetts, on the first of February it's a huge stretch to imagine that spring will ever arrive.

My father, wearing a cow's head left over from someone's

long-ago Halloween costume, walked around with the basket of cut grass from the nearest saltmarsh. When I reached in to grab a handful of the long, elegant grass, it was partially covered with melting ice. It smelled like the ocean.

"Our Polly held the basket and the flashlight," our dad said, "while I did the cutting with my pocket knife. A lady can never be too careful when she's in a delicate condition."

Everybody looked at Polly. She blushed.

I caught Polly's eye. *Ignore them*, I mouthed. I'd spent most of my life doing just that, so I knew it was excellent advice.

The adults and older kids paired up with the younger kids and we all got ready to make our St. Brigid's Day crosses. When we finished, we'd burn last year's crosses in the fireplace. We'd hang the new crosses we made over the inside entrances of our houses, so that Brigid would protect our homes from fire in the new year.

Then we'd pass out the threadbare embroidered lace-edged handkerchiefs that had once belonged to our grandmothers. We'd leave them outside tonight, flung over some snow-dappled shrubbery or a frozen clothesline, for St. Brigid to bless as she rode by on her cow. We'd bring the handkerchiefs inside tomorrow morning, put them under our pillows, and they'd keep us safe from headaches and sore throats. It was a pretty big suspension of disbelief, but it seemed like a good backup for a flu shot, which I also had my doubts about, so we all went along with it.

Maeve sat on one side of me, and Polly sat on the other, our lengths of marsh grass piled on the floor in front of us.

I clicked into teacher mode. "Okay, pick up a piece of grass and hold it upright. Now take a second piece of grass and fold it in the middle, then wrap the second piece around the first piece at the center so that it opens to your right. Pull it tight."

"Why do the boys have to do this?" Sydney's older brother Sean asked.

"Because boys secretly like to do this stuff but will never admit it," my brother Michael said as he reached for another piece of marsh grass.

"Good answer," I said.

"He's practically a sister," Carol said.

"Thanks," Michael said. "I think."

Our dad looked longingly at the refrigerator and his beer within.

"Not yet, Dad," my brother Johnny said. "Unless you want to get me one, too."

"Now," I said, "rotate the whole thing 90 degrees counter-clockwise, holding it at the center. Then take a third piece of grass and wrap it around the second piece so that it opens to your right. Pull it tight, then rotate the entire thing 90 degrees counter-clockwise again."

"Where's Dennis?" I asked Carol.

"Traveling," Carol said.

"What else is new," Maeve said. She lit up when she got a big laugh.

Where's Joe?" Carol Said.

"Working," Christine said.

"What else is new," Sydney said. She got an even bigger laugh.

"Where's Phoebe?" Christine said.

"Reading," Michael said. "She says we tell too many old stories."

I bit my tongue before I said, *Kevin used to say that, too.* Michael and Phoebe's marriage was still hanging on, sometimes by a thread. My ex and I were history, and I was getting better at keeping my mouth shut.

"Where's John?" Michael said.

"Looking for something green," I said.

"Before he gets pinched?" Christine said. "Remember that? If you forgot to wear green to school on St. Patrick's

Day, the other kids would pretend to be leprechauns and pinch you when you walked by in the hallway."

"Come on," Carol said. "Let's take it one holiday at a time here."

"Oh, now I see how this gets to be a cross," Polly said after we added the fourth or fifth piece of grass. "At least kind of a square cross. The kids at school would love this."

"Ha," I said. "In my early teaching days, I tried it with them. A couple of the kids got papercuts from the edges of the marsh grass. When they brought their finished master-pieces home, which by the way were barely recognizable as crosses, pagan or otherwise, I got two dinnertime phone calls about the separation of church and school. An irate parent even called the school the next day to say I was teaching the preschoolers how to make swastikas."

"What an idiot," Christine said. "Even I know you're a better teacher than that. Eww, I think there's seagull poop on my marsh grass." She pushed herself up and jogged in the direction of my father's guest bathroom.

"Anyway," I said in Polly's direction, "I have a watered-down version we'll do tomorrow that will hopefully keep me out of preschool prison."

"Well," Polly said. "I am definitely doing this with my baby every year. It's a beautiful tradition."

"Have you started childbirth classes yet?" Carol asked Polly.

"Mind your own beeswax," I said.

"I'm going to take the classes online," Polly said. "I thought it might be less intimidating that way."

"What?" my brother Johnny said. "I told you I'd go with you."

"I thought you were trying to get back together with Kim," I said.

"Mind your own beeswax," Johnny said.

"Does that mean you're going to have the baby online?"

Carol asked. "I could have gone for that, especially by my fourth one."

I checked my hands for signs of seagull poop. When Christine came out of the bathroom, my father went in. Ian stood off to the side, shuffling from foot to foot and inspecting his own hands. I should have thought to bring the bathroom pass from Polly's and my classroom.

My father came out of the bathroom and headed straight for Polly. He got down on one knee. He took her hand in his and held out a ring.

"There is no cure for love other than marriage," he said.

"Yeats?" Michael said.

"Anonymous," I said. "I looked it up once, just out of curiosity."

"Jesus, Dad," Christine said. "That's my engagement ring. I took it off to wash my hands."

"We can't be leaving this baby to be born on the internut," our father said without taking his eyes off Polly. "We'll have a quick wedding serendipity in Las Vegas, then you kids can throw us a big shindig as soon as we get home."

The smoke alarm went off in the other part of the house.

"Saved by the bell," I said.

Chapter Five

"Once the smoke cleared out last night, those casseroles weren't half bad," I said to Polly as I caught up to her in the school hallway. "I might have to encourage my dad to date Dot again. Maybe Franny, too. Maureen, not so much—I can still taste the metallic cream-of-chicken-soup-tang from that casserole of hers."

Polly was staring at a sepia vintage postcard taped to our classroom door. A man with slicked-back hair was leaning over a woman in a flapper dress lying on a fainting couch. The woman's hair was in spit curls. Their lips were about to touch. Taped to the woman's left ring finger was another conversation heart.

"OOH LA LA," the heart said.

"I like it," I said. "If John ever speaks to me again, I think I just might have to ask him to reenact this postcard."

I peeled the postcard off the door, worked the conversation heart off without ripping the postcard.

I didn't even bother to throw the candy up in the air. I just handed it to Polly.

I turned the postcard over. "Paris, It's Never A Bad Idea"

was stamped next to a sketch of the Eiffel Tower. No post-mark, no handwriting.

"Score one for the Arts Barn display," I said. "Whatever else comes in, we'll always have Paris."

"Who do you think it's from?" Polly asked.

"I have no idea. Hey, are you okay? Sorry about my dad last night. But do you really think you should take your child-birth classes online? I meant it when I offered to go with you."

"I'm already signed up," Polly said. "They start Valentine's Day week, last for a month, so that means I'll be finished a month before my due date, which all the books say is the optimal timing."

"Optimal," I said. I searched for something to add, the perfect balance of tough love and being supportive, came up blank. I mean, what did I really know about anything to do with having babies, online or otherwise?

The outside door opened. Pandora pulled off her faux fur hat as she trudged in. She was wearing a heart-shaped sticker on her forehead like a bindi.

"Valentine's Day rule infraction?" Polly whispered.

"I think she's got us over a barrel," I whispered back, "since we put heart-shaped stickers on the circle. If we tell her to take it off, she'll probably hire a lawyer. I think our best bet is to just pretend we didn't see it."

"Got it," Polly said.

A bunch of the kids had postcards in their backpacks, so we shared them all at circle time.

Celine held up an oversized postcard, maybe 18-inches by 24-inches, of a frozen landscape. "Everyone should go to RickyRick, Icyland once before they die," she said solemnly.

"I had my birthday party there," Millicent said.

"You can come to my birthday party," Gulliver said.

"You can come to *my* birthday party," Harper said. "My house is impectable."

"Reykjavik, Iceland," I said, pronouncing it slowly. *Rake-*

yah-vick. Ice-land. Polly found Iceland on our classroom globe and walked around with the globe so all the kids could see.

"Have you been to Reykjavik, Iceland, Celine?" I asked.

Celine shrugged.

"She didn't die yet," Gulliver said.

"My grandpa died," Juliet said.

"My guinea pig died," Jaden said.

Before we got into a group death knell, I moved things along. Millicent held up a postcard from Dubai, a high-rise luxury hotel with two camels riding by in the sand. "Dubai is everything," she said.

We moved on to postcards from Aruba, Jamaica, Bermuda, Key Largo, Montego, Martinique. In some cases, the kids had actually visited. In others, they'd missed the trip and all they got was a postcard or a T-shirt or a designer accessory.

By the time we finished postcard sharing, most of the kids had peeled off the heart-shaped stickers they'd been sitting on and pressed them onto their foreheads like Pandora.

Polly and I looked at each other, then peeled off our own stickers and put them on our foreheads. Good preschool teachers know when to just go with the flow.

"Freeze-dancing," I said as I pushed myself up off the floor. The kids cheered.

The first song I played was "Kokomo," which seemed only fitting given the postcard origins. We danced and danced and sang about Aruba and Jamaica and all the rest. I hovered near the music and got ready to press Pause when the kids least expected it. I was thinking about all the places I'd never been. And I was wondering why I hadn't accepted John's invitation to Timbuktu. Or Tulum. Or wherever it was.

━━

The morning kids had gone home. Polly and the full-day

students were eating lunch in our classroom. I decided to hang up today's postcards in the Arts Barn on the way to the teachers' room and my own lunch.

Just inside the entrance, a massive bulletin board framed in hardwood was neatly covered with burlap, dotted with red construction paper hearts.

I tacked up our postcards, took a minute to scan the others. The destinations were eerily similar to the ones I'd collected in my classroom. Did all these families live the same life? Or did they just think the same postcards would be impressive? Maybe they'd never been to any of these places— they'd just ordered the postcards online and paid a ridiculous amount of money to have them shipped overnight.

"There she is," an all-too-familiar voice said behind me.

"I'm working," I said without turning around.

My wasband Kevin stepped up beside me. Hasbeen? He was wearing a new cologne or aftershave or something or other. Underneath it, he still smelled like himself, which triggered a quick but disagreeable stroll down memory lane. I shivered.

"Here you go," he said as he held out some postcards. "Nikki had a pile of them one of her home sellers left behind in a box in a closet. You wouldn't believe what people don't bother to take with them when they move."

"Well, I'm certainly not going to tack them up for you," I said. "Give them to your kids' teacher."

Kevin grinned. "There's the sunny Sarah I remember. I thought it might be safer to give them to you since the twins' teacher is even scarier than you are."

I told him to go f-bomb himself, quietly so it couldn't possibly echo in the cavernous space. Then I gave a quick silent thank-you to the universe for landing his twins in Lorna's class, since Lorna was a good enough friend to delight in torturing my whatever-he-was on my behalf. My name deleted?

Kevin laughed. "It's nice to talk to another sane adult. Nikki's pregnancy is driving her nuts, which means she's driving me nuts."

"Karma is a boomerang," I said sweetly.

"So what's new?" he asked.

I handed him the rest of my tacks, sharp sides down. "What is your problem? You never once asked me *what's new* when we were married." It might have been a slight exaggeration, but it had the feel of truth.

The artsy postcard from Sedona he'd finished tacking to the bulletin board was crooked. I resisted the urge to straighten it out. I tried to remember if I would have straightened it out for him back when we were married. There was possibly a metaphor about growth in there somewhere, but I had no intention of thinking about it long enough to figure it out.

My hasbeen blew out a mouthful of coffee-tinged air, shuffled his postcards like a poker deck. "Do you ever wonder what we'd be doing right now if we'd stayed together?"

My jaw might literally have dropped if it wasn't attached to the rest of me.

Kevin fanned out his cards so I could see them. "You know, traveling the world, no kids, no responsibilities, footloose and fancy free."

"Right," I said. "You stay with me just long enough to make sure it's probably too late for me to have kids of my own, and now you're telling me you don't really want the two and a half kids you decided to have with *Nikki*?"

My ex dropped his head. No, not my ex, my X. Because he wasn't anything anymore. "Sounds pretty lame now that you put it that way," he said to his postcards.

"Ya think?" I said.

"We had some good times," Kevin said.

"I'll take your word for it," I said.

Kevin tacked up a postcard of the Roman Colosseum. I

entertained a quick satisfying fantasy of him being thrown to some lions.

He ruined it by turning around. "I guess Valentine's Day around the corner and all that is just making me sappy."

"Right," I said. "Do you remember that year you gave me a heart-shaped toilet seat?"

"That wasn't cheap, you know. It was solid hardwood. Plus, I was planning to do the installation myself, which was part of the gift." He shrugged. "If you think about it, it was kind of rude that you returned it. I thought you'd think it was funny. And sweet."

"Sweet," I said as I walked away.

"Hey, you don't want to have a drink after school one day, do you?" he said to my back. "Nikki doesn't like to be around the smell of alcohol when she's pregnant."

I flashed my idiot ass-HAAT and his missing sensitivity chip my favorite finger, right next to the one that used to wear his ring.

———

"Nice heart," Lorna said when I walked into the teachers' room. "But I'm afraid I'm going to have to report you to the Valentine's Day authorities."

I reached up to peel the sticker off my forehead, decided to live dangerously and leave it there. I bypassed the refrigerator where I'd stashed a slab of leftover casserole I'd packed in my mother's ancient Tupperware this morning. I headed right for the contraband chocolate.

I grabbed a tin of Dove chocolates and plopped it down in front of me on the long table. It was a red heart-shaped tin that said *Dove* in chocolate-colored doodles. The shape of the tin was kind of loopy, slightly off-kilter in a way that was either charming or seriously distorted. Possibly a lot like me.

I pried it open and popped a milk chocolate peanut butter

heart into my mouth. Lorna peeled off a heart-shaped sticker on the tin that said *40 pieces* and stuck it on her own forehead.

I did the math. "Thirty-nine," I mumbled through a mouthful of Dove.

"Are you okay, Sweetie?" Gloria asked from her seat next to Lorna.

"Tell me this," I said. "Are there any circumstances at all in which a heart-shaped toilet seat might be an appropriate Valentine's Day gift?"

"Sure," Ethan said. "If you're trying to get rid of someone."

"Thanks," I said. "I needed that."

"Let me guess, honey," Gloria said. "John gave you an early valentine and it was a toilet seat?"

"No," I said. "It was pre-John."

Ethan reached for a chocolate. "Once I gave someone an elephant dung flower bouquet."

I nodded as that sunk in.

"Where did you even find it?" somebody said.

Ethan held up one finger while he finished chewing. "The Great Elephant Poo Poo Paper Company."

We all burst out laughing. When it comes to humor, most preschool teachers eventually sink to their students' level.

Ethan reached for another chocolate, so I did, too.

"Okay, I'll bite," Lorna said. "How do you make flowers out of elephant shit?"

"Elephant dung," Ethan said, "is basically full of short to medium grained fibrous materials from the elephant's diet, which makes excellent paper. You spread the dung cakes evenly over a mesh-bottomed tray and lean the tray up against a tree in the sun and let it dry. Then you cut it into petals."

"OMG," Lorna said. "We should totally have the kids make Valentine's Day poop bouquets to take home. Obviously, we won't tell them what the secret ingredient is, but *we'll* know."

"Not that she's bitter," I said.

"I thought it was unique and innovative," Ethan said, "Plus I thought she liked gifts that give back."

"Who exactly are you giving back to?" I asked as I popped yet another chocolate in my mouth. "Do the elephants get to keep the money?"

"By the way," Gloria said. "Do you have a date for Polly's baby shower yet, honey?"

"Polly's baby shower," I repeated.

Chapter Six

I'd hired Polly right before the school year started when Kate Stone had pulled a last-minute switcheroo, sending June, the assistant I'd spent an entire year training, off to work with Ethan.

Polly had been a total train wreck at the interview. She had absolutely no experience with preschools, or even children. But my heart went out to her because she'd left her husband, moved across the country to Marshbury, and found a tiny winter rental on the beach. She was trying to figure out what the next chapter of her life might be, and whether or not it would include having a child by herself.

So against my better judgment, as well as the objections of my bossypants boss, I chose Polly instead of a more qualified applicant. And except for the fact that it turned out Polly was already pregnant and wouldn't quite make it to the end of the school year before her baby was born, she'd ended up being a great assistant.

After lunch, Polly and I got the students settled in around our long classroom table. Polly eased herself down to one of the kiddie chairs, her baby bump wedged between the rest of her and the table edge. I sat beside Polly in another kiddie chair, casually reached under my seat to measure how much of my thighs were spilling over the edges. It was the best fitness motivation I knew. I took a moment to be grateful that my chocolate lunch hadn't caught up to me yet.

"In Ireland," I said once the students had settled down, "today is the first day of spring."

The kids looked out our frost-painted window doubtfully. Two black-capped chickadees, down feathers puffed out to create space between their tiny bodies and the cold air, were doggedly working their way through the wafts of snow that covered our classroom bird feeder to get to the black sunflower seeds.

"And to celebrate springtime in Ireland," I continued, "we're going to make Irish Spring Catchers."

Marshbury, Massachusetts, is part of what is affectionately known as the Irish Riviera. Marshbury is even on record, or at least internet record, as the most Irish American town in the United States. If you weren't Irish when you got here, it didn't take long to pick up the vibe—big families with bigger mouths, a propensity for corned beef and cabbage beyond St. Paddy's Day, enforced Irish step dancing classes at some point in your life, banging an illegal U-ey whenever possible like any respectable Masshole driver, calling the water fountain a bublah and the basement a cellah, buying your booze at the packie, spewing wicked pissa swear words in your wicked awesome Boston accent, having no problem calling anybody who doesn't agree with you a loozah or a chucklehead. The joke was that even the Marshbury dogs start to think they're Irish Setters after a while.

More and more, the Bayberry parents might consider themselves gentrified, too cool for school, but this was still the Irish Riviera. Which meant that the teachers could pretty much get away with anything as long as they called it Irish and it didn't look too religious.

St. Brigid is the patron saint of babies, blacksmiths, boatmen, cattle, chicken farmers, children whose parents aren't married, milk maids, mariners and poets. For all I knew she was the patron saint of preschool teachers who needed to stay out of trouble, too. At the very least, I was pretty sure St. Brigid was too busy to worry about me leaving her out of this next activity.

I felt a little bit guilty about taking us one more step in the direction of a Hallmark card world. St. Valentine's Day had already become saint-free Valentine's Day, and now I was helping to make St. Brigid's Day disappear. Before I knew it, St. Patrick's Day would be shortened to Pat's Day, or even just P-Day.

"Can you say Irish Spring Catchers?" I said, mostly to bring myself back to the classroom.

"Irish Spring Catchers," the kids and Polly roared.

I walked around the table, counting out furry green and white pipe cleaners, placing a small pile in front of each of us.

When I was back in my chair, I picked up two green pipe cleaners, folded them in half.

The kids imitated me perfectly with their stubby fingers. I looped one pipe cleaner through the other, pulling the ends in opposite directions.

Polly and most of the kids stayed with me. I folded a white pipe cleaner in half and looped it over the intersection of the green ones at a right angle. Then I folded a second white pipe cleaner in half and looped it over the green ones facing in the opposite direction.

I looped a new green pipe cleaner over the last one I'd added. Then I gave the whole thing a quarter turn.

"This is a lot harder than it looks," Millicent said.

"It sure is," I said. "But we're all doing a great job."

We kept going until we'd used up all our pipe cleaners. The results were a bit wonky, but the good news was that I didn't think we could be accused of making St. Brigid's Day crosses on school grounds.

I reached for some more pipe cleaners and cut them into small pieces. We used them like twist ties to keep the centers from unraveling, then spread the ends out like fans.

"Ta dah," I said. "Irish Spring Catchers."

I wasn't exactly sure who started it, but before I knew it the kids were all rubbing them under their armpits. I'd been imagining the spring version of dream catchers. Leave it to the kids to go in the direction of deodorant soap.

"Singing in the shower," Jaden sang.

"Singing in the shower," the rest of the kids parroted.

"Don't forget to wash your armpits," somebody sang. Everybody repeated that, too.

"Okay," I whispered to Polly. "So maybe there are still a few kinks to work out in this one."

I felt The Feared One's presence before I saw her. Kate Stone walked in on silent Birkenstock feet, stood at the back of the room. A really good-looking guy I'd never seen before was right behind her. He was wearing a blazer over slim-cut gray dress pants and a nice button-down shirt. His shoes—deep gray suede wingtips with blue soles—added just the perfect bit of flash. He had dark skin and shiny deep brown eyes, and his hair was cut in what my nephews called a fade, where the hair gets gradually shorter on the sides and back as it gets closer to your neck. He looked a little bit like Blair Underwood. He was possibly even better looking than Blair Underwood.

I accidently caught his attention, possibly because I was staring at him. When he smiled at me, his teeth sparkled, but the smile didn't quite reach his eyes.

There were Bayberry parents who weren't even embarrassed to deck out their fancy SUVs with bumper stickers that said FUTURE IVY LEAGUER. Somehow, probably because of all those stupid bumper stickers in the drop-off and pick-up lines, Bayberry had gotten a reputation as the preschool that could take you there. *There* being the right private elementary school that led to the right private high school and maybe a detour to the right prep school before going Ivy.

This was delusional thinking on so many levels, the biggest of which was that while Bayberry was a great preschool, none of the teachers, or even our bitch of a boss, had any interest in pushing the kids anywhere other than to kindergarten.

Still, parents had been known to actually call from the hospital to leave a credit card deposit to get their just-born child on the Bayberry admissions list to help unlock those distant Ivy gates. Occasionally, they'd follow up with a professional headshot of the baby for our files.

All by way of saying that each new class of rising three-year-olds at Bayberry Preschool was full by the time we started taking applications in December for the following September. The only way there might be an opening for a four- or five-year-old was if another family moved.

Still, it certainly wasn't unusual to have the Type A parents of future students come in to check us out in February to make sure they'd made the right decision. If they decided they didn't like Bayberry after all and wanted to try to jump to another Ivy-track preschool, they'd lose their deposit. If they wanted to request one Bayberry classroom over another, Bayberry didn't take requests. We didn't have to. Our waiting list was a mile long.

Unlike me, Polly was actually paying attention to the kids and hadn't even noticed our visitors.

I sidled over to her. "Hot dad alert," I teacher-whispered.

Apparently, my teacher whisper was on the fritz.

"Hot dad alert," Pandora said. Loudly.

"Hot dad alert," Millicent said. Even more loudly.

Polly choked back a giggle. I bit my lower lip.

"Hot cross buns," Pandora sang.

"Hot cross buns," the other kids sang.

Polly and I both lost it.

The kids kept singing. "Hot cross buns, hot cross buns, one a penny, two a penny, hot cross buns."

The Great Demotivator crossed her arms over her chest. The sleeves of her boysenberry tunic hung like bat wings, never a good sign.

I pulled it together as quickly as I could. I handed Polly a ball of yarn and a pair of our teacher scissors. She cut long strips of yarn and I helped the kids tie them around one end of their creations. We wrapped the other end of the yarn around tiny suction cup hooks that we'd pressed on the window. Our Irish Spring Catchers dangled in the window, looking a lot like pipe cleaner spiderwebs.

"Good job," I said to all of us anyway.

By the time I dared to look over again, Kate Stone and Hot Cross Buns had disappeared.

***

The kids had all gone home, and Polly and I were sitting across from each other at the kiddie table.

"I can't believe I didn't pee my pants," Polly said. "It's a challenge now even when nothing funny happens."

"I'm sure one of the kids would have let you borrow a change of clothing from her Oops bag."

"Ha. I was sooooo close. The pressure is the hardest thing about being this pregnant. And that's when the baby isn't even trying to kick a hole through my bladder."

It was pretty pathetic that even baby bladder kicks made me feel wistful. I opened our Three Good Things notebook and turned it to the first blank page, slid it over to Polly.

"You didn't pee your pants," I said. "Go ahead, write it."

Polly smiled, wrote it in purple pen, slid the notebook back over to me.

"HOT CROSS BUNS!" I wrote in huge purple letters. I drew a big heart around it.

We laughed and laughed. After a day spent with preschoolers, it doesn't take much to get you going.

"Out of the mouths of babes," Polly said. "I barely saw him or his buns though. I was too afraid to look over there."

"Ohmigod," I said. "That guy was so gorgeous. I can't decide whether or not I want his kid in our classroom next year. I mean, on the one hand, we'd get to drool over him on a regular basis that way. But on the other hand, it might ruin the fantasy when he's sitting on the other end of the conference table with his wife. Especially if they both turn out to be wicked losahs, as my brothers would say."

There was a beat of silence. Maybe mentioning my brothers made Polly think of my brother Johnny, who I was pretty sure still had the hots for her. Maybe it was none of my beeswax.

"I won't be in this classroom next year, remember?" Polly said. "I'll be working in childcare."

The thought crashed over my head like an ocean wave. During gale warnings.

At least in part because of Ethan's nudging, Kate Stone had offered Polly a full-time job in childcare once she came back to work after having her baby. The upside was that Polly could bring her baby to work with her. The downside was that I'd have to train another assistant teacher, my third in three consecutive school years.

I felt a pity party coming on. So I took a deep breath, forced myself not to start whining in front of Polly. She had enough on her plate.

"It'll be fine," I said. "We can visit each other all the time. Plus, you're not going to move out of my house at least until the baby goes off to college, right?"

Polly's eyes teared up. "Seriously, Sarah, you have no idea how much your support means to me. I don't think I could have gotten through all this without you. And your family."

I rested one hand on her hand, pulled it away quickly before things got too mushy.

I slid the notebook back over to her. "Come on, you chucklehead. One more good thing that happened today and we can go home."

"I have plans for dinner. So you don't have to save any casserole for me tonight." She smiled and wrote NO CASSEROLE.

Chapter Seven

February days are ridiculously short, so it was dusk by the time I pulled into the parking lot at Marshbury Provisions. I crunched my way over sand-sprinkled ice, my toes already cold under my boots, my breath spewing steamy clouds out in front of me. Somebody had plowed a small mountain of dirty snow into three adjoining parking spaces that probably wouldn't be car-friendly again at least until the first real day of spring.

The plow had left tire tracks in the snow that looked exactly like two side-by-side hearts. I stopped walking for a moment to take them in. Even I thought those hearts had to be a good omen.

I grabbed a cart outside the store, wiggling my hands up into the sleeves of my down coat first so they wouldn't freeze to the handle. Then I bumped my way over more sand-strewn ice to get inside. I headed straight for the produce section, zeroed in on a clear plastic box labeled *Power Greens* because if I was actually going to cook for a change, I could use all the power I could get. I picked up a still-hot rotisserie chicken, a package of shredded pepper jack cheese, tortilla shells, guacamole, salsa.

A perky Muzak rendition of "Hey, Good Lookin'" filled the grocery store.

"Whatcha got cookin'?" I sang along, perhaps a bit too loudly. My father used to sing the Dean Martin version of the Hank Williams song to my mother when we were kids. Decades later, when Jimmy Buffet came out with his own recording of it, one of us gave our dad the CD it was on, *License to Chill*, for Father's Day. We played "Hey, Good Lookin'" over and over on our old boombox at family barbeques for the rest of the summer, my father flipping burgers and sounding like Dean doing a duet with Jimmy as he sang to my mother.

Even after hearing the song a gazillion times, or perhaps because of it, I still hated to cook, but maybe there was hope for me yet. I danced my way down the aisle, singing along and faking the lyrics when I had to. I leaned on the cart for balance as I got ready to click my heels out to one side like I was in a grocery store music video.

Just before I was actually going to try the heel click and probably wipe out the cart, I pulled it together. I made a beeline for the wine section. Found a bottle of Educated Guess, John's and my special cabernet. Grabbed a boxed wine to use as a decoy for my father, so he didn't commandeer the good stuff if he happened to wander over from his new mancave. Assuming, of course, my dad wasn't Polly's dinner date.

On my ride home, I played Nancy Drew, sleuthing out possibilities like the wannabe keen investigator I was. One, Polly was having dinner with my father. Two, Polly was having dinner with my brother Johnny. Three, Polly was having dinner with Ethan. Four, Polly was having dinner with someone else who wasn't old enough to be her father or technically still married or trying to work things out with an ex.

Five, Polly was having dinner solo to give John and me some space. I pictured her eating a lonely dinner at a fast food booth, a straw stuck into her carton of milk. There weren't many fast food options in Marshbury. Dunkin' Donuts was the only chain the Marshbury Board of Selectman had voted to allow in, but the dyamic duo of Micky D's and Burger King were perched just past the town line. I flipped to a less pathetic image of Polly having an enjoyable unaccompanied dinner at a charming independently owned watering hole like Oceana or High Tide. Wondered if I should drive around to see if I could find her. Decided that if I didn't get things sorted out with John, I'd be the one eating solo dinners. Permanently.

When I pulled into the driveway of my new old house, Foreigner was singing "I Wanna Know What Love Is." The grocery store had put me in a singing mood, so I turned up my radio and belted out the part about how in my life there's been heartache and pain and how I don't know if I can face it again.

I knew I should kick off the evening with something better than that sentiment, so I waited until The Romantics jumped in with "What I Like About You" before I turned off the radio. I kicked my partially frozen car door open and slid out, leaned back in to grab my groceries. I detoured over to one of the ancient rhododendrons that flanked the side of the house. Even by the yellow light over the kitchen door, I could see that the overgrown bush had curled its leathery leaves in protest to February.

"I'm with you," I said as I retrieved the lace-edged handkerchief I'd thrown over the rhododendron last night. "I'd curl my own leaves if I had any."

I warmed the stiff handkerchief on my cheek, hoped St. Brigid and her cow had found it overnight and that now it really would protect me from sore throats and headaches. I closed my eyes, upgraded the handkerchief's power to protect me from Foreigner's heartache and pain, too.

Saintly defense and groceries in hand, I walked in through the kitchen door. Horatio and Scruffy Dog barked. Pebbles meowed. The four kittens mewed and rolled around like puppies.

The scarred pine trestle table of my childhood was set, with cloth napkins and everything. Two fat pillar candles flickered on top of the tall chunky modern candle holders that formerly decorated the fireplace mantle in John's Boston condo. A huge tossed salad was waiting in John's Dansk wooden salad bowl that always made the salad taste urban chic and sophisticated. John was standing at the stove, stirring a big metal pot with a wooden spoon.

"Oh, I'm sorry," I said. "I must have the wrong house. Can I stay anyway?"

"Sure," he said. "There's plenty. Beef bourguignon—stew beef, bacon, onion, garlic, a bouquet garni, carrots, mushrooms, beef stock, two kinds of wine."

I held up my grocery bags. "Make that four kinds of wine. Plus non-marsh grass green stuff and non-casserole quesadilla ingredients."

"Be still my heart." John put one hand on his chest and opened his Heath bar eyes wide. "You were really planning to cook?"

I plopped the bags on the kitchen table, slid out of my coat, gave him a kiss. "Yeah. From scratch. Well, kind of from scratch. Although I will admit to feeling a certain amount of relief knowing that now I don't have to."

I took the wooden spoon out of John's hand. The beef bourguignon was amazing, rich and comforting and tender, almost enough to make you glad it was February.

"Orgasmic," I said.

"Let's hope," John said.

We gave each other *the look*.

John started doling out food for the animals. As soon as I put my groceries away, I jumped in to help him. The animals lined up at their dishes and began gobbling away. I found two wine glasses, and John poured us the wine that hadn't made it into the beef bourguignon.

John turned the heat down under the stew pot. "The extra simmer will be good for it."

"The extra simmer would be terrible for us," I said as I reached one arm around his waist. "We're hot enough already."

━━

John reached down and pulled the comforter up over us.

He kissed my shoulder. "Well, that was long overdue."

I nuzzled his neck. "It certainly was."

I reached for the handkerchief I'd managed to stuff under my pillow during the heat of passion and gave St. Brigid a silent thank you. Maybe she was the patron saint of good make-up sex, too.

John and I flopped back on our pillows, stared up at the ceiling.

"I can't believe the animals left us alone the entire time," John said. "That's a first."

"Yeah," I said. "There's nothing like making love with two dogs and five cats watching."

"Or scratching at the door," John said.

The kittens had figured out how to get up the stairs on their own, but so far the only way they knew to get back down by themselves resulted in tumbling, arse over teakettle, as my father would say, down the old maple stairs. So we'd started strategically blocking off the stairs with the baby gate when we needed to. Gloria had handed it down to Polly along with all the other baby paraphernalia Gloria had no intention of ever using again.

I felt a little bump of sadness every time we set up that baby gate. Before we knew it, the kittens would outgrow it along with their kittenhood, and then Polly would use it for her baby. The likelihood that Polly would ever hand it back to John and me for a human baby seemed lower than low.

I pushed the thought away, happy that at least John and I didn't have to deal with any of it until after we'd finished the garage, the final stage of our renovations. Burying our parenthood quest until some chirpy day in spring seemed infinitely preferable to having to face ice cold winter reality.

"Do you think they're all okay down there?" I said.

"They're fine." John slid his arm behind my neck and around my shoulders. "If you don't count the fact that some of them may have eaten slightly more than their fair share of food."

"Whatever." I wiggled closer to him. "We'll just give them all some more food when we get back downstairs. We have to do that at school sometimes, when one of the kids goes on a carrot stick binge and starts raiding everybody else's stash when they're not paying attention. Often, by the way, to stick said carrots up his or her nose. Sorry, TMI, right?"

John smiled. We both looked around our new old room. The original 1890 maple floors, lightly sanded and refreshed with two new coats of polyurethane. The Agreeable Gray-painted walls that we'd chosen mostly for the name. The Simply White trim we'd picked from the surprisingly confusing array of whites to make it easy, because after all it was *white paint*, not rocket science.

Adjacent to our bedroom, my sister Carol's former bedroom had been turned into a generous master closet with custom organizers, as well as a master bath with modern dual vanities and retro faucets. The huge walk-in shower had been tiled in Coastal Dew, a gorgeous tumbled edge frosted glass elongated subway tile that looked like seafoam green sea glass.

For the bottom of the shower, we'd chosen a mosaic tile made from individual beach pebbles attached to a mesh square that gave you a foot massage every time you stepped in. The porcelain tile on the bathroom floor looked like weathered driftwood planks, but also had hints of the maple tone of the wood on our original bedroom floor.

Under and around us was the new sleek modern bed we'd bought, deep espresso wood and topped with a new comfy latex mattress and John's crisp white, high-thread-count sheets from his condo. We'd thrown out my old pillows and kept his, which were Goldilocks-esque not-too-firm and not-too-soft, better quality than I'd ever dreamed existed. We'd bought a new beachy turquoise bedspread and left the patchwork quilt my mother's mother had made for my mother's sixteenth birthday folded and draped over the foot of the bed.

Someday, we'd get around to putting things on the walls, negotiating placement for his, mine, ours. For now, I liked the way the clean, bare walls gave us space to breathe, a blank slate.

"It's not that I don't love our fancy-schmancy new master suite," I said, "but it's still bittersweet. Half my childhood was spent in one half of a part of this room, pretending that my sister Christine wasn't in the other half. Sometimes when I wake up, I still see Christine's and my dressers, her David Bowie poster on her side of the tiny old closet."

"We should talk," John said.

"Said no man ever," I said.

It was one of those moments that could have gone either way. A laugh. A round of battle.

John took his arm back and leaned away from me to grab his wineglass from the bedside table. I leaned in the opposite direction and grabbed mine, took a long fortifying sip.

"How do you like your chowdah?" a loud voice yelled from downstairs.

"Hot, hot, hot!" more loud voices roared. Fists pounded to mark each word.

"Whose turn is it to do the dishes?" somebody else yelled.

"Not, not, not," the voices and fists rumbled.

"You can't do this," I said when we got down to the kitchen.

My father, my brother Johnny, and my sister Carol were sitting around the kitchen table, eating John's beef bourguignon. They'd completely ignored the decoy boxed wine and had helped themselves to the Educated Guess.

"You were just here last night," I tried.

"No we weren't," Carol said. "We were at Dad's."

"Same difference," I said.

"Remember," Carol said, "when we used to say samesies when we wanted to wear the same thing as someone else? I think now samesies just means that you agree with something. Kids don't even hosey things anymore the way we used to."

"You're changing the subject," I said. "And by the way, it's not chowder."

"If you can eat it with a spoon," Johnny said, "that means it's fundamentally a member of the chowdah genus. Don't worry, we saved you plenty. It's a work night, so we couldn't wait any longer."

"Work is the curse of the drinking classes," my father said.

"Oscar Wilde," Johnny and Carol said at once, as if there'd been any doubt.

"Owe me a Coke," they said at the same time.

"Jinx," they both said.

Belatedly, I combed my fingers through my hair, straightened out the school clothes I'd thrown back on.

"Have a nice synergistic energy exchange?" Carol said.

"Huh?" I said.

"S.E.X.," she mouthed.

"We'll have none of that talk in my house," my father said, even though she hadn't said it out loud, and it wasn't technically his house anymore.

"Excellent chowdah, by the way," Johnny said. "Not even half bad for a stew."

"Thanks," John said. "It's actually beef bourguignon."

"See," Carol said. "I told you there was no way Sarah made it."

"Help yourself," Johnny said in my direction. "We even left you the napkins."

"Gee, thanks." I picked up my bottle of Educated Guess, held it up to the light to see if there was anything left.

"Pardon my pa here, he's a wicked whore for the drink," Johnny said as if he were one of our ancestors just stepping off the boat from Ireland.

"Your pa takes that as a compliment, Sonny Boy, and raises you one." My father and Johnny toasted each other over the scratched pine trestle table with John's and my special wine.

"There's a box of wine sittin' over there on the counter if you kiddos want to open it," my father said.

I put the bottle back down on the table, perhaps a bit harder than necessary. I grabbed two bowls, ladled in John's beef bourguignon. John topped off our glasses with the stew wine, tore off two pieces of what was left of the baguette.

Horatio and Scruffy dog were camped out under the kitchen table, waiting for spills. "Some watchdogs you are," I said. The cats must have relocated to the family room. I couldn't blame them.

I didn't have to be Nancy Drew to read John's face. He no longer glowed like a guy who'd just had make-up sex. He looked pissed off. Politely pissed off.

"Next time you show up uninvited," I said, basically because I knew I had to be the one to say it since it was my family, "there's casserole in the freezer, you guys. Anything else is off limits."

"Limits," my sister Carol said.

"Define your terms," my father said.

"John and I will be in the dining room," I said.

"Good idea," Johnny said. "This kitchen table was a lot bigger when we were kids."

As I ate my beef bourguignon, I tried to pretend my family hadn't followed us into the dining room, but it was useless.

"So what are you doing here anyway?" I asked Carol.

Carol dunked some of John's baguette into his bourguignon. "I dropped off some old postcards for you."

I dunked, too. "And you decided you might as well eat your way through our dinner while you were here?"

"I left frozen macaroni and cheese in the oven and told Dennis to feed the kids if I wasn't back in half an hour." Carol woke up her phone and checked the time. "Which should be. Just. About. Now."

"Fiendish," Johnny said.

"'Women are meant to be loved, not understood,'" my father said.

"Byron?" I tried.

"Oscar Fingal O'Flahertie Wills Wilde," my father said.

"No fair," I said. "I thought I had to guess someone new. You didn't tell me it was Oscar Wilde night."

"Where's Poppy?" Johnny asked.

"Her name is Polly," I said. "And I thought you were getting back together with your wife."

"We're working on it," Johnny said. "But I think Kim likes dating me better than being married to me."

"I get that," Carol said. "I would love, love to date Dennis again. Go out with my friends the rest of the time. Or just stay home and read a good book. While taking a bubble bath."

"And your four kids would be . . ." I said.

"Buzz kill," Carol said. "Wait, they'd be with Dennis."

"I hope you saved me some stew," my sister Christine said as she walked in. "And you can't date Dennis. The girls are still ahead of the boys in the divorce department. Sarah's the only girl whose marriage has tanked so far, but both—"

"Women," I said. "We're women, not girls." Although I had to admit that whenever my sisters and brothers and I were together, we had a tendency to regress to about twelve.

"My marriage isn't even close to tanking," Johnny said. "We're just working our way through our disillusionment period."

"What period is after that?" I asked, because I really wanted to know.

"The hang in there period," Carol said, "which is basically till death do you part."

"The point is," Christine said, "that thanks to the girls, as a family we're still ahead of the national divorce average. But we don't have a lot of wiggle room left for shaky marriages."

Chapter Eight

"My marriage wasn't shaky," Michael said. He walked in with a stew bowl, dropped some postcards on the dining room table. "It was marginally wobbly. Temporarily. Past tense." Mother Teresa, Michael's St. Bernard, got low and wiggled under the table to join the other dogs.

There was a natural law in my family that once one person showed up, the rest weren't far behind. If we ever got around to renovating the rest of the house, maybe John and I could install a revolving door, so they'd merely circle around and end up back outside again.

"Right," Christine said. "Sure, your marriage wasn't shaky. Which is why you all chased Phoebe to Savannah without even inviting me."

"Don't start," Carol said. If she lived to be one hundred, Christine would never forgive us for accidentally leaving her out of our Savannah/Hilton Head escapade.

My father stuck out a beefy index finger and did a head count. "One of you might want to give Billy Jr. a ring-a-ling on the ting-a-ling so he doesn't get the extinct impression he's been forgotten."

"Don't you dare," I said. "I was counting on bringing left-over beef bourguignon to school tomorrow for my lunch."

My father took a long sip of my wine. He was wearing a red T-shirt with a pink heart that had writing on it. I squinted. "What does your shirt say, Dad?"

My father stretched out the shirt so we could read it: YOU GIVE ME A HEART ON.

"Jesus, Dad," Carol said. "Don't you dare wear that around your grandchildren."

Our dad grinned. "Don't look at me. It was a gift from a lady friend."

"That friend is no lady, Dad," Carol said. "You might want to class it up a notch."

"The whole Valentine vibe works against my astral plane, or maybe it's my emotional aura," Johnny said, slipping into hippie talk the way he did these days when he was feeling insecure.

"Maybe it's your chi balls," Michael said.

"We'll have none of that talk under my roof," our dad said.

I took a moment to be thankful that at least my brother Johnny had dropped the dashiki and started dressing like himself again. He'd also cut his hair so he could no longer pull it into a man bun even if he wanted to.

"Nothing," Johnny continued, "flips me out the way Valentine's Day does. I love spreading the Aloha, but I always get it wrong."

"Maybe because you're not in Hawaii?" Christine said.

"I'm with ya, bro," Michael said. "All the screwups I've had over the years. No matter how hard I try, I can never come up with the right Valentine's Day present for Phoebe."

"Your mother," our father said, "was always bowled over by a bouquet of red roses. I'd pull the reddest ones out of the arrangements at the supermarket and have the girl tie them up again with a fancy red bow."

"They love it when you take apart the bouquets at the grocery store," I said. "Even more than they like being called *the girl.*"

"Phoebe hates it when I give her roses," Michael said. "She says they drop their petals all over the place and then one day the vase is filled with swamp water and it smells up the whole house."

"Phoebe is a bitch," Christine said.

"Takes one to know one," I said.

"Just ask Phoebe what she wants," Carol said. "That's what Dennis does every year."

"Thanks," Michael said. "I didn't even think of that."

"The real problem," Carol said, "is that all the longing comes out around Valentine's Day. It's like your high school self is still lurking around just under the surface."

"Not me," Christine said. "I don't need to look back. I live a charmed life."

"Right," Carol said. "Like those people on Facebook who post about how much they love their perfect spouses, who just so happen to be in the next room. I mean, if you love them that much, why not just open the door and yell it to them. People who live charmed lives don't need to post in public forums that they live charmed lives."

"Take it back," Christine said. "And just in case you didn't notice, this is a dining room, not a public forum."

"Oh, grow up," Carol said.

"You grow up," Christine said.

"What is the national divorce average these days anyway?" Carol said. "I've been so busy chasing kids I haven't really kept up."

"Almost fifty percent of marriages end in divorce or separation," I said without glancing at John. "Every thirteen seconds there is one divorce in America. Not that I've checked into it or anything."

"Not that I've looked into it either," Michael said, "but the average first marriage that ends in divorce lasts about eight years."

Everybody turned to look at me. Except for John, who kept eating his beef bourguignon.

"Stop staring at me, you guys," I said. "Whatshisname and I made it to ten."

"You're such an overachiever," Carol said.

"Russia has the highest divorce rate in the world," Johnny said.

"All that tree juice they drink over there doesn't help," our dad said. "And when you live in darkness six months of the year, things can get a little cray-cray, as my old friend Sugar Butt was wont to say."

"Sugar Butt," Carol said. "Speaking of classing it up."

"Basically," Johnny said, "it's because in a typical Russian apartment there are a lot more bodies than there are rooms. Many people in Russia spend their entire lives living with their parents."

Everybody but John was looking at me again.

"We don't live together," I said. "Dad lives way over there in his mancave. And don't forget that you live here, too, hotshot."

"I do not," Johnny said. "I'm out back in the trailer. Which, by the way, Kim happens to find really romantic when she visits me."

"Ooh," Carol said. "Maybe I can borrow the trailer to date Dennis."

I sighed. "Forty-one percent of first marriages end in divorce. Sixty percent of second marriages end in divorce. Seventy-three and a third percent of third marriages end in divorce. Give or take."

John took a long drink of wine.

"Let me point out again," Christine said, "that we're still Girls 2, Boys 1 for intact marriages."

"No way," Johnny said. "It's Girls 2, Boys 3. Michael and I are still intact."

"We're talking about marriage," Carol said, "not circumcision."

"Funny," Michael said. "So funny I forgot to laugh."

John pushed himself away from the dining room table. I tried to catch his eye.

"Was it something we said?" Johnny asked as my Valentine-to-be walked away.

Horatio and Scruffy Dog followed John. Mother Teresa circled the table once, conflicted, then plopped down next to Michael.

"I should go, too," Carol said.

"I'm glad you've finally reached that conclusion," I said.

Carol ignored me. "But first, speaking of daunting odds, since it looks like Polly isn't going anywhere right now, what are your plans? Besides keeping Dad and Johnny away from her?"

"Yeah," Christine said. "If she ends up with Johnny, they won't have a prayer. It'll totally ruin our family standing in the national divorce averages."

"Hello," Johnny said. "I'm right here."

"And if she ends up with Dad," Carol said, "it'll totally ruin our inheritance."

"Tell me you didn't really just say that," I said.

But she had. And worse, Polly had just poked her head into the dining room. She'd taken off her burgundy blanket-like poncho and her gray slip-on shearling ankle booties with buttons on the side. Her black maternity leggings were tucked into her socks. Her cheeks were red, too red, and her freckles popped against the rest of her face, which had gone simply white.

"Darlin'," my father said.

"Poppy," Johnny said.

But Polly was gone.

"Okay," I said. "That's it. Make sure you load your stuff into the dishwasher, everybody. Don't let the door hit your butts on the way out. And next time call before you show up. Or at least text."

"Right," Christine said. "So you can pretend you didn't get the text."

"Geez Louise," Carol said. "I was only going to ask you whether you've planned a baby shower for Polly yet. After all, I *am* an event planner. Not that you can afford my rates, but I could consider taking it out in babysitting services."

"Of course, I've planned a baby shower," I said, even though it was a slight exaggeration. "I'm having it at school. And don't any of you dare show up."

After everybody left, I considered running upstairs to apologize to Polly and John for my family. Or maybe to John first and then to Polly. But then again, if I apologized to Polly first, I could crawl into bed and go to sleep as soon as I apologized to John. But, then again-*again*, everything looked better in the morning, so maybe I should wait.

In the end, the only conclusion I came to was that I had a true talent for overthinking.

I found the cats in the family room. Pebbles was stretched out nursing her kittens on the lowest bookshelf, the place she'd picked the day we rescued her, once she'd stopped running around the house breaking things. Time flies when you have kittens, and now Catsby, Oreo, Sunshine and Squiggy were so big that when they nursed, the back half of their bodies overspilled the lowest shelf and ended up on the floor.

The kittens were eating enough cat food these days to survive on that alone, but John and I figured Pebbles would know when it was time to wean them. At that point, we'd have Pebbles spayed and her four sons neutered. But right now, they were a snuggly, mother's milk-intoxicated little family, and it was hard to tell where one fluffy ball of fur ended and the next one began.

I watched them, trance-like, my eyes half-closed. Pebbles stared at me with full eye contact, her emerald eyes twinkling, as if to say, *Relax, you and John will figure it all out. Polly will figure it all out. You'll get through Valentine's Day. You'll get your family out of your house, at least some of the time.*

Pebbles gave me a long slow languid blink, closing her eyes completely, which is a cat's way of saying I love you. I trust you. I'll never judge you. I'll always be there for you. I'll never try to change you. Just feed me and I'm in. Until death do us part.

I slow-blinked back, letting Pebbles know I trusted her, too, and that I posed no threat to her or her kittens, and I would always take care of them. Everything was pretty simple with cats. You didn't have to worry about flashbacks to your first marriage, for one. You didn't have to worry about divorce rates. Cats didn't mind if you never cooked. They didn't care whether you ever had a baby or not. Maybe I was missing something, but it seemed like it was a helluva lot easier to love someone with four legs as opposed to two.

When Pebbles and the kittens had finished, I fed them all again in the kitchen. The signature sound of a can opening never fails to rally any and all animals in the immediate vicinity. Sure enough, Horatio and Scruffy Dog came running, nails scratching on the hardwood stairs, so I gave them a bonus meal, too.

By the time I went upstairs to bed, it was too late to knock on Polly's door. I left a post-it note on it instead. *Sorry about my family*, it said.

John didn't open his eyes when I tiptoed into our new old room. I stared at him for a moment, trying to tell if he was really sleeping or fake sleeping.

Sorry about my family, I whispered as I climbed in beside him.

Chapter Nine

Thirty days hath September, April, June and November. All the rest have thirty-one, except for February, which has one thousand eight hundred and forty-three.

Today was only the second day of the month, which didn't make it feel much shorter. And so far, February hadn't gotten off to such a great start. The post-it had disappeared from Polly's door when I walked by this morning, and Polly was already gone by the time I made it down to the kitchen.

John was gone, too. He'd left me a note on the refrigerator:

Meetings at work. Back late. Fed animals breakfast.

Not exactly a Valentine. To anchor his note, he'd chosen a square vintage magnet from a surplus of decorative magnets that had landed on the front of the old refrigerator over the years. Salmon background, a brunette woman in a harvest gold dress sitting on an avocado green sofa, pressing the receiver of a beige corded phone to one ear. The magnet said in white block letters: *I was just sitting here overthinking the joy out of everything.*

If John had intended the magnet as a second message to
me, I certainly didn't appreciate it. On the other hand, maybe
he'd just grabbed the first magnet he saw.

And here I was, overthinking the overthinking magnet.

My sister Carol had given me that magnet a long time ago.
My marriage to my hasbeen had been getting increasingly
rocky, and I couldn't figure out why. It just seemed that at first
so much of our time together was taken up by when and
where and how often we'd have sex. Then after that, there was
all that planning for the wedding. Then looking for a house,
and finding it, and decorating it, and having people over to
see it.

Until one day, we looked at each other across the kitchen
table in the little ranchburger we'd bought, and I realized we
had absolutely nothing to say to each other. I suppose it was
probably just time to have children. We'd talked about it some,
but Kevin was never quite ready. I was way past ready and
getting close to too late. And then, instead of children, Kevin
decided to have Nikki. Before we even officially broke up, she
was already pregnant with the twins that should have been
mine.

But before I knew all that, there was a time when I
thought I just had to find the missing piece of the relationship
puzzle to get us on track again. After years of lapsed Catholicism, the fact that my seventeen-months-older sister Carol
knew everything was the one miracle I still believed in. So one
Saturday morning, I showed up early at Carol and Dennis's
house with coffee from Morning Glories for the three of us
and a six-pack of blueberry muffins for the kids.

I hung around for hours and watched Carol and Dennis as
they ran about, outside and in, mowing the lawn and vacu-
uming and throwing load after load of laundry into the
washing machine and dryer. I read some books to Maeve,
played catch with Trevor and Ian. When Siobhan finally
rolled out of bed, I helped her pick a topic for a term paper.

"What the hell are you still doing here?" Carol finally said.

I shrugged. "I'm trying to figure out how normal people live."

Carol laughed. "I think it was Tina Fey who said that you can't be that kid standing at the top of the waterslide, over-thinking. You have to go down the chute."

"But which chute?" I said.

Eventually, Carol kicked me out. And all I got from the whole experience was this stupid refrigerator magnet, which she dropped off about a week later.

At least John had made coffee before he'd taken off this morning. But when I finished pouring what was left in the pot, my coffee mug was still half empty. I swore softly, tried my hardest to pretend my mug was actually half full. Realized I could never be that much of an optimist without more caffeine.

The burning desire for more coffee propelled me to school earlier than I'd arrived in ages. I stretched forward and wiped the inside of the frosty windshield with one mitten as I drove so I could see my way up the long drive.

When I pulled into the parking lot, Loretta Lynn was singing "You're the Reason Our Kids Are So Ugly."

"Not helping," I said. I sat in the car and waited for Loretta to stop.

Bryan Adams was up next with "(Everything I Do) I Do It For You."

"Yeah, right," I said. "Sure you do, pal. I bet you don't even make a full pot of coffee before you leave the house in the morning."

When the Beatles started singing "Love Me Do," it felt safe to leave the car. There wasn't a lot of wiggle room with those lyrics. Love me do, new, you, true. You didn't need a roadmap to get there. Not for the first time, I wondered why my life couldn't be an early Beatles song.

When I opened the main door to the school, I heard Kate

Stone laughing from her office. It was enough of an unusual occurrence that my inner Nancy Drew kicked in and was dying to know who was in there with her.

I'd worked at Bayberry long enough to have figured out that if my boss's door was open and you stopped just outside it and looked at the fair-trade handcrafted wall mirror from Ghana on the opposite wall, you could see right into her office. I'd just give it a quick peek before I headed to the teachers' room and a full cup of coffee.

For impromptu camouflage, I pushed my wool scarf up over my chin and nose and then tiptoed over in my purple faux UGGs. I peered into the mirror, pretending I was fluffing up my hair from a distance.

Polly and Hot Cross Buns were sitting side by side, laughing with Kate Stone across her gargantuan desk.

"Can I help you?" I heard my boss say. Apparently, the mirror trick worked both ways.

I whipped my head away from the mirror and hightailed it to the teachers' room.

My heart was still beating like crazy while I spun the coffee carousel. I almost chose a decaf pod to calm down, decided I needed more caffeine to handle the day and picked a medium roast breakfast blend instead. While the Keurig was gurgling, my paranoia kicked in full throttle. Why was Polly, the teaching assistant, instead of me, the lead teacher of long standing, in that before-school meeting? Did Kate Stone accidentally call Polly instead of me? Or had Hot Cross Buns specifically asked to meet with Polly? Was he complaining about me to my bitch of a boss, maybe even saying it was too bad Polly wasn't the lead teacher, because then he'd have no problem with his precious child being in our class?

Spiraling from there, I pictured Kate Stone banishing me to a job in childcare while Polly took over my classroom. But wait, the whole point of working in childcare was so that Polly could have her baby at work with her. Even my feared leader couldn't send me to childcare to watch Polly's baby, at least I didn't think she could. And Bayberry didn't even take classroom requests from parents, so who even cared if Hot Cross Buns liked Polly better than me. I sure as hell didn't need Hot Cross Buns to like me.

As I poured cream into my coffee, a quote popped into my head: "What other people think of you is none of your business." I'd seen it attributed to everyone from Deepak Chopra to Jack Canfield. Maybe whoever said it is also none of our business. In theory, it was a great quote. In reality, I still wanted to know why I wasn't in that meeting.

I gulped my coffee and pouted my way to my classroom. This time, instead of a tiny conversation heart stuck to the door, there was an oversized one. WINK WINK it said in big pink letters.

I was so not in the mood for this. I grabbed a thin marker, crossed out the WINK WINK and wrote KISS OFF over it.

"Too much?" I said as Polly walked up beside me. Her coat and boots were nowhere to be seen, so clearly it had been a premeditated meeting.

"Maybe a little," Polly said. "Especially for the kids who can read."

I yanked the candy heart off the door. "These hearts are starting to creep me out. And speaking of creepers, sorry about my family."

"Thanks, I got your note," Polly said. She didn't quite look at me. She didn't quite tell me about the meeting she'd just left either.

We drifted away from each other, greeting kids, getting everything set up for the day.

"Happy Groundhog Day," I said once the kids had arrived and we were all seated for circle time.

"I saw the movie," Max said. "It was over my head."

A chorus of *I saw the movie, too* and *it wasn't over my head* followed.

"As long as you remember never to swear or kill yourself, it's okay to watch *Groundhog Day* with your babysitter," Pandora said. "Just don't tell anyone."

I wasn't going to touch this conversation with a ten-foot pole, so I pulled the groundhog puppet I'd had since my first teaching days out from behind my back.

"It's a woodchuck!" one of the kids yelled.

"Actually," I said. "A woodchuck and a groundhog are the same thing."

"Are you sure?" somebody else said. Polly looked like she didn't quite believe me either. But I was a good teacher, a really good teacher, and I knew my groundhogs and woodchucks.

"I'm sure," I said. It was nice to be sure about something.

"How much wood could a woodchuck chuck if a wood-chuck could chuck wood," I chanted as fast as I could. As I said it, I pretended I was holding one side of an imaginary ear of corn and the puppet was holding the other, and we were both chomping away from one side to the other as fast as we could.

"Now your turn," I said.

The kids giggled and chanted and chomped as they repeated it.

I stretched out on my stomach in the center of the circle with my puppet and rolled over and over. "How much ground could a groundhog hog if a groundhog could hog ground," I chanted.

The kids rolled around inside the circle like a litter of kittens, giggling away while they repeated the line. Granted, preschoolers were a great audience. But I knew how to make them laugh. And not only did I know my groundhogs and woodchucks, I'd made up the last part myself, my unique and original twist on the traditional woodchuck tongue twister. Take that, Hot Cross Buns.

Polly and I got the kids untangled and back to their spots on the circle again.

"Can you say Punxsutawney Phil?" I said as I moved the groundhog puppet's mouth.

"Pachydermia Phil," Jaden yelled. It was a step up from Pedophilia Phil, which one of the kids had blurted out a few years ago. Punxsutawney was a tough word for preschoolers.

"Groundhog Day," I said, "comes from a Pennsylvania Dutch tradition. Punxsutawney Phil is the most famous groundhog of them all. Legend has it that if the groundhog sees its shadow because the weather's clear when it wakes up today, which is February 2nd, the groundhog goes back to its den and hibernates some more, and we'll have wintry weather for six more weeks. If the groundhog doesn't see its shadow because it's cloudy, we'll have an early spring."

This always seemed counterintuitive to me. I mean, if it's a sunny day, spring should be on the way, right? But the kids didn't seem to have a problem with Groundhog Day logic.

"Shadows are made when something blocks the light," I said. "And now, we're all going to be groundhogs and see if we can find our shadows."

It was too cold to go outside, so Polly and I divided the kids into teams of two and gave each team a flashlight. Polly closed the blinds while I turned off the lights in the classroom. The flashlight holders shined the flashlight on their partners so they could find their shadows.

"I found it!" Depp yelled as he turned around fast and jumped on his shadow. "I'm having an early spring, baby."

After everyone took turns holding the flashlight and finding their shadow, Polly and I held a flashlight in each hand and pointed them at the kids, moving them up and down fast like disco lights. We all sang "Heads, Shoulders, Knees &

Toes" as the kids and their shadows touched the appropriate body parts.

Then we moved on to shadow freeze dancing and the kids busted some moves to Frank Sinatra and Sammy Davis Jr.'s version of "Me and My Shadow," which I'd borrowed from my father. A few years ago, I'd downloaded Cat Stevens' "Moonshadow," but all that talk about losing hands and legs scared some of the kids, so I'd taken it off our Groundhog Day playlist.

When the kids were all sweaty and exhausted from jumping around, we took a break for snack.

"My cheese cube can see its shadow," Juliette said before she popped it into her mouth.

"My pee can see its shadow," Griffin said. Unfortunately, Griffin didn't wait to go to the bathroom but tested out his theory in his pants. Polly helped him find his Oops change of clothing bag. That's what assistant teachers do, while the lead teachers do the heavy lifting. It wasn't my finest moment, but I had to admit that this morning this particular assistant teacher duty made me happier than it should have.

"God hates ugly," I could almost hear my mother say, although I'd lost the precise sound of her voice shortly after she died. That and the sophisticated crunch she made when she chewed cornflakes, a sound I tried my whole childhood to imitate. *God hates a smarty-pants* and *God hates glib* were also part of our family lexicon. Quoting God this way was not at all about religion, but about bringing in enough clout to give the speaker irrefutable authority on a subject.

God hates ugly. If my mother were still alive, she'd straighten me right out. She'd know whether it would be pushing my luck to marry John. She'd have Polly's baby shower all planned. Although, come to think of it, even my mother would probably like Polly better than me.

After snack, we made groundhog puppets. We glued pre-cut green felt rectangles, the top edges fringed with scissors to look like grass, around bathroom-sized paper cups, fringe side up. Polly and I had cut a slit in the bottom of each cup. Polly had also already cut out little groundhogs for every-body from brown felt, complete with little groundhog ears sticking up. And she'd cut notches out of one side of tiny squares of white cardboard to make buck teeth. The kids glued the teeth and some googly eyes to their groundhogs. Then we glued popsicle sticks to the backs of the ground-hogs. We all placed our groundhogs in the cups and threaded the stick down through the slit in the bottom of the cup.

I let my groundhog puppet hold my popsicle stick and move my felt groundhog up and down so it appeared and disappeared in the green felt grass. "My groundhog can see its shadow," I said.

"My groundhog can see its shadow, too," the kids yelled.

We danced our groundhogs up and down and up and down again. Preschoolers love repetition, but eventually even dancing groundhogs get old. So we tucked the groundhogs into their paper cups and lined them up across the windowsill until the kids could bring them home at dismissal.

When we moved on to individual work, we even had a Groundhog Day activity for the kids to choose along with the wooden puzzles and sandpaper letters and trips to our reading boat.

Polly had drawn a series of cute groundhogs in a variety of poses with easily distinguishable characteristics—holding flowers, wearing a hat, waving, hands overhead, hands on hips, etc.—on rectangles of white poster board. She'd also drawn a matching gray shadow card for each groundhog.

The kids took turns spreading the big white cards across the long kiddie table and matching the shadows to the ground-hogs. It was brilliant and simple, and the kids loved it. And I couldn't take any credit at all for coming up with the idea.

Okay, I had to admit it. Polly had skills.

I offered up a silent apology to my mother for my earlier ugliness, vowed to be a better person.

"Great job on those," I teacher-whispered to Polly as the kids circled around the table, waiting for a turn with the groundhog shadow cards.

"Thanks," Polly said, but she still didn't quite look at me.

Chapter Ten

I raced home at lunch to feed the cats and give the dogs a treat. They met me at the kitchen door, dogs barking, cats mewing, Pebbles circling around me and head-butting my shins to mark me as her own. Standing at the kitchen counter in my winter coat, snow melting off my boots onto the worn linoleum floor, I was grateful for the opportunity to woof down some beef bourguignon myself. Technically, I knew was *wolf* down, but when you lived with dogs you were allowed to woof things down.

When I took Horatio and Scruffy Dog out for a quick pee, the wind howled and the icy air bit into my cheeks. The dogs tugged at their leashes to get back inside.

I jumped in my car and was back at Bayberry before my lunchbreak was even over. According to my teacher watch, I had almost three minutes to spare, so I swung by the teachers' room for some dessert.

The Valentine's Day confiscated candy stash had grown significantly, towering piles of gold and red-boxed decadence squatting wherever they could. I grabbed a Godiva box, checked to make sure I was getting a piece that hadn't already been pinched, popped a dark chocolate candy into my mouth.

"That better not be a dark chocolate truffle," Lorna said.

I opened my mouth. "You want it?"

Ethan caught up to me as I walked back to my classroom. "Do you and Polly have time to meet after school today? We really should get going on packaging those materials for preschools if we're actually going to do it in this lifetime."

High on the success of *A Howliday Tail*, the Bayberry performance we'd put on just before winter break, I'd complimented Ethan once again on his amazing set design.

"Right back at you," Ethan had responded, lighting up the room with his surfer boy smile. "Having the kind of creativity you have that allows you to pull something like this together in a fun age-appropriate way is a big deal. And Polly has told me about how you can rewrite lyrics to any song at the drop of a hat. You should think about packaging materials for other preschool teachers."

We decided to collaborate. It had sounded like such a brilliant idea at the time. We could take it holiday by holiday, working our way through the school year, then spin off into other categories, like seasons and skills and subjects. I'd do the writing and Ethan would make diagrams and instructions for building props and sets. Polly could draw anything, so we'd bring her in, too, to draw whatever needed to be drawn and to help with the overall packaging.

Once we had a few units finished, we'd share them with teacher friends and ask for feedback. We'd test the waters by setting up a website. We'd rent a table at a teacher conference, maybe the NAEYC, or The National Association for the Education of Young Children, which hosted the largest early childhood conference in the world, or maybe a local event put on by BAEYC, the Boston Association for the Education of Young Children. Or even one of the kindergarten conferences, because our materials would be so amazing that they could easily age up. The opportunities were endless. The whole thing might be so brilliantly successful that someday we'd even have no choice but to quit our day jobs.

We'd planned to get going on it during our winter break, but somehow it never happened. And then before we knew it, we were back at school and January had slipped away, too.

When I was first teaching, I assumed that all the other teachers' brains swarmed with new ideas the way mine did. When I least expected it, taking a shower or a walk on the beach or in the middle of the night, a fresh idea would pop into my head. Nothing earth-shattering, but just a new way of making it fun to learn basic skills like shapes and colors and letters and numbers and cooperative play and fine and gross motor skills. But then, somewhere along the way, I realized that there were lots of great preschool teachers whose brains didn't work like that, who didn't have that particular kind of creativity.

I had lots of good ideas, plenty to share. I knew that just from this morning alone, there was enough material to put together a Groundhog Day package. And my Valentine's Day materials were locked and loaded and ready to go.

But for me, buyer's remorse had somehow set in. You get this great idea and decide you want to buy into it. And then all the reasons you shouldn't do it pop up. It feels too big, too overwhelming. What if everyone else thinks it's a stupid idea? What if I'm not good enough to pull it off? The energy dissipates, like air from a balloon.

As Langston Hughes once asked in one of my favorite poems, "What happens to a dream deferred?"

I was pretty sure it frets in a February freeze until one cold sad day it's just gone.

I realized that Ethan was waiting for me to actually say something.

"I can't today," I lied. "There's somewhere I have to be."

"No problem," Ethan said. "Polly and I can meet, and we'll catch you up later."

When Ethan disappeared into his classroom, I just stood there. Great. Ethan and Polly would do the project without me. They'd become rich and famous and quit their day jobs. And years from now I'd be this hunkered-over preschool teacher with a cane I'd bedazzled in sea shells. John would have escaped to greener pastures, and even I would have to admit that technically I lived with my father. I'd take up crocheting lace doilies, and priests would come visit us once a month for dinner. We'd eat casseroles dropped off by a series of increasingly younger women who had the hots for my dad.

Ethan's classroom door opened again. June, my former and his current assistant, appeared. She flipped her long blond twenty-something hair, which sent it shimmering in summery waves down the full length of her back.

"Hey, Sarah," she said. "Great to see you." Like I didn't spend my work life in the classroom next door.

"Really?" I said.

June laughed. I'd forgotten how much I liked her, other than the fact that she was far too young and pretty, and back when we worked together, she used to disappear to meditate when I least expected it. But she always came back.

"Hey," I said as June started to walk away. "How's your puppy doing? Creases, right?"

June stopped, turned. "Wrinkles."

Belatedly I remembered that Creases was another pup born to the same litter of Labrador-shar pei crosses at the Marshbury Animal Shelter, adorable puppies that looked like black labs crossed with raisins. I'd actually once borrowed June's unsuspecting puppy to meet a hot guy I was stalking at the time, who just so happened to be the owner of Creases. I'd ended up dating the guy and almost sleeping with him. The guy had eventually smartened up and dated June instead.

I would have asked how this guy I'd almost slept with was doing, but I was such a horrible person I couldn't even remember his name.

"He's awesome," June said. "He's all grown up now."

I looked at her, puzzled. I wasn't the best judge, but this guy hadn't seemed like the type that was likely to grow up.

"Wrinkles," she said. "He's like a full-blown dog now."

"Got it," I said. "That's great." Maybe I could invite June out for coffee or to walk the beach. I'd become the big sister she'd never had. Or another big sister if she already had one. I'd teach her everything I hadn't already taught her when we worked together, and when she looked back on her life, I'd be her favorite mentor ever. And when I could no longer see to crochet my lace doilies, she'd take me shopping and buy me a new pair of glasses. And a magnifying glass with a stand to use as backup to the glasses.

"So, how are things going with Ethan?" I asked in my most sympathetic mentor voice.

Her blue eyes sparkled. "Ethan is amazing. I don't know how I got so lucky."

She took a few steps down the hallways, flipped her hair again and looked back over her shoulder. "He's like the big brother I always wanted but never had."

Children flourish when given the freedom to learn through self-directed activity, so it behooves us as educators not to overschedule their school day.

All by way of saying that when I limped my way back to my classroom after running into June, it didn't look like anybody there needed me either. Polly was working with a couple of the students on a counting game. A few of the kids were drawing on big sheets of white paper spread out on the floor. Everybody else was curled up in or around our reading boat, either reading or pre-reading.

I grabbed today's postcard donations, waved them at Polly, pointed in the direction of the Arts Barn.

One entire huge bulletin board in the Arts Barn was completely covered with postcards. Another bulletin board had been rolled over next to the first one and was partially covered already. I still didn't get what postcards had to do with Valentine's Day, but I had to admit that this project was turning out to be good busywork for the parents.

I tacked up my classroom contributions, stood back to take it all in.

As I scanned the postcards, I realized that a cluster of them were almost identical. They all had the exact same sepia shot of an entrance to the beach marked on either side with weathered wood storm fencing, the kind used to protect sand dunes. They all began with *Greetings From*. The only thing different was the destination—*Block Island, Scituate, Nantucket, Kauai, Ipswich, Clearwater Beach, Santa Monica State Beach, Seven Mile Beach, East Beach, South Beach, Coast Guard Beach*. All with the same generic beach shot.

A crazy feeling came over me that there was a message in these postcards that would help me, if only I could figure it out. *Pick a beach, any beach? It really doesn't matter where you go as long as your toes are in the sand? Travel the world, beach by beach? Collect the same postcard? Stay home and start a postcard business? Wherever you go, there you are?*

"How's it going?" a familiar voice said behind me.

"Beachy keen," I said.

The voice clicked. I whipped my head around. "Are you *stalking* me?"

The X was sitting on the floor, leaning back against the low lip of the stage, open laptop on his lap.

Kevin chewed the edge of his lower lip as he pushed himself up off the floor. "Of course not. I'm here to pick up the twins."

"You're two hours early," I said sweetly. "And we don't allow loitering."

I started rearranging all the *Greetings From* postcards into their own area in case that might help me figure out what they were trying to tell me. And also to avoid looking at my hasbeen, since I'd already spent far too many years of my life doing just that.

"I'm working remote," he said. "And Nikki likes having the house to herself while she naps."

"Try Morning Glories," I said. "They have great internet." Actually, I had no idea if that was true, but whatever. Maybe the postcards were telling me not to forget to plan a beach day for the kids, assuming the groundhog was right and spring actually arrived.

"Lately," Kevin said, "I have these days when it would feel good to have another adult to talk to."

I forgot myself and turned around. "You want to talk to adults, so you came to a *preschool?*"

My name deleted sighed. That Man? Bastardmobile on Wheels? "Nikki doesn't like the same music. She hasn't even *heard of* some of my favorite bands. Essentially, she's from a different generation."

"She's not that much younger than us," I said. "I mean, it's not like she's twelve or anything. Plus you have crappy taste in music anyway."

He smiled a sad smile. "See, you could always make me laugh."

"No, I couldn't. You hated my sense of humor."

I could only surmise that things must be pretty bad with wife number two if I was starting to look good to my whatever-he-was. I allowed myself a little smile.

"Well," I said without even bothering to glance at my watch. "Will you look at the time. I've got a classroom to run. Brilliantly, I might add."

"Did I ever tell you," Kevin said quietly, "how Nikki and I met?"

I averted my eyes. I covered my ears. "Lalalala," I sang.

I waited till I was almost out the door before I turned around.

I pulled my hands away from my ears and put them on my hips. "I have absolutely no interest in that story. Or in anything else you might possibly ever have to say to me. Stay away from me, Kevin. Period. Full stop. Double space. No, wait, single space. Only dinosaurs still use double spaces. And I, for one, am not a dinosaur. I have every intention of continuing to evolve. As soon as I make it through February."

"Wait," my wasband said.

"Don't hold your breath," I said.

Chapter Eleven

Carol's minivan was taking up prime real estate in my driveway when I pulled in after school. A new white decal in the lower corner of the rear windshield read: I USED TO BE COOL. I noticed she still hadn't added the bumper sticker I'd given her for Christmas: CONDOMS PREVENT MINI-VANS. Maybe less is more.

I considered backing right out of the driveway again, decided she was probably looking out the window. And even if she wasn't, it was no use. Carol was whatever was beyond persistent, so she'd manage to track me down again in no time at all.

"Three days in a row," I said to her by way of greeting as I kicked off my boots in the kitchen. "That's completely over the line. And remember how you were going to start calling before you came over? Or at least texting?"

"Sarah, Sarah, Sarah." Carol shook her head once for each repetition.

"That's my name," I said, "don't wear it out. All that head-shaking can't be good for your brain either."

Carol crossed her arms over her chest. "When are you going to find homes for some of these animals?"

"They have a home." I squatted down to pet my way through everybody. "It's okay, babies. She'll be gone soon."

Carol grabbed my arm, yanked me back up to a standing position.

"Ouch," I said. "That pinches."

She ignored me and hauled me out to the center hallway. Then she dragged me about halfway up the stairs until we reached the step that, after years of childhood trial and error, we'd all discovered was low enough to spy on the floor below but high enough to keep the conversation private. Nobody else was home right now, at least as far as I could tell, but old habits die hard and all that.

Mismatched picture frames stretched along both sides of the staircase all the way up to the new locked door that Christine's contractor husband Joe had installed at the entrance to the second floor to protect John's and my private quarters. Actually, semi-private, since Polly and her baby-to-be had taken over my parents' former bedroom and sitting area.

Dozens of family photos surrounded my bossy big sister and me like a group hug. Our grandparents' wedding photos. Our parents' wedding photo. The adult Hurlihy kids' wedding photos. Except mine.

I'd taken down Kevin's and my wedding photo the day our divorce had become final in a ceremony that involved my father's biggest hammer and the sound of breaking glass while my family cheered me on.

"Good riddance to bad rubbish," we'd all yelled.

There were so many photos on the walls that you almost didn't notice the gap that remained unless you knew where to look. But the gap was gone now. Just after John and I bought the house, I'd finally gotten around to printing out a selfie I'd taken of John and me and taping it up in the empty space.

"Jeez Louise, get a real picture, will you?" Carol had said to me about eight gazillion times since then. "Like maybe taken by a professional photographer when you two actually get around to marrying each other."

I waited for her to start in on me again, to tell me I should at least invest in a decent frame for the selfie in the meantime. She didn't even glance up.

"You are *not* going to believe this," she said, digging her fingernails into my thigh.

"Ouch," I said. "Is it really necessary to make every conversation so painful?"

Carol stopped hurting me long enough to grab her phone. "Remember Brendan O'Donoghue?"

"Italian kid?" I said.

"Funny," Carol said. "So funny I forgot to laugh. Anyway, he had a huge crush on me in high school."

"You think everyone had a huge crush on you in high school."

Carol looked up from scrolling. "Your point?"

"Ohmigod, you are so conceited."

"Aww," Carol said as she tucked a hunk of hair behind her ear. "I forgot we used to say *conceited*."

"Yeah, usually about you, as I remember." I tried to resist tucking a hunk of hair behind my own ear, but I couldn't. I'd spent my whole life looking to Carol for direction.

"Actually, it's all your fault," Carol said. "I shared your Facebook post about needing postcards for school, and other people must have shared it from my timeline, and so on and so forth until it was totally out on the old high school grapevine—"

"Old being the operative word."

Carol ignored my ageist dig. "Brendan sent me a friend request, and then he sent me a private message saying he had some postcards for me. And did I want to get together for coffee so he could give them to me."

"I hope you didn't fall for it," I said. "If we were still back in high school, he'd be trying to trick you so he could push you into a bathroom to make out and/or grope you. And it would turn out that there weren't any postcards."

"This is my stroll down memory lane, not yours," Carol said. "And how many times did I tell you that if a guy tries to cut you off from the pack at a party, you kick him in the balls."

"You always made that sound so easy. I had no idea how hard guys cry when you do that."

"Smooth seas do not make skillful sailors," Carol said. "African proverb."

"Am I the sea or the sailor?" I said. "Sisterly question."

Carol ignored me. Horatio and Scruffy Dog galloped up the stairs. Horatio was holding his favorite stuffed squirrel in his mouth, and Scruffy Dog had a tennis ball in hers. I bounced the tennis ball down the stairs, then sent the squirrel flying up the stairs. The dogs went after them. It doesn't take much to make dogs happy.

Pebbles was sitting in the wide center downstairs hallway, grooming herself. The kittens started climbing the stairs. I debated whether or not it was worth setting up the baby gate, but I really didn't want to hear what Carol would say about that. And since Pebbles didn't seem the least bit concerned, I decided I'd just scoop them into my lap once they got close enough.

"So should I do it?" Carol said.

"Kick Brendan What's-His-Name in the balls?"

"Meet him for coffee." Carol tucked another hunk of hair behind her other ear.

I sat on my hands so I wouldn't do it, too. "Did the post-cards sound like they were any good?"

"God, you're so self-absorbed."

"Takes one to know one," I said.

Carol pulled up Brendan O'Donoghue's Facebook profile on her phone.

"He looks exactly like Dennis," I said.

"No, he doesn't." Carol sighed. "He, Brendan, told me I hadn't aged at all. I feel a tiny bit guilty since my profile picture is from before I was pregnant with Siobhan. Not that I don't believe that true sexiness comes with maturity. You know who you are and you're not trying to be anyone else. There's real power in that."

I wondered if I could get Carol to text that to me so I could write it down later. My sister has read a lot of self-help books, which could be a real time-saver for me.

"Plus, he'll be looking at me through high school-colored glasses," Carol said. "But that's not completely reliable, so maybe I shouldn't meet him for coffee unless his photo is eighteen years old, too."

"Why would you want to do that?" I said. "Coffee, not using the old photo. Actually, coffee *and* the old photo. But, I mean, couldn't you just tell him to drop them off at Bayberry? Or put them in the mail? They *are* postcards, after all, which means they're highly mailable."

Squiggy and Oreo reached me at the same time. I scooped them up, handed Oreo over to Carol because he was the toughest.

Carol put Oreo over her shoulder and started patting his back like she was burping a baby. Catsby reached me next, so I dropped him into Carol's lap, then scooped up Sunshine, the runt of the litter.

"It's just," Carol said, "that I don't want to spend the rest of my life in this godforsaken little town in the middle of nowhere, driving a minivan and married to the same man for centuries."

"Coulda, woulda, shoulda," I said.

Carol blew out a gust of air. "Not helping."

"You can't put the toothpaste back in the tube?" I tried.

Carol and I both started to laugh. Then we laughed and laughed, that crazy out of control kind of laughter that doesn't happen often enough once you're a grownup. Or at least theoretically a grownup.

"Ohmigod," Carol said. "Remember when Dad used to use the toothpaste line on our dates as he glared at the crotches of their parachute pants? It was so humiliating."

"Yeah, like parachute pants weren't humiliating enough all by themselves. The one that got me was when the nuns at school used to tell us to picture Jesus, or maybe it was Mary—"

"Standing outside the car crying, to give us the strength not to have sex with a boy in the backseat."

"I know, right?" I said. "It completely ruined car sex for me."

"Liar, liar, pants on fire."

"Fine," I said. I tried to cover Squiggy's and Sunshine's ears at the same time. "It partially ruined car sex for me." I stood up, carried the two kittens down to the bottom of the stairs.

"No wonder we're screwed up for life," Carol said. She carried her two kittens down the stairs.

"Yeah," I said. "Let's blame it on Dad and the nuns." By the time I sat back down on our step, the kittens had climbed halfway up to me again. "And having coffee with a guy from high school is going to help you not be screwed up for life how?"

Carol sat down next to me. Oreo and Catsby headed up the stairs in our direction, too.

"The romance is gone," Carol said. "I think I just want a Valentine's Day like Dennis and I used to have."

"I thought you said you just tell Dennis what to get you for Valentine's Day. So, tell him you want romance."

"It's not just the romance. I miss the days when he'd get me a Valentine's Day present that I hated, and I loved him enough not to tell him."

"That's really profound," I said. "Either that or I'm even more screwed up than I thought I was."

Carol leaned back on her elbows. "One Valentine's Day he left a heart he made out of condoms on my pillow."

"Eww," I said. "Wrapped or unwrapped? Not used, I hope. Wait, don't tell me."

"Grow up. They were in cute red packages. I think they were called Cupid Condoms."

"Or Stupid Condoms."

"It was a joke. You know, because of the Saran Wrap thing."

Carol and Dennis couldn't find a condom once, so they used Saran Wrap. Nine months and five days later, Siobhan was born. It was my least favorite story Carol had ever told me, and there was plenty of competition. I closed my eyes against a horrifying vision of Dennis's Saran Wrap-covered penis.

Carol sighed. "And once he gave me a toy monkey that pooped candy."

"Ooh, can I borrow it if you still have it? The kids at school would love it. Wait, I'd have to find something to fill it with instead of candy. Do you think it would work with carrot sticks? Never mind, I could leave it in the teachers' room instead."

"And then one year, the romance died. I casually mentioned something about getting a step-on trash can so Maeve would stop eating the trash. And boom, that was my Valentine's Day present from Dennis. He didn't even wrap it."

"And a trash can is that much worse than a monkey that poops candy how?"

"I guess," Carol said. "I'm just dying to do something rebellious. And having coffee with a guy I went to high school with is the only opportunity that has come up."

"Just make sure he wears Saran Wrap."

"Get your head out of the gutter," Carol said. "What I

mean is that my life is so pathetic, I can't think of anything besides coffee and postcards that I could do and still be back in time to drive afternoon carpool."

The massive oak front door creaked. Polly took a step in, stopped.

My father was right behind her. "I'll have you know it's snowing cats and dogs out there. A true gentleman walks a lady right to her doorstop, and then he escorts her up to her boudoir in case there are roof leaks."

"Excuse me," Polly said. And then she raced up the stairs, one hand on her baby bump.

Chapter Twelve

Another jumbo pink conversation heart was stuck on my class-room door. I pulled off a mitten with my teeth, fumbled in my canvas teachers' bag for my reading glasses.

WHY NOT, the heart said in red letters.

I grabbed a marker, crossed it out and wrote, IT'S NOT YOU, IT'S ME.

Decided that didn't have quite enough bite, so I ripped the heart off the door, turned it over, wrote, SCREW LOVE, I'D RATHER FALL IN CHOCOLATE.

It was a lot of words, even for an oversized conversation heart. But the sentiment was what mattered, not the legibility. And chocolate was exactly what I needed.

I threw the candy heart away in our classroom wastebasket. Decided I could get in serious trouble if one of the kids found it and either ate it or read it. Fished it out again and headed for the teachers' room to dispose of it there.

The truth was I couldn't wait until Valentine's Day was over. It was like I could feel Cupid's arrows shooting all around me, but the navigation was defective, and none of the arrows were hitting their mark.

While Cupid was misfiring, I was trying to step things up

at my end. Once I'd managed to get rid of Carol and my father yesterday, I'd actually cooked quesadillas for dinner instead of leaving the ingredients in the refrigerator where they could make me feel guilty as they rotted.

John wasn't even all that late coming home. He complimented the quesadillas. I asked him how the traffic was. We queried each other about our days. We kept the conversation safe, neutral, boring, like an old married couple that had had the same stupid fights so many times over the years that they couldn't be bothered getting into it all again.

I took another bite of salad.

John took another bite of quesadilla. "This is actually really good."

"What do you mean by that?" I said. "I mean, seriously, how patronizing can you get?"

John wiped his mouth, crumpled his napkin on the plate.

"If you ever want to have a conversation about what's really going on," he said as he slid his chair back from the table, "let me know."

John went to bed early. I waited until I was pretty sure he was asleep before I tiptoed into the bedroom.

"If you ever want to have a conversation about what's really going on," I whispered to the ceiling over and over again, "let me know." It was like my own twisted version of counting sheep. Except that sheep probably lead to better sleep. And I'm a poet and I don't even know it.

When my alarm woke me up, I felt sleep-deprived and grouchy. John was still in bed, sleeping or pretending to be asleep. Must be nice to work remote. I made my own coffee, fed all the animals myself, decided to wait to have a chocolate breakfast at school, because that might well be the high point of my day.

Ethan was standing in the teachers' room when I pushed the door open, shoveling chocolates into his mouth.

"Breakfast," he mumbled.

"I'm with you," I said. I took in the piles of confiscated chocolate. There was candy for days. Weeks. Maybe years.

I opened an expensive looking gold box, popped a fluffy chocolate something or other into my mouth. Closed my eyes while it melted.

"Do you think we can donate this stuff somewhere?" I said when I opened my eyes again. "Like maybe a gym, where they might have a better chance of working it off?"

"I could bring some to my next 12-step meeting," Ethan said. "You have no idea how much crap people eat at those meetings."

I opened another box, this one red, made my best guess and picked a chocolate. It was disgusting, like a mini fruit cake dipped in chocolate. I spit it into the wastebasket. If you're going to drown yourself in a sea of chocolate, it should only be the best. I remembered I was still carrying the conversation heart, threw that in the wastebasket, too.

"I know," I said. "How about if we jam as much as we can into the freezer. The first rule of chocolate is that once it's frozen, it's off limits."

Ethan opened another box of chocolate. "I'm not sure I concur with that rule. Three Musketeers are definitely better frozen."

"Good point," I said, "though I have to say I prefer frozen Thin Mints. I think we should try it anyway. At least being frozen slows down the eating experience. You know, the dose makes the poison and all that."

Ethan and I both grabbed a stack of chocolate boxes. I shoved a teacherly pile of Lean Cuisines way into the back, and we packed as much of the confiscated chocolate into the freezer as we could.

"Sugar high, sugar high," I said as the chocolate kicked in.

"Sugar high, sugar high," Ethan said. We jumped up and down like preschoolers.

"That felt good," Ethan said when we finished. "I always wondered why the kids did that."

I nodded. "Yeah, it totally intensifies the chocolate experience. Those kids have some pretty good tricks up their sleeves."

I spun the coffee carousel. I closed my eyes while I picked a pod. Because life was a crapshoot. Either you got lucky or you didn't.

"So," I said while the Keurig was spitting my coffee into a mug. "How did your planning meeting go with Polly after school yesterday?"

"She had other plans." Ethan closed his eyes and spun the coffee carousel. "You don't happen to know what they were, do you?" He said it like it was a casual question, but I could tell it wasn't.

"She and my dad came home together," I said. "So I wouldn't worry about it. He was probably just proposing to her again. You know, so her baby can have a good Irish name."

"Great," Ethan said. And then he walked out the door without even waiting for his coffee.

Polly smiled politely whenever I looked her way. When you really like your teaching assistant, this is as insulting as if she had stuck out her tongue at you. Or given you the finger.

I wasn't the only one not having a good day.

"Do you have any kings?" Max asked Pandora, who was seated across from him at the other end of a rolled-out mat.

"Go Fish," Pandora said.

"I don't want to Go Fish," Max said.

"You have to," Pandora said. "That's why they call it Go Fish."

Teacher radar alerted, I sidled up to them, far enough

away to give them space to work it out on their own, but close enough to swoop down if I saw signs of impending bloodshed.

I glanced at Polly. She ignored me.

"Somebody call my Nanny Meghan on her cellphone so I can win," Max yelled.

I swooped. "Remember our rule," I said calmly. "Whining stops the game, and everybody loses."

Max let out a yelp like he'd been kicked. "I don't want to stop the game. I want to WIN!"

"We all want to win," I said. "But life doesn't work that way. Now shake hands and tell Pandora that next time you look forward to being a good sport."

"Poop face," Max said as he stuck out his hand. It was unclear whether this was directed at Pandora or me. Possibly both.

"You do you, Boo," Pandora said as she shook Max's hand.

I thought this was pretty philosophical for a five-year-old, even if she'd probably gotten it from a movie she wasn't technically old enough to watch. It was like whatever Max said couldn't touch her—because while Max was doing Max, Pandora was on her side of the mat doing Pandora. *You do you, Boo.* Maybe that could be my new mantra. As opposed to *You screwed up, Sarah.*

"Max . . ." I said. "We're waiting."

"I look forward to beena good sport," Max said.

"Good job," I said.

"Poop face," Max said. This one was definitely directed at me.

Pandora looked up at me. "I hope you get paid good money for this," she said.

I kept my mouth shut, since I knew it would be unprofessional to say *I wish.* It would be even more unprofessional to sit down on the mat beside a five-year-old and tell her that not only did the money suck, but the truth was that teaching was getting more challenging every year. It wasn't the kids that were the real problem. All my students were doing as well as they could be, given the parents they had to work with. It was the parents whose issues appeared to be escalating.

Helicopter parents, who used to hover over their kids to protect them, seemed to have given way to snowplow parents, who barreled through every obstacle in their kids' way so the kids didn't have to do it themselves. If their kids didn't play well with other kids, they plowed right over those kids and found more kids. If a game was too challenging, they, or the nanny, made it easier by letting them cheat.

If these kids didn't like their potatoes touching their meat at the restaurant, the parents sent it back and the kid got a new meal. That the waitperson had probably just separated the same meat and potatoes on the plate and then spit on it before bringing it back isn't the point, although maybe it should be. There are always consequences, even when parents try to snowplow them away to protect their children.

Children need to face obstacles. They have to get mad, frustrated. They need to know that life can be tough, and bad behavior has penalties. When they don't have these experiences, when everyone around them enables them, they manage to grow up without really growing up. Until one day they run head first into cold hard truth. It's a lot less cute at forty than it is at four.

If a child never loses at Go Fish, what happens when she or he gets out in the real world?

Chapter Thirteen

My brother Michael texted me just as I was starting up my car in the school parking lot.

Dropping kids at library. Need 2 kill time. Meet me at Morning Glories in 5 min.?

I decided not to be insulted by being chosen as his designated time killer. Instead I could look at it as the universe's way of keeping me from having to go right home to deal with John and his bad attitude.

Michael never asked me to get together with him unless something was wrong. So if I looked on the bright side, maybe whatever was going on with him would make me feel better about how I seemed to be hell bent on messing up my own life.

"Not bad," I said to my steering wheel. "See, I can be positive after all."

When I turned on the radio, The Hollies were belting out, "He Ain't Heavy, He's My Brother." I yelled along with the part about how the road is long with many a winding turn, exaggerating my turns as I sang. Not a smart February move. I skidded on a patch of ice, started to slide into the bushes, veered back to the road just in time. The Hollies were already singing the part about his welfare being of my concern, a good reminder that Michael was family, and I needed to be there for him. As far as fortune telling by radio went, it could be a lot worse.

Thinking about being there for someone made me think about John. Why was he so stuck on us getting married? It seemed to me we had enough on our plates already. Buying my family house together had been substantially less risky. Especially since my siblings had made us ask the guy we'd lawyer-shared with my father to add a clause saying that if John and I split up, I'd be able to buy him out by using the money that our dad had deposited into an account to automatically pay rent to us. John knew my sisters and brothers were just looking out for me, so he'd signed on the dotted line, no problem at all.

"It's not like it'll ever happen," he'd said. I wondered if he was still so sure.

The Temptations jumped in with "Ball of Confusion."

"Exactly," I said to the radio. I mean, a family house was one thing, but marriage was a whole other ball of confusion. I mean, if John and I split up now, I'd get to keep the house, not that I would necessarily want it, but it would be devastating. But if we split up after we got married, I'd have to face the humiliation that, as Britney Spears once sang, *oops, I did it again*. It would be mortifying, soul-crushing, proof positive that I wasn't good enough.

And for the rest of my life I'd have to hear from my sister Christine that I'd screwed up the girls' standing in the Hurlihy Family Divorce Race. Twice. I pictured all six adult Hurlihy kids lined up in the backyard on the 4th of July, one ankle tied to their spouse's ankle with torn strips of white sheets to make it a three-legged race. I'd be the only one without a spouse, so my family would tie my legs to each other. As soon as our dad yelled *Go*, I'd fall flat on my face as my nieces and nephews cheered and the dogs barked.

I pulled into the Morning Glories parking lot, skidded into a space, jumped out fast before "Ball of Confusion" stopped playing and I had to face another song.

The smell of late afternoon hot chocolate and freshly baked pie enveloped me like a hug as I walked in. It was toasty warm inside, so I slid off my puffy down coat as I walked toward Michael's button-top table.

"Holy cowser," I said as I got closer. "That's an aggressive shade of pink."

Michael looked down at the parka he was still wearing. "Phoebe gave it to me for Christmas. She says it's raspberry. She thinks I'm manly enough to pull it off."

"Of course, you are," I said, because it seemed like my best option.

Michael pulled his arms out of the parka. "How bad is it?"

"It's fine," I said. "If another guy walked in wearing it, we'd only make fun of him for a brief interlude."

"Thanks," Michael said. "I'll wear it for another week or two and then hide it in the back of the coat closet."

"Or stop by and I'll trip and spill some of the decoy boxed red wine we leave out for Dad on you. That stuff is rot gut— nothing gets it out."

"Rot gut," Michael said. "I remember when we used to say rot gut. I think it was about Boone Farms apple wine in high school though."

"That'll be our next step in the decoy department," I said. "Although I don't think Dad will fall for it. He has great radar when it comes to zeroing in on the most expensive alcohol he didn't pay for."

I leaned over to scratch Mother Teresa's chest. "Sorry, I didn't even see you, girl. I must have been blinded by all that pink." Mother Teresa wagged her tail so hard the button-top table almost went over.

Michael and I both grabbed the table top.

"How'd you get her in here?" I said. "I thought only the outside courtyard was dog friendly."

Michael shrugged. "Nobody said anything. I guess they didn't notice her. Right, Mother Teresa?"

Given that Mother Teresa was a St. Bernard rescue who weighed approximately two tons, with half that weight in drool, this was highly doubtful.

I leaned forward over the table and lowered my voice. "Well, if the waitress says anything, tell her she's an emotional support animal. One of the kids at school just tried that with his hamster."

Michael reached down to scratch behind Mother Teresa's ear. "Thanks for the tip. Did it work?"

"Almost," I said. "I'm pretty sure he'll be back with his lawyer tomorrow."

"The kid or the hamster?" Michael said.

"Both. They have separate representation."

The waitress came over. Michael ordered hot chocolate. I went with tea since I'd already eaten my weight in chocolate at school today.

"No dogs allowed," the waitress said when she came back with our orders. She bent down to put a bowl of water and a dog treat on the floor in front of Mother Teresa.

"Thanks," Michael said.

"Don't worry," I said. "She's an excellent tipper."

Michael and I sipped our drinks and looked at each other.

Michael leaned across the table and gave the top of my head a hard grind with his knuckles. If I had a nickel for every time one of my brothers showed their love by giving me a noogie, I'd be a wealthy woman.

"Ouch," I said. I mean, it was amazing I wasn't bald by now. "Mom, Dad, he's touching me," I added in my best retro whine.

Michael smiled his crooked smile, which always reminded me of my mother. That and his hazel eyes.

"What's up?" I said.

"I can't do it," he said.

"Can't do what?"

He shook his head, ran a finger around the mouth of his mug. "I asked Phoebe what she wanted for Valentine's Day so I wouldn't screw it up again, and she said she wants me to get a vasectomy."

I started to choke, spit a mouthful of tea back in my mug. "Wow. How do you wrap *that*?"

"Funny."

Growing up, Michael used to call his penis Duckie. He would talk to it while he played in the bathtub, and Christine and I giggled from the other side of the bathroom door. Sadly, I could already see the now grown Duckie tied up with a big red bow. Another horror to place next to the image of my brother-in-law's penis wrapped in Saran Wrap. I pictured St. Brigid and her cow handing them embroidered handkerchiefs to cover up. That helped a little.

Michael reached down to scratch behind Mother Teresa's ear. I leaned over to scratch her chest. Dogs were so much easier than brothers.

Michael hunched over, drummed the table lightly with his knuckles. "Annie and Lainie are getting older. We're not planning to have more kids. Phoebe's the one who's done the heavy lifting—two pregnancies, two births. She doesn't want to be on the pill anymore. It's my turn."

I nodded.

"I get it," Michael said. "And I thought I could do it. But when I was sitting in the examining room at Seaside—"

"Seaside," I said. "I thought that was an OB/GYN group."

Michael shrugged. "That plus everything that has anything to do with fertility, infertility, procreation, donation, whatever. Phoebe said it's like one-stop shopping, but with different waiting rooms, like the way they separate the dogs from the cats at the vets. And I figured it's a few towns away, so theoretically it's more private, and you won't walk in and realize you went to high school with half the waiting room."

"Except," I said, "that everyone you went to high school with is there, too, for exactly the same reason. When you live your life in a small town, you're always chasing the elusive myth of privacy."

"Exactly," Michael said. "I hadn't seen Swag Shaunessy in a dog's age. Three marriages, six kids. Said he was way past ready for the big snipperoo."

When my seventeen-year-old niece Siobhan found out she was pregnant, she'd decided to carry the baby and give it up for adoption. She also decided that John and I would be the perfect parents. Despite enough red flags to open a car dealership, eventually John got onboard.

We'd taken Siobhan three towns away to her first appointment at Seaside. We sat in the waiting room, not quite Siobhan's parents and not quite the parents of her baby-to-be. But I breathed a huge sigh of relief that even if it turned out to be too late to get pregnant myself, we'd end up with a baby after all.

And then we all found out that Siobhan had a tubal pregnancy, which needed to be terminated. She'd be fine, and I'd be fine, but I knew that every time we looked at each other, maybe forever, we'd both think of the baby that didn't make it. And every time someone mentioned Seaside, the memories would all flood back.

I shook my head to make them go away. "So what happened?" I asked Michael.

"They called me in for the initial consultation, and the nurse handed me this paper to sign saying that I understood that a vasectomy is a permanent solution. And it hit me right between the eyes that I couldn't do it. I mean, what if something happened to Annie and Lainie? How could I possibly live the rest of my life without kids?"

I bit my lower lip so I wouldn't react.

"Sorry," Michael said.

"No problem," I said.

Michael brought his mug halfway to his mouth, put it down on the table again. "It's not that I think anything's going to happen to them. But we're always just one phone call away from being brought to our knees, you know?"

"I know," I said. "Further proof that the Irish worldview is encoded in our DNA."

"And I know another baby couldn't possibly replace them. They're everything. There are parts of me in Annie and Lainie that are so much better in them than they are in me. That's a pretty incredible thing to get to see."

My eyes filled with tears. I casually looked up at the ceiling and blinked them away.

"And what if," Michael said softly, "Phoebe and I end up splitting up after all?"

"Or Phoebe dies," I said, just to be an active contributor. I mean, Phoebe was fine, but even when they were getting along, I never quite thought she deserved my sweet brother.

"Or she dies. And one day a long way down the road I meet someone else who wants to have kids." Michael cleared his throat. "It might even be a little boy this time. Not that I don't love having two girls."

"Shit," I said. "So what are you going to do?"

"I've got time," Michael said. "I don't think Phoebe was picturing me getting a vasectomy *on* Valentine's Day. Lots of guys schedule them for March Madness, you know, the NCAA Men's Basketball Tournament, so they can binge watch it on TV while they're packed in ice."

It was an oddly sexy image. I really was screwed up.

"I've even considered," Michael said, "that I could just pretend to get one and take my chances."

Even I could tell this was a really bad idea. "You can't do that. Faking a vasectomy isn't exactly like faking an orgasm."

Michael sighed. "Yeah, I guess."

"Just tell Phoebe you're not ready and then cook her a really nice dinner for Valentine's Day. Flowers and champagne might be a good idea, too. You have to go with your heart, Mikey."

Michael tilted his head. "Speaking of going with your heart, I saw John. At Seaside. He was just disappearing into an exam room, so he didn't see me. But it was definitely him."

"What?"

"I know it's none of my business, but are you and John really sure you don't want to keep trying to have kids?"

Chapter Fourteen

I was so freaked out I couldn't even answer my brother.

"Oops," I said instead. "I have to go. I forgot I have a . . . a thing."

I reached for some money.

"I got it," Michael said.

I threw a five-dollar bill on the table. "Mother Teresa's tip. She has a reputation to uphold." For the Hurlihy clan, glib was our family shield. We polished it until it shone. No matter what life hurled at us, no matter how upset we were, we always fired off a glib crack before we fell. Even if it wasn't a particularly good one.

"Sarah," Michael said. "Wait a minute."

But I was already halfway out the door. I made it into my car before I started to cry, which was a good thing. In February in Marshbury your stupid tears can turn into icicles on your cheeks in no time at all.

I drove along the already pitch-black backroads, the occasional yellow streetlight barely making a dent, pulled into the empty beach parking lot. Snowplowed piles of dirty ice dotted the asphalt like mini glaciers. Or like mountains of obstacles temporarily pushed away but still there, lurking until they could get a better shot at you.

When I opened my car door, I got a mouthful of frigid salt air. A gust of wind almost pulled the door out of my hands. I fought for control, finally managed to shut the door again. Even if I could remember how to find the flashlight on my cell phone, I knew a walk on the beach was out of the question. Too dark. Too cold. Too windy. I settled for banging my head against the steering wheel a few times for exercise.

At least Scruffy Dog wasn't still out there on the beach, trying to stay alive through the winter. Horatio had fallen in love with her the minute they'd set eyes on each other. I was completely onboard with making Scruffy Dog part of our pack. John, not so much. He'd been fantasizing about choosing a breed as a way of choosing desirable charac- teristics.

I knew I had lots of undesirable characteristics. I was a bad girlfriend, for starters. I was probably a worse wife, so there was that.

But I'd thought John loved me, the way he'd learned to love Scruffy Dog despite her lack of pedigree. John had agreed with me about taking a break from all the stress of trying to get pregnant until the final stage of the renovations was completed. As soon as we had enough of a thaw, my brother-in-law Joe would get that new garage built in the blink of an eye, because if he didn't, I'd make sure Christine was all over him.

Then John and I would have a separate staircase that led from the new garage up to our private quarters, a foolproof way of avoiding my family when they showed up uninvited. Maybe we could even add a kitchenette and we'd never have to go downstairs again unless we were feeling particularly chipper.

We'd live happily ever after in our own little cocoon. And

I'd be able to commit, fully commit, to trying my hardest to get pregnant. If it didn't happen, I'd find a way to deal with the loss. Because being too frozen with fear to really try didn't seem to be working so well for me.

Last I checked, we'd just pressed Pause. So how had John given up on having a baby before I did? He wasn't exactly a go-off-and-get-an-impulsive-vasectomy kind of guy. Or maybe I only thought I knew him. If he was having baby doubts, couldn't he just wear a condom until they passed? Or ask me to dust off my diaphragm?

A pair of headlights lit up my rearview mirror. Great, probably a couple of teenagers pulling in to make out. Sure, they'd have fun tonight, footloose and fancy free. But wait till they found out what the rest of their lives had in store for them.

The car pulled in right next to me. My life being my life, it would be just my luck to end up next to a pair of exhibitionists. I hoped they'd at least have the decency to keep the lights turned off when they had car sex.

Out of the corner of my eye I saw the passenger window lower. The interior light came on.

I lowered my own window.

"Seriously?" I said into a mouthful of frosty air. "You're stalking me *again?*"

"Of course, I'm not stalking you," my former marital misstep said. His lips kept moving, but the wind blew the next words away. There were times in our marriage when I would have killed for that.

I fanned out one hand behind my ear and shook my head.

Kevin pointed across me to the passenger seat of my car.

I hit my lock button, shook my head some more. I actually found my cellphone flashlight by swiping up on my phone screen, turned it on, pointed it at him like a weapon. *Whatever it is*, I mouthed, *text it to me.*

In the circle of light, I watched Kevin write a text message on his phone, hunting and pecking with one index finger instead of using his thumbs, which probably drove Nikki crazy. I bet she hadn't realized what a dinosaur, a luddite, he was when she first started screwing around with him.

His text beeped into my phone.

You've been in my thighs.

WTF, I texted back. My car was still running, or I'd be frozen solid by now. I got ready to slam it into reverse and hit the gas, just in case Kevin had completely lost it. *Wasband Gone Wacko*, the headline in the *Marshbury Mirror* would read.

I watched him read my text, look up at his own. He started shaking his head and trying to write another text at the same time. He gave up, shoved his car door open, ran around to my passenger door.

I lowered the window maybe an inch.

"Thoughts," he yelled. "Thoughts. You've been in my *thoughts!*"

"Gotta love Autocorrect," I said. "It's like karma on steroids."

Kevin grabbed my door handle. I imagined his bare hand freezing to it like a tongue to a Popsicle, me driving through the dark streets dragging him along beside my trusty Civic. It didn't give me quite as much pleasure as it once would have. It was hard to tell whether this was a sign of growth or lethargy.

I unclicked the passenger lock. Kevin opened the door.

"Try anything and I'll kick you in the balls," I said.

"Got it," he said as he climbed in.

We sat there for a moment, the windows fogging up some more from my ex-hole's hot air.

This beach parking lot had history. When we were growing up, it had been practically a Marshbury High School graduation requirement to go parking there at least once. I was a late bloomer, just as happy to daydream about the ordinary boys I imagined into something more, than to actually talk to one of them. My sister Carol found this endlessly annoying, so she harassed me nonstop until I finally agreed to let her fix me up with the younger brother of some guy she was dating.

The moment he showed up in his parents' car to pick me up, I could tell his brother had badgered him into it, too. We drove around listlessly until it was dark, then pulled into the beach parking lot. And spent the rest of the night identifying the couples in the cars that pulled in, like we were contestants on some kind of pathetic game show for losers. Finally, he pulled out the condom his brother had donated to the cause and blew it up like a balloon. We batted it back and forth to each other, the high point of the night. And then he drove me home, kiss-less.

So sitting there in my car with my biggest mistake wasn't even the oddest thing that had happened to me in this parking lot.

"I tried to find you at dismissal," Kevin said.

"Thanks for missing me," I said.

"At dismissal," I added. I'd meant it as an insult, but it had come out sounding a little bit weird.

"I found this postcard." He pulled it out of his coat pocket, handed it to me word-side-up.

The flashlight on my phone had somehow disappeared again, so I flicked the switch on the overhead light.

Hey, I really miss you—how 'bout that?
Love, S

"Remember?" Kevin said. "That teacher conference you went to in Boston that summer? I thought it was pretty romantic that you sent me a postcard from twenty-five miles away."

"Especially for me," I said.

"Especially for you," he said.

I turned the postcard over. *Greetings From Boston.* Same generic beach scene—a sepia shot of an entrance to the beach marked on either side with weathered wood storm fencing, the kind used to protect sand dunes. With all the tall buildings and historic monuments and gorgeous waterfront in Boston, this is what I'd picked.

Kevin swiveled his head to face me. "Nikki found it rolled up in some gym shorts I never have time to wear to the gym anymore. She thought you might want to add it to the post-card collection at school."

I shook my head. "That's just disturbing on so many levels." Once, when Nikki was trying to find John and me a new house to buy without being asked, she'd returned some old CDs to me via John. They were my finds, my special songs, and I'd left them behind because Kevin had ruined them for me. Back before our marriage had crashed and burned, Kevin and I used to dance around our bedroom before we made love. Old standards always, slow and roman-tic. Diana Krall singing "I've Got You Under My Skin." Eva Cassidy's version of "Cheek to Cheek." Bonnie Raitt's "I Can't Make You Love Me," which turned out to be truer than true.

"Nikki's not so good with limits," Kevin said.

"Ya think?"

I turned on the radio to push those old songs out of my head. Al Green was singing "Let's Stay Together." I turned the radio off again, fast, so it wouldn't count as fortune telling by radio. And before Al got to the part about why people break up, then turn around and make up.

"Hey," Kevin said. "I like that song."

"My car, I control the radio, pal."

"Fair enough. Hey, you don't happen to know how to get rid of a text message, do you? That thigh thing isn't going to fly too well with Nikki next time she goes through my phone."

"Change your password and don't give it to her."

"Like that would ever work with Nikki."

I held out my hand for his phone, deleted the whole thread. "Next time try Googling how to do it. Or ask your three-year-olds. They're probably pretty phone savvy by now."

"Thanks. Nikki insisted on getting me a new phone for Christmas. I'm barely functionable on it."

"Functional," I said. "There's no such word as functionable. Unless my father says it."

"You always said the only thing your dad and I had in common was a creative vocabulary."

"That didn't make him like you any more."

"Even after we were married, I was never quite sure if he really didn't remember my name or just pretended not to."

"Good riddance to bad rubbish," I said in my best Billy Boy Hurlihy imitation.

"Yeah, well, he totally ripped me off when he showed up with that check to buy me out on our house for you."

"Oh, puh-lease," I said. "Nikki got a hefty commission when she sold it for me without being invited, so I'd say you made out in the end."

"Yeah, I have to admit I felt pretty good about that. Nikki's got her issues, but she sure knows how to close a deal."

"Given the history," I said, "I am so not going to touch that line."

We sat for a moment in an oddly companionable silence, something we'd never been able to master for long when we were married. Just for a split second, I almost liked him.

"Hey," I said. "This is purely theoretical, but would you ever consider going off and getting a vasectomy without telling Nikki?"

"Hell, yeah."

"Really?"

Kevin yawned. "I should have done it after the twins. My body, my decision. If I'd talked to Nikki first, she never would have let me do it. She has this thing about how having three kids is on trend right now."

I yawned back. "It's important to follow the dictates of fashion when it comes to your progeny."

"Progeny?"

"Offspring."

"See, how could I ever compete with that vocabulary. You know, I should have had those babies with you. You just never made things easy."

"That's my jam," I said.

I pictured Nikki dying from the complications of an après-third-child tummy tuck. Not my kindest fantasy, but since she'd screwed around with my hasbeen while we were still married, even St. Brigid and her cow would probably cut me some slack. Not that Kevin wasn't ultimately culpable, since he was the one who was married to me during said screwing around, not Nikki.

But I loved kids, so once Nikki was dead and buried, I pictured Kevin talking me into getting back together and helping him raise the twins and the new baby. We'd have to find a workaround for the twins' names though, since calling one after each of their parents was the ultimate in vanity. And those kids were out of control, even the baby, but I had exceptional skills and I was pretty sure that with firm, clear limits, I could turn them around.

Another car pulled into the parking lot, its headlights passing over my car as it pulled into a slot closer to the beach entrance. I followed the action as if Kevin and I were watching a giant movie screen at one of the last remaining drive-in theaters.

John jumped out of his car, followed by Horatio and Scruffy Dog.

"Holy insert swear word here," I said.

I closed my eyes, as if I might luck out and it would make me invisible.

Horatio caught the scent of my car first and started barking like a maniac. Scruffy Dog joined in.

John turned the big flashlight he was holding right at my wasband and me.

Chapter Fifteen

"Get down," I yelled.

For what it was worth, Kevin ducked.

I jumped out of my car like I'd been shot out of a cannon.

I jogged over to John. "Hey," I yelled into the biting cold. "You'll never guess who I just ran into."

The dogs jumped up on me, their claws digging into my quickly freezing thighs. *You've been in my thighs* flashed into my head, and I smiled before I could stop myself. I wondered if there would ever be a time that I could tell that story to John and he would think it was funny. Probably not.

John's flashlight was still pointing at my car. "Your car is still running," he yelled over the wind. "And do you want to tell me why your ex-husband is in it?"

Horatio and Scruffy Dog started pulling John toward the nearest vertical surface so they could pee on it.

"Sure," I yelled. "As soon as you tell me why you scheduled a vasectomy without discussing it with me first. Last I checked we were hoping to have children."

"Last I checked you were still making excuses about why it wasn't the right time."

"Yet," I yelled. "It wasn't the right time *yet.*"

"And so you called your ex to rendezvous in a dark parking lot?"

Even though we were standing practically nose-to-nose, it was still almost impossible to hear each other. It occurred to me that some of this might have been about the February wind, and some of it might have been about us.

The dogs dragged John in the direction of the boardwalk entrance to the beach. I jogged a few steps to catch up. I almost reached for one of the leashes, but it seemed too civilized a move. Or maybe too domestic, something I was apparently never going to be able to pull off.

I glanced over my shoulder instead. Kevin must have turned off the engine because my car was dark now. Under the dim parking lot lights, I could just make out my wasband's car rolling toward the street with the headlights off.

"Who told you I'd scheduled a vasectomy?" John yelled.

"My brother Michael," I yelled. "He saw you going into an exam room."

"Of course he did," John yelled. "And it made the rounds to the rest of the family within, what, nanoseconds?"

I thought about defending Michael. I was actually pretty sure he hadn't told anyone but me. Unlike Christine, and maybe even Carol, who would have called their way right through the family tree with a tidbit that juicy.

But it seemed to me that the bigger point was that John hadn't denied it.

Yelling in the freezing cold is probably a great antidote for frostbite, but it only lasts so long. Anxiety rose in my chest, fighting the cold for space.

John and the dogs trudged ahead. I turned back toward the parking lot. Turned around again. Considered spinning like a top until I figured out which way to go.

I would have loved to look up and find the north star for direction. But there weren't even any stupid stars in the sky.

"Anyone?" I yelled to the vastness, like the preschool

version of the economics teacher in *Ferris Bueller's Day Off.*
"Anyone?"

The dogs reversed direction and started pulling John back
toward the parking lot. I bent down, gave them each a quick
scratch behind the ears.

"You poop head," I yelled at John. And then I ran back to
my car.

———

It wasn't my best parting line, although to be completely
honest, it probably wasn't my worst either.

I drove straight home and threw a casserole in the oven
because it seemed to me that the least of my problems was
what John thought about my inability to commit to cooking.

I fed Pebbles and the kittens, curled up with the kittens on
my lap in the family room, Pebbles sitting off to the side of us
at a comfortable formerly feral distance. I flipped through the
channels, finally settled on an ancient episode of *I Dream of
Jeannie.*

Jeannie was definitely objectified, but she didn't seem to
mind it, and that pink and red harem costume was skimpy but
flattering. I'd once read that Barbara Eden had actually been
pregnant during the first ten episodes, which explained all
those extra veils they kept piling on. The sexual tension
between Jeannie and Tony was pretty hot, too, at least until
they got married and ruined the whole show.

The cats and I finished watching one episode and jumped
right into the next one, "The Americanization of Jeannie."
Jeannie is obsessed with a magazine article that explains how
to become the perfect American woman. She hopes to impress
her Master with her amazing domesticity, but everything she
tries turns into a catastrophe. It was her own damn fault for
reading that stupid article in the first place. And I had to
admit that I also had a real issue with the whole Master thing.

"Get over him, Jeannie," I said. "No matter how hard you try, he's only going to go off and get a vasectomy without telling you anyway."

Pebbles looked over at me with her shimmery emerald eyes.

"I don't have to tell *you* it's a tough world out there," I said. I mean, Pebbles got her kittens, but it's not like the father even stuck around to help her out.

I paused *I Dream of Jeannie*, put the kittens down on the floor to play, checked the casserole. I figured it was warm enough, so I scooped some into a cereal bowl, grabbed a big spoon, carried it back to the family room to watch the rest of the episode.

The casserole turned out to be some kind of ground beef and broccoli concoction. There might have been cream of mushroom soup involved, too, but I was able to mostly ignore that because the whole thing was topped with about a million Tater Tots and sprinkled with cheese. It somehow managed to straddle the line between disgusting and delicious in a way that kept me teeter-tottering from bite to bite.

A gust of frosty air traveled all the way into the family room when John slammed the kitchen door. When I brought my empty bowl out to the kitchen, he was sitting at the kitchen table eating a solo sub from Maria's. I opened the refrigerator door to double check that he hadn't bought one for me, too. Nothing.

It was a low blow. In my family, you don't go to Maria's Sub Shop without buying for everybody. Plus extra to bring to school for lunch the next day.

I stood there, debating whether to throw my empty bowl in the sink or at John.

"I'd appreciate it if you'd put that in the dishwasher," he said.

"Oh, go vasectomy yourself," I said. And then I grabbed

the casserole from the counter and headed for my dad's mancave.

"Make sure you tell your father," John said. "Oh, wait, I'm sure he's already heard all about it by now."

The good news was that the vasectomy story seemed to have taken precedence over John finding me sitting in my car in the dark with the motor idling and my ex-hole in the passenger seat.

My father and I met, with perfect timing, in the tiny mudroom that separated his new quarters from the rest of the house.

"What a lovely surprise, darlin'," he said. "Fancy meeting one of my very favorite daughters here on this frosty winter's eve."

"Dad," I said, "you look like the Abominable Snowman." His nose and his cheeks were bright red, and his bushy white eyebrows had frosted over. "Come on, let's get some lukewarm food inside of you."

I opened the door to my father's place, plopped the casserole on the little kitchen counter. My father held out an open bottle of champagne and two champagne glasses in my direction, so I relayed those to the kitchen counter, too.

My dad kicked off his boots and hung his coat and scarf on a hook. Once he settled into the new recliner we'd given him for Christmas, I pulled the throw off his round bed and wrapped it around him.

I found an ancient cereal bowl in one of his new kitchen cabinets, scooped some casserole in, found a spoon, handed it to my father.

"Goodness gracious sakes alive," he said. "Do I detect the delectable aroma of Tater Tots?"

I plopped down next to him in the old recliner that he'd decided to keep after all. I imagined us giving him a new recliner every year until he had a whole row of them, one for each adult kid, while his grandchildren all circled around the edge of his round bed with the flashing LED lights. The inlaws and dogs would stake out seats on the new couch.

"You do indeed," I said. "And now I truly understand the meaning of *sinfully delicious* as it pertains to Tater Tots-topped casseroles."

"You always were the smart one, weren't you now," my father said. "Anything you put your pretty little head to, you could figure out lickety-split."

"Right, Dad. Not that I doubt your memory of my brilliance, but what's my name. Fast."

"We'll have none of that nonsense, Christine."

"You're good," I said. "Even I can't tell if you're kidding or not."

My father took a bite of casserole, closed his eyes while he chewed.

"Where did you get the champagne and the glasses?" I asked. "Tell me you didn't crash another book club meeting."

"Bite your tongue, darlin'. One of those shindigs was enough for me. Half those Hotsy-Totsies didn't even finish the book."

My father got another bite loaded onto his spoon, pointed to the champagne. "Be a good girl and pour me another glass. Get yourself one, too, while you're up and moving."

I had no problem being a good girl when champagne was involved.

As soon as I handed it to him, my father held up his glass. "'Ever tried. Ever failed. No matter. Try again. Fail again. Fail better.'"

"Wow," I said. "The story of my life, although I'm not quite sure I have the failing better part down yet. Samuel Beckett, by the way. Who knows her Irish writers?"

We clinked glasses, and then I met his Samuel Beckett with my own. "'Where I am, I don't know, I'll never know, in the silence you don't know, you must go on, I can't go on, I'll go on.'"

My father winked. "Well done, Carol."

"Ha." I took a sip of champagne. It had little crystals of ice in it. "Does this champagne have a story, Dad?"

"It most certainly does. I brought it to drink with your mother."

"You sat outside at the cemetery drinking champagne in this weather?"

"Your mother and I like to stretch our Valentine's Day to fill the entire month. So I wear my long johns on a regular basis and keep a lawn chair and a camp heater handy for just these peccadillos."

I tried to imagine John still drinking champagne with me after I was dead. I had a hard-enough time imagining him ever drinking champagne with me again while I was alive. I tried to picture myself ever forgiving him for taking my hope away by planning a vasectomy. I tried to imagine having the guts to ask him why, but I was pretty sure I didn't want to hear his answer. In theory, I was all for the idea of talking things through, but once I found myself in a worst-case scenario, it felt safer to keep my head buried in the sand.

"Dad, how did you and Mom manage to stay so crazy about each other? What was your secret?" I'd asked my father this question so many times.

"Well, I can't say I haven't cast an eyeball at that question a few times in my life," my father began like he always did. "It's one of the great mysteries of the world, how a saint like your mother ever fell for a flutter bum like me."

My father paused to sip his champagne and let the suspense build.

"But if I had to put it down to any one thing, the magic for me was that I never once stopped wanting to know what your mother thought about something. Couldn't wait to get home to tell her some silly thing or other. All day long, I'd be saving up stories to razzle-dazzle her with at night. Even now, when something happens, I think about how I'm going to tell it to her as soon as I crawl into bed. But I have to say that the best part now is remembering the good ol' times together, when every day was like the grand opening of a fresh new start. When it was all still in front of us."

He wiped a tear from his eye, took another sip.

"Tonight," he said. "I'm going to tell your mother all about this casserole. I won't mention the lovely lady that delivered it to thank me for our date. You mother's fine with me dating, she just doesn't like to hear all the terrifics."

Chapter Sixteen

Carol and I were sitting in her minivan in my driveway, eating heart-shaped chocolate lollipops I'd pilfered for us from the confiscated candy stash in the teachers' room.

"You called John a poop head?" Carol said. "And to think I was worried about your ability to sustain a mature relationship."

I shrugged. "In my defense, when you hear a phrase like that all day long at school, it does have a tendency to come out when you need it."

"I wouldn't worry about it," Carol said. "Nobody gets along in February. That's why they stuck Valentine's Day smack dab in the middle of the month—so you can patch things up with kisses and chocolate."

It had been a long kiss-less night last night, the chill in John's and my new old house giving the bitter cold outside a run for its money. At school today, Polly seemed to have retreated inward, there but not there. Even the kids were well-behaved and low-energy, almost as if they were hibernating. Midway through the day, another Samuel Beckett quote popped into my head.

The sun shone, having no alternative, on the nothing new.

I nibbled another piece off my chocolate lollipop to bring myself back to Carol's minivan.

Carol wrapped her lollipop up in its cellophane again, put it down, picked it up again, unwrapped it.

"I can't believe you brought me this," she said. "I should at least have a flat stomach when Brendan O'Donoghue sees me again after all this time."

"You're not really going to do this," I said. "It's ridiculous."

Carol put the lollipop down again and reached for her phone. "Of course, I am. I said I'd text him when I was on my way."

"Tell him he's been in your thighs," I said.

"What?"

"Never mind. Autocorrect joke. Listen, it's not worth the risk. I mean, what if Dennis just happens to show up?"

"Dennis is out of town on business. Dennis is always out of town on business. Where he could be doing anything with anyone."

"You don't really think that, do you?"

"Of course I don't, or I wouldn't still be married to him. But the point is that he could. While I'm trying to find a way to fit in my own work while spending my entire life driving the kids around in this stupid minivan because he's not home."

I pointed to an array of unidentifiable food objects in various stages of decay behind us. "You might want to clean it up a little before you get naked with Brendan O'Donoghue back there."

"Don't even say that. It would be just my luck to go through all this only to end up having minivan sex."

I smiled sweetly. "Just picture the nuns and Jesus standing outside the minivan crying. You'll be fine."

Carol put the phone down. She unwrapped the lollipop again and nibbled off a piece. "You're right. I'm far too evolved for this. It's just that sometimes I wish I'd met Dennis a little bit later, you know? I was still such a child back then."

"Judging by your recent behavior, you're still such a child now."

"Not helpful." Carol reached for the rearview mirror, angled it to get a look at herself. "Do I look okay?"

"Your lipstick's leaning a bit too much in the direction of dark chocolate, but other that you look great."

Carol flipped open a door on top of the console between us, rummaged around until she found a lipstick. While she wiped off the chocolate and touched up her lips in the mirror, I turned on the radio to get a reading on the adventure to come.

The Rolling Stones were singing "Wild Horses."

"Couldn't drag us awaaaaay," Carol and I sang at the top of our lungs. Apparently, we had our answer.

John came out the kitchen door, dogs on leashes. They all climbed into his car. John backed around us in the driveway as if he didn't see us. Drove off.

"Poop head," Carol and I sang in perfect sibling harmony.

"Okay then," I said. "We might as well go inside for a minute to thaw out. Maybe we can come up with a healthy alternative for you to this immature acting out. Wine or more chocolate?"

Carol put the whole lollipop in her mouth and made her eyes bug out. "There's not enough wine and chocolate in the world," she mumbled around the lollipop.

She kicked her minivan door open, so I kicked mine open, too. It felt a little bit like the suburban version of kicking open a saloon door in an old Western. Or like we were minivan vigilantes off to take matters into our own hands and kick some butt.

"What if you plan a big romantic Valentine's date with Dennis?" I said once we'd made it into the kitchen and I started handing out treats to the cats. "Siobhan will babysit the younger kids, right?"

"Dennis and I don't go out on Valentine's Day. It's total amateur night. Overcrowded restaurants and overpriced meals."

My hope was that if we kept talking long enough, I'd forget about my screwed-up life by focusing on my sister's.

"We could go get our bellybuttons pierced as an act of rebellion," I said. "Except that Siobhan and I already did that, so the whole idea has kind of lost its luster for me."

"I'm pretty sure she let hers close up."

"Yeah, me, too." I rested one hand on top of the layers of winter clothing that covered my bellybutton. "And honestly, it wasn't really worth the excruciating pain. How about a tattoo? Maybe on the inside of our forearms?"

"Or between two toes. That way my kids wouldn't see it."

"My feet are way too ticklish for that. And what's the point of getting a tattoo if nobody can see it?"

Carol was shaking her head again. "You're right. And it's not like my kids ever look at me anyway. Dennis doesn't even look at me anymore."

I could tell she was heading into wallow-world again, so I tried to redirect her. "What if you got a word or phrase tattoo? You know, sort of a mantra or a theme for your life. That's pretty hip right now."

"Yeah, you're such an authority on hip. What would you get?"

I closed my eyes to try to picture it. "I used to think I'd get TEACH PEACE. Lately it's more like I WILL SURVIVE."

"WANDERLUST," Carol said.

"I like it," I said. "It just hints at lust without being too in your face about it."

"Thanks for ruining my tattoo," Carol said. "Okay, how 'bout NEVER TOO LATE? That might be a little bit classier."

"What about ALL YOU NEED IS LOVE?" I said. "Although it would never fit between two toes. LOVE would definitely be a lot less painful. Or even AYNIL as an acronym."

"Funny," Carol said. "I am so not anal, by the way. My minivan wouldn't be this messy if I was."

I took a moment to get my own joke. I decided I could take credit for it even if it was unintentional. A joke was a joke, even a stupid AYNIL/anal joke. Like a horse was a horse, of course, of course, unless you were Mr. Ed.

"A cup of coffee at Morning Glories couldn't hurt," Carol said. "Lots of people reconnect with friends from high school."

"You were friends in high school?"

"No, but we could have been. I just didn't want to lead him on—"

"Because he had such a massive crush on you."

"Exactly. Plus, you need the postcards."

"Assuming the postcards even exist," I said.

Carol wrapped up her lollipop again. "Of course they exist. Who invents postcards?"

It was a good point. And if the postcards were real, I wanted them. "Okay, fine, but I have to go with you. I can be your wing woman."

We sat for a moment trying to imagine it.

"I think I'd like Sandra Bullock to play me in the movie," Carol said.

I considered this. "I don't think Sandy's doing movies like this anymore. She's upped her standards now that she has kids."

"Well, goody for her," Carol said. "My standards have always been high. Even before I had kids."

"Right," I said. "I've always said that about your movies."

Carol circled her head and did a major hair flip. "Maybe we should make a music video instead."

I'd been a preschool teacher so long I couldn't help myself. Carol whipped her hair around while I came up with the lyrics. I wrote them on a piece of paper I tore from the pad that John and I used to write notes to each other back when we were actually speaking.

Carol and I positioned ourselves in the wide center hallway, which had been the stage for countless plays and handstand and hula hoop contests while we were growing up and still got plenty of use from my nieces and nephews. The cats gathered around, hoping for more treats.

Yo, Yo, No, Go
You Keep the Valentine
I'll take the love

Tulum or Timbuktu
Whatever happened to me and you

Rappin' to the miss
Holdin' out for the kiss

breakup
makeup
shake up
screw up
wake up
throw up
sit up
turn up
giddy up

Yo, Yo, No, Go
You Keep the Valentine
I'll take the love

Tulum or Timbuktu
Whatever happened to me and you

Rappin' to the miss
Holdin' out for the kiss

breakup
makeup
shake up
screw up
wake up
throw up
sit up
turn up
giddy up

Carol stopped dancing. "Whoa, Nellybelle," she whispered. "Heads up."

"I think we already have that one," I said. I did a couple of bumps and added a long, slow hip circle.

When I looked up, John was standing in the doorway to the kitchen with the dogs.

"Oh, hi," I said.

"Excuse me," John said as he walked by us to get to the stairs.

"That was for our music video," I said to his disappearing back. "It wasn't about you."

Chapter Seventeen

Because Carol was an event planner, her occupation had a tendency to spread all over everything. It was a lot like the ocean at high tide, but more unwavering.

Once we got to Morning Glories, Carol cased the place as if we were planning a robbery. She made sure we were fully ensconced at the best available table with the most flattering muted lighting coming in through the nearest window. Carol dragged a third mismatched ice cream parlor chair over to our tiny round button table. She pulled out a mirrored compact and added another layer of lipstick. She checked her teeth, then put the lipstick and mirror away. She fluffed her hair.

She ran out to her minivan, came back with a single yellow rose, draped it across the table.

"Really?" I said.

Carol grinned. "It worked for Dad when he dated you."

The fact that I'd once accidentally answered my father's personal ad would never go away. I mean, like it couldn't have happened to anyone.

"Funny," I said. "So funny I forgot to laugh."

Carol was too busy texting Brendan O'Donoghue to hear me.

He must have been cruising around waiting for her text because he arrived almost immediately. We watched him park his shiny red midlife crisis convertible where we couldn't possibly miss seeing it from anywhere inside Morning Glories. When he got out, he was coatless. His plaid flannel shirt was tucked in and he was wearing a scarf in a clashing plaid over it. He scooped a blob of slush off the hood of his car with one bare hand and flicked it into the parking lot. Even from here, I could tell his Facebook profile picture was even older than Carol's.

Brendan O'Donoghue ambled in like he owned the place, the waist of his man jeans cinched where his waist used to be. He walked toward us with no hesitation at all. He grabbed the empty chair we'd left for him, turned it around and straddled it. It was not a good look.

"Hey, girls," he said.

"Hay is for horses," Carol and I both said at once, without even planning it.

Brendan O'Donoghue looked a little bit like Dennis crossed with a troll. Not the internet variety, but the kind of troll with hair that stuck straight up that we used to put on the end of our pencils.

Nothing against old trolls. I still had some of mine packed away. But what was left of Brendan's over-processed dyed orangey hair was less than appealing, even if you looked at it through the rose-colored glasses of high school. In and around his troll hair, what looked like little Xes were sewn into his scalp. I pulled up my phone surreptitiously and Googled it under our tiny button table. Just as I'd suspected, his patch-work scalp was the result of a failed hair transplant. I wondered if his doctor had made the fatal mistake of using actual trolls as hair donors.

"Wow, two for one," Brendan O'Donoghue was saying when I looked up again. "So which one of you is Carol?"

Carol pointed to me.

"Cute," I said.

Carol held out her hand. "I'm Carol. Nice to see you again, Brendan. And this is my sister Sarah."

"Order what you want," he said. The highest priced item on the Morning Glories menu was a sandwich. "It's on me. Even though I was only expecting one of you."

We threw fiscal caution to the wind and ordered hot chocolates all around.

Brendan held up his mug. "To the best times of our lives. May the memories live forever."

We clanked our mugs to his, in spite of the fact that I didn't exactly echo the sentiment. As far as I was concerned, high school had been just something to try to live through.

We all sipped politely, except for Brendan, who actually grunted like a troll with his first slurp. When he put his mug down again, he had a full-on whipped cream mustache.

Carol and I both handed him a napkin at the same time.

"Thanks," he said. He took them both, wiped his mouth with one, blew his nose with the other.

If I'd had a nose-hair trimmer with me, I would have handed him that, too. The good news was that there was no way my sister was going to screw up her marriage by sleeping with this guy.

"So," he said. "Divorced or on your way?"

"Happily married," Carol said. She picked up the yellow rose from the table, held it against her heart. "He still sends me flowers."

"Can I have my postcards?" I said.

Brendan took another troll slurp. It might have been my imagination, but his ears even looked a little pointy.

"Gotcha," he said when he came up for air. "No postcards."

I glared at him.

"Don't worry about it," he said to Carol. "I just signed up for a Tinder account anyway. Maybe you girls can help me out. I keep swiping left by mistake and losing the good ones."

"I think there's an undo button if you have the paid version," I said. "Not that I would know from personal experience."

"Much," Carol said.

We helped Brendan O'Donoghue swipe right on a few possibilities, women we all might have gone to high school with. I was hoping we'd find someone more troll-like for him, maybe with straight-up pink or purple hair, but he seemed satisfied, so I didn't pursue it. Mostly I was thankful that, at least for the moment, I no longer had to try to stay up-to-date on dating. Or even, horror of horrors, had to go out there and date again.

"Well." Carol reached for her purse. "We'd better get going. We have a—"

"—a thing," I said.

"You girls can leave a tip," Brendan O'Donoghue said.

"I have a tip," I said. "You might want to lose the slurp before your next date."

"He meant money," Carol said as she dropped some bills on the table.

"Oops," I said.

Carol and I waited until he pulled away before we climbed into her minivan.

"It's just," she said, "that there's no sense telegraphing the fact that I drive a minivan."

"Yeah," I said. "You wouldn't want that to get out."

We buckled our seatbelts, lost in our own thoughts.

"Sorry Brendan O'Donoghue didn't pan out," I said.

"Bummer," Carol said. "It was like a romantic comedy with the wrong ending."

I sighed. Even in the minivan, I could see my breath. "What I'm really afraid of is that it's going to turn out that all of life is like a romantic comedy with the wrong ending."

Carol unwrapped the rest of her chocolate lollipop. "I don't know, the good news is that Dennis is looking pretty hot to me now."

"Yeah," I said. "Next to that guy, Dennis is a total Hunkasaurus Rex." I didn't even like Dennis, so coming from me this was high preschool teacher praise indeed.

"See? So you could say that, in a way, Brendan O'Donoghue gave me my life back."

I reached for the rest of my chocolate lollipop. "Sure, let's go with that."

"'Yesterday is gone,'" Carol said. "'Tomorrow has not yet come. We have only today. Let us begin.'"

"Sister Sledge?" I tried.

"Mother Teresa," Carol said.

I squinted. "Michael's Mother Teresa?"

"No, the real one. And Michael needs to find a new name for that dog. One that isn't blasphemous."

"It's probably only a venial sin, if that," I said. "And I bet the first Mother Teresa would think it was sweet to have a St. Bernard namesake."

Polly's car drove in, crossed the parking lot and pulled into a space in the back corner. She got out, pressed both palms against her lower back for a moment. A wave of guilt washed over me. Polly was pregnant and alone. I was supposed to be there for her, and I'd been practically ignoring her at home and at school. I couldn't even remember why I'd aimed my bad February attitude at her in the first place. I should be planning her baby shower, making sure she had everything she needed, pulling together a village to help raise her baby once it was born.

"Is that Polly?" Carol said.

Before I could answer, the passenger door opened. And the really cute guy Polly had been sitting with in Kate Stone's office climbed out. The guy who should have been meeting with Kate Stone and me instead. He walked around to the driver's side, crooked an elbow. Polly smiled and looped her arm through his.

"Hot Cross Buns," I said.

"He certainly does," Carol said.

I could already feel myself spiraling, faster and faster, lower and lower, like riding the Whip-o-Whirl when we were kids and the Marshbury Carnival came to town in the summer. I hated that ride. Why was Polly in that meeting? If not for me, the goodness of my heart, she wouldn't even have her job. She had absolutely no experience, no qualifications, no business being a teacher assistant. And, I mean, who simply goes out there and gets pregnant, just because she wants a baby? And how about all those men swirling around her, lining up for a chance to step in and play Baby Daddy. My own father, for sure. Probably Ethan. Maybe my brother Johnny, if it didn't interfere with date nights in the trailer with his wife Kim. And now this new guy. How unprofessional. How extremely unprofessional to loop your arm through the arm of a possible parent-to-be at the school where you were lucky enough to have a job. Thanks to me.

When I tried to swallow down my rage, it only gave me heartburn. Or maybe that was all the chocolate.

"Wowser," Carol said. "He looks just like Blair Underwood. Why couldn't I have gone to high school with *him*?"

"Because he doesn't appear to be Irish American?" I said. "I mean, what were there, maybe three kids in your graduating class that weren't Irish?"

"He could be black Irish," Carol said.

I nodded. "If he hangs around Marshbury, he will be soon enough."

"Yeah," Carol said. "I noticed that even John is starting to look a little bit like a leprechaun these days."

"Better than an orange-headed Irish troll," I said.

Carol executed a perfect troll grunt.

I made a slurping sound.

The guy held the door for Polly as they walked into Morning Glories.

"Well," Carol said. "I guess the good news for our inheritance is that it doesn't look like Polly will be marrying Dad anytime soon."

Chapter Eighteen

Polly and I gathered the kids for circle time. Most of the heart-shaped stickers had disappeared by now—lost to foreheads and hands and pockets—so we'd gone with the flow once again and peeled off the rest of them. The kids and I were sitting on the regular brightly colored stickers that marked our places on the fluorescent pink circle.

Polly dragged one of the kiddie chairs to the circle, looked over her shoulder to gauge the distance, sat down with a thud.

"You're the beach ball of love, baby," Depp said to Polly's baby bump.

"You're having a beach ball?" Juliette said.

"This is how rumors get started," I said to no one in particular.

We began with Show and Tell. When it was her turn, Violet picked up a guitar that was worth more than a Bayberry teacher made in a month. Possibly even a year. It also appeared to have been signed by Taylor Swift, which I could only hope was just a joke.

Violet strummed the guitar. "When I was four years old, I got my first guitar. It changed my life."

Violet had just turned five. She strummed some more,

stretched her stubby fingers to try to make a chord. "I have what it takes to be the youngest contestant on *American Idol*. My mommy and daddy say that if I get good enough, they'll make them change the rules for me. Because the world shouldn't have to wait until I get to be thirteen."

Let's hear it for the snowplow parents.

Julian was next. He held out a postcard. GREETINGS FROM PROVINCETOWN, it said. Same beach scene.

"This is a rare postcard from A-B-C-town," he said.

I was pretty sure he meant P-town, but it was too cute to correct.

"My Uncle Bob wrote a love letter on it to my other Uncle Bob," Julian said.

"I have an Uncle Bob," Harper said.

"I have an Uncle Bob," Josiah said.

"Do you ever think you'll write a love letter like that to someone someday, Julian?" I said, partly to break up the chorus of *I have an Uncle Bob* from the rest of the kids.

"I think I'll just text her," Julian said.

The other kids nodded in agreement.

After Show and Tell, we passed around a big red stuffed heart and took turns telling everyone what we loved.

Depp held the heart to his chest and pumped it back and forth. "I'm the lover of love, baby."

"Thanks," I said. "But can you tell us all *what* you love, Depp?"

"Love, baby," Depp said.

Pandora was next. "I love my Barbie Jeep and my Barbie high heels. And my babysitter Megan, the good Megan who makes YouTube videos, not the other Megan. And imported chocolate truffles from the south of France, because when it comes to calories, you should never settle. And I'm worth it."

When it was my turn, I said, "I love the smell of my kittens when they're all curled up together in a sun puddle."

I passed the heart to Gulliver. ""I love the smell of my

hamster when it has a clean cage," he said. His lawyer sat behind him taking notes.

When Gulliver passed the heart to Polly, a tear rolled down her cheek.

"Are you okay?" I teacher-whispered, since Hot Cross Buns wasn't here to jump in and rescue her.

Juliette brushed a tear from her own cheek. "Are we sad crying?" she asked. "Or ugly crying?"

"I'm happy crying," Polly said. "I love listening to all of you. I love the way my baby gets to hear you, too. It's all too beautiful."

It's all too beautiful. It had been a long time since I'd heard those lyrics.

And for the rest of the stupid day, *Itchycoo Park* played over and over in my head like an endless loop.

⊏⊐

Even though I was relieved that my work day was almost over, I had to admit I wasn't all that crazy about the idea of going home. To bridge the gap, I grabbed a small box of chocolate from the teachers' room and brought it back to the classroom.

Polly had our Three Good Things notebook out and ready to go. Big deal.

I pulled up a kiddie chair across the table from her.

"You go," I said.

The kids were amazing, Polly wrote. She slid the notebook over to me.

There are only 6 gazillion days left in February, I wrote.

I slid the notebook back over to Polly.

I love working here, she wrote.

When I looked up, The Great Mighty Poo Poo was standing there.

"That makes one of us," I said.

"Sarah," Kate Stone said. "May I speak to you in my office?"

In the history of the universe, there was never a good conversation that began with *May I speak to you in my office.*

I took the box of chocolates with me for emotional support. If Gulliver could have an emotional support hamster, I figured I was more than entitled.

Kate Stone's desk was made from a massive freeform slab of redwood. Whenever I saw it, I imagined a long-ago chain gang of Bayberry teachers cutting down the entire tree with tiny preschool scissors during a hell-on-earth inservice program that would only end when they finally yelled *Timber!* The top of the desk had been polyurethaned until it was so shiny you could see how nervous you looked in the reflection. Which was probably the point.

I sat down, slid my chair a little closer to the desk, but not so close that the sweater my sister Christine had given me for Christmas would get snagged on the rough bark that still edged it. I'd promised myself that I wouldn't add the sweater to my work clothes rotation until next winter. But then I'd run out of clean clothes, so all promises were off. It was a decision I'd regret with the first splotch of preschool paint—if somebody ever tells you preschool paint is washable, don't believe it for a second.

I looked up, faked a smile, held out the heart-shaped box. "Chocolate?"

My boss pushed up the sleeves of her elderberry batik tunic, rested her elbows on the desk, laced her fingers together. "Let's get right to the point. Your new assistant teacher will begin training with you tomorrow."

"It's only February," I said. "Polly's baby isn't even close to being due. At least not *that* close. Wait, you're not vetting the resumés and giving me a choice, like you did with Polly?"

Super Bitch reached for her desktop Magic Eight Ball and turned it over with an obnoxious flourish. "It has already been decided," she pretended to read. She put it down again and brushed her hands back and forth once, punctuation for a done deal.

Already, Polly's perceived value was growing, like an old boyfriend, or even a wasband, whose faults faded more with each passing year. Polly was sweet and conscientious and hard-working. The kids were crazy about her. She had mad art skills. When she sat down, her thighs spilled over the edges of the kiddie chairs more than mine did now—granted she was seven months pregnant, but still. Polly never disappeared at the drop of a hat to meditate, like my former assistant June used to do. Sure, Polly was a bit of a man magnet, but every-body had something.

If I wasn't even allowed to get a vote, my new assistant could be anyone. She could be anything. My life could go downhill as fast as a waxed toboggan on a ski slope.

Kate Stone slid a resumé across the vast expanse of her desk to me. "Take some time to look it over this evening, Sarah. And make sure you're here on time tomorrow. I'm counting on you to set a good example."

I found Lorna in the teachers' room, pinching the bottoms of a box of chocolates.

"Don't judge me," she said. "Just start pinching."

"You are not going to believe this," I teacher-whispered as I put the resumé down on the table. "The Great Mighty Poo Poo just hired Polly's replacement without consulting me." I pinched the bottom out of some disgusting chocolate berry thing, tossed it in the wastebasket. "She starts training tomor-row. She could be anything. *Anything.*"

"The Great Mighty Poo Poo is mine," Lorna said. "I want full credit for that name." She popped a chocolate into her mouth, grabbed the resumé.

"Watch it," I said. "You-know-who will probably find a way to check it for chocolate fingerprints to make sure I haven't passed it around."

Lorna stuck out her chocolate-covered tongue. "So sue me. Half my students are doing it."

I tossed another faulty chocolate in the wastebasket.

"Wow," Lorna said. "Wow, wow, wow. She did it. Poo Poo Platter friggin' did it."

"Let me see that," I said. I grabbed the resumé away from Lorna, actually looked at it.

I could feel my mouth making a great big O without me even telling it to.

"Holy roly-poly cannoli," I said. "I can't believe she found a male applicant. What do they make up, like three percent of preschool teachers and assistant teachers in the country?"

"I think it's less than two-point-five," Lorna said. "A male preschool teacher is like a unicorn. The only reason we got Ethan is that he's her godson."

"And because no one else would hire Ethan," I said. "Which doesn't bode well for the new guy."

"First things first," Lorna said. "Not to be sexist, but I hope he's good-looking. I get a little bit bored drooling over Ethan all the time. Damien's a nice drool-worthy name."

"Sure," I said, "if you rule out *The Exorcist.*"

"I thought the Damien from *The Exorcist* was hot," Lorna said. "Too bad it's probably not the same one. A troubled priest who's also a psychiatric counselor might come in handy around here, especially for the teachers."

I was already Googling the new Damien's full name. I pulled up his profile picture on Facebook.

It was Hot Cross Buns.

Chapter Nineteen

"What's rarer than a unicorn?" I said.

"I don't know," Lorna said. "What *is* rarer than a unicorn?"

I was so overwhelmed I could barely speak. "A male preschool teacher who's also black. And extremely good-looking."

"I don't think there are even statistics for that," Lorna said.

"Especially the good-looking part," I said.

Lorna pinched a chocolate, lobbed it into the wastebasket. "It's like the perfect trifecta."

"Technically," I said, "it's a quadfecta."

Lorna counted out my new assistant's attributes on her fingers. "You're right. We should look into getting him cloned —we could make a fortune."

"He probably has no experience at all," I said. "I can't believe our bitch of a boss hired him. I'm the one who's going to have to train him."

"You made that sound so sexy," Lorna said. "Especially when I added the silk handcuffs in my head."

"Come on," I said. "Don't objectify him. Just because women have had to put up with being objectified for centuries."

"Fine," Lorna said. "I'll hold off until we're sure we don't like him. But I'm keeping the silk handcuffs."

In a big old new house in the middle of February, it's easy to prepare for the next day at work. Especially when your significant other isn't exactly speaking to you. And your father appears to be out on a date, or maybe even two. And your teaching assistant, who is soon to be your ex-teaching assistant and didn't even give you a heads up about her replacement, isn't home either.

John seemed to have relocated to the family room, so I sat in the kitchen at the pine trestle table and dug through my teacher bag for a notebook and a pen. Before I got started, I took a moment to trace my finger over the graffiti we'd all carved in the table as rebellious teenagers. Our initials. Our crushes. Our former crushes, crossed out. *Help, get me out of here. Take a chill pill. You're adopted, I'm not. Grounded for life. Wicked cool. Buzz off. Who cut the cheese?*

February sucks, I carved in an empty space with my pen. When I finished, I felt almost better.

I was sure Kate Stone had given the new guy the official Bayberry Preschool teacher assistant job description. But I wanted him to know that I had expectations, too, and this job was serious business, even for good-looking male unicorns of color. And it went well beyond the fact that most of his day would be spent cleaning up poop and puke and scrubbing Play-doh off tabletops. And eating lunch with the students, so the lead teacher could eat lunch with more intellectually stimulating company, theoretically anyway, in the teachers' room.

I began writing:

- *Our students will learn to recognize, identify, and express their emotions.*
- *Our students will learn to feel and express empathy.*
- *Our students will learn to engage socially and to build healthy relationships with others.*

I stopped then, because it hit me like a ton of bricks that I might really need to go back and be a preschool student again myself.

———

When I turned on the radio, The Surfaris were playing the original instrumental version of "Wipe Out." The fact that it didn't have lyrics seemed like I might be able to dodge a bullet as far as fortune-telling by radio went. But the lack of lyrics steered me back to the song title, and it was hard to read that as a good omen.

I actually made it to school early, so I had time to find my reading glasses and consider the conversation heart attached to the door. SNOW DAY, it said in pink writing on a tiny white heart. Oh, if only it were true.

Polly and Damien came strolling down the hallway together, not even pretending that they hadn't already bonded behind my back. I peeled the conversation heart off the door, handed it to Damien.

Damien held it out so Polly could read it, too.

"Eat it fast," I said, "before the word gets out and the teachers start stampeding the exits."

"No problem," Damien said. He threw it up in the air and caught it in his mouth.

I held out my hand. "Nice to meet you, Damien. I'm Sarah. I see you and Polly have already met."

He shook my hand like he wasn't afraid of women. When he smiled, it still didn't reach his eyes.

Damien sat in a kiddie chair in the back of the room for the first part of the morning. He was dressed in navy pants and wearing a dove gray sweater over a paler gray shirt with a collar. His face was recently shaved, and his hair was freshly gelled. His dark eyes were wideset, and his skin was the most gorgeous shade of chocolate brown. Even the small Blair Underwood-esque scars on his forehead and chin were sexy.

Polly kept herself a careful distance from both Damien and me. She worked the rest of the room, checking on kids, scrubbing surfaces. I sent her pathetic telepathic messages: *Why didn't you give me a heads up about him? How come you got to meet him first? Do you like him better than me?* Clearly, I hadn't gotten over being a middle child in my family.

When Damien crossed one leg over the other, Max ran over and tried to sit on his foot. "Can you be my new toy?" Max asked.

"No," Damien said calmly as he uncrossed his legs. "But you can probably help me with a wooden puzzle after I finish watching for a while."

"Watch carefully," Pandora said. "We're very important."

"I can see that already," Damien said.

"I got my first guitar when I was four," Violet said. "It changed my life."

"It's good to have a dream," Damien said.

"I'm the dreamer of dreams, baby," Depp said.

"Great to hear," Damien said.

"I have nightmares," Gulliver said. "My hamster does, too. That's why he sleeps in my bed."

"It sounds like the two of you are working things out together," Damien said.

I hated to admit it, but Hot Cross Buns had good instincts.

Then Polly went down to practice working at childcare while Damien practiced being Polly. For what it was worth, I practiced not feeling sorry for myself that I was losing Polly.

After I mastered that, I'd work on finding my inner empathy and the rest of the preschool classroom expectations.

"When in doubt," I teacher-whispered to Damien, "just clean something."

"Got it," he said.

A few minutes later, Max pushed himself up off the floor where he was helping Damien with a wooden puzzle.

"Sometimes I throw up," he said. And then he threw up all over Hot Cross Buns and the puzzle.

Damien climbed to his feet. He and Max stood there, vomit dripping off their faces. I handed them each a bunch of paper towels. Then I race-walked to the supply closet, grabbed our spillage and biologically hazardous materials bucket. I found the labeled spray bottle of bleach-and-water solution to spray on all contaminated services. I slid on a pair of disposable non-latex gloves, looped a big white chef's apron over my head. Grabbed a box of baby wipes.

"You're doing great, Max," I said as I race-walked back.

Damien held out his hand. "I've got it."

I'd already wiped up a career's worth of puke, plus Hot Cross Buns was already covered in it, so I didn't fight him. I grabbed him another pair of gloves.

While Damien cleaned up Max and himself, the other kids looked on, their faces alternating between empathy and glee. I found Max's Oops change of clothing bag. I stepped out into the hallway to call Max's mother Millie on my cellphone. Technically, we were supposed to keep our cellphones off for the school day and use our old-school wired classroom phones, but it was one of those antiquated rules that we pretty much ignored. The upside was that cellphones were much easier. The downside was that the parents had the teachers' cell numbers.

"Are you sure it was Max who threw up?" Max's mom said when she answered.

I rolled my eyes. "A hundred percent."

"I'm just about to step into a big meeting," Max's mom said.

"I'm just about to step into a classroom that reeks of vomit," I said.

"Twenty minutes?" she said.

"Make it ten," I said. "Or Max will be waiting for you in childcare."

"Good job, you guys," I said to Max and Damien as I stepped back into the classroom. "My bet is that one of you has kids of your own."

"Not me," Max said. He looked a little bit better, but I'd been fooled by student nausea that came in waves before.

"I do indeed," Damien said. "Two boys, two and three."

Damien was casually holding one finger in front of his nose to block the smell. It didn't have a wedding ring on it. Lots of married guys didn't wear wedding rings.

"Go," I said. "Go home and change and then come back. Make sure you jump in the shower first. Take it from me, don't make the change-only mistake—or you'll be holding your nose all afternoon. And so will the rest of us."

"Are you sure you'll be okay?" Damien said, as if we had another option here.

"I'm sure. Max's mom will be here in a few, and I can call Polly if I need her."

I reached out my hand. "Here, give me your phone."

He peeled off a non-latex glove, fished his phone out of his pocket, handed it over. I typed my number into his Contacts list.

"Okay," I said. "Now call me so I can save the number on my phone. Just in case we have to reach each other. Or if I feel an overpowering need to check to make sure you're not running for the hills."

Damien called me.

"What do *you* want?" I said when I answered.

The kids all laughed, even Max. Then they walked around the room, imaginary phones pressed to their ears, saying *Call me* and *What do* you *want?*

Max's mom Millie picked up Max with less than a minute to spare. She was dressed for success and tried to hug Max without actually touching him. I handed over his change-of-clothing bag, which now contained his pukey clothes. She hesitated for a moment, then took it.

"You're welcome," I said as they walked away. "Feel better, Max," I added.

I cracked a window and put shallow bowls of white vinegar wherever the kids couldn't spill and/or drink them to absorb the lingering smell of vomit. It worked-ish.

Polly came back without me even calling her. When it was time to take the morning kids outside for dismissal, I volunteered. I was grateful for the fresh air, even in February. I kept my puffy down coat unbuttoned, flapped it around a little to air me out.

Polly and Damien were sitting at the long table eating lunch with the full-day kids when I got back inside. Everybody was laughing. I felt left out, as if I wasn't in on some joke. Or as if I was suddenly invisible.

I thought about inviting Damien to eat the rest of his lunch with me in the teachers' room so I could introduce him to some of the teachers. But I was still feeling a little bit rocky, and I wasn't sure I could stomach leftover casserole. Or even confiscated chocolate.

I grabbed my teacher bag, put my coat back on, headed for the beach. I parked at the opposite end of the lot from last time, as if that might erase any residual memories of that visit.

The beach was beyond freezing, empty except for a few diehard dogs and dog walkers. But the wind was wild enough to blow the smell of vomit away. The sun was strong. I walked quickly, swinging my arms. The tide had turned and was getting higher with every wave.

By the time I'd jumped back in my car, I was hardly even depressed anymore. Which might be as good as it gets in February.

Chapter Twenty

Polly went back to childcare after lunch. Damien worked with some of the full-day students on a math game while I did a writing activity with the rest of them. Then Damien curled up with all the kids in and around our reading boat. He picked up *Hugs and Kisses for the Grouchy Ladybug*. It was a story about making the world a kinder place, one friend at a time.

It probably wouldn't have hurt me to hang around and listen to the book, but instead I gave Damien a thumbs up. I picked up today's small pile of postcards, pointed to the hall-way, held up my phone so he could see that I had it with me. It was important to let my assistant-to-be know that he was doing a good job. I'd leave him alone just long enough to tack up the postcards in the Arts Barn. Then I'd come right back for a rousing game of freeze dancing.

A third bulletin board had been rolled into the Arts Barn to make room for all the postcards that were coming in. I grabbed some unoccupied tacks, sorted through today's contributions.

One was labeled FUN FACTS and said that a letter written by a Maine teacher in 1931 to her mother 150 miles away had finally been delivered to the family 83 years later.

And everybody wondered why the post office was having issues.

Another postcard said GREETINGS FROM MONTANA. Same beach scene—a sepia shot of the sea with an entrance to the beach marked on either side with weathered wood storm fencing. My geography had some significant holes in it, but even I was pretty sure that although Montana was a beautiful place, it didn't have an ocean.

I felt his presence behind me before I saw him.

"Don't think I won't call the police," I said without turning around. "Because I will. And I'll probably even enjoy it. A lot."

"Hey there," my hasbeen said from his space on the floor by the lip of the stage. He closed his laptop, pushed himself up, took a few steps in my direction.

"That's far enough." I turned around and held out one hand like I was a traffic guard. Or one of the Supremes singing "Stop (In the Name of Love)."

"Relax," Kevin said. But he stopped. "I just wanted to check in to make sure I didn't get you in trouble at the beach."

It was an odd phrase to hear, since when we were growing up, the only girls I knew who got in trouble at the beach ended up with exactly what I wanted all these years later: a baby.

"Are you okay?" my wasband said.

"Huh?" I said.

"Do you want me to man up and go talk to John for you?"

"No, I don't want you to man up and do anything," I said. "Don't be so condescending. I can hang out at the beach with anybody I want to. And if anyone talks to John about anything, it's obviously going to be me." And, I didn't add, I have every intention of doing just that one of these days. Soon. Real soon.

"Fine," Kevin said. He took another step toward me, held out his hand, open palm up.

I unhooked my reading glasses from the front of my sweater, put them on, leaned forward.

MY FUNNY VALENTINE, a tiny pink conversation heart said in red letters.

"Did you leave the SNOW DAY one on my door this morning?" I said. "That was cruel."

He shrugged.

"No way. You're the conversation heart cupid?" I'd been so sure it was one of Polly's bevy of admirers.

Kevin nodded. "The one and only. At least as far as I know."

"Wait a minute. What about the PARIS, IT'S ALWAYS A GOOD IDEA postcard with the OOH-LA-LA heart?"

He shrugged again. "Yup."

"We never went to Paris," I said.

"Maybe we should have," he said.

"Sit down," I said.

We sat on the lip of the stage, our feet dangling over the edge like we were preschoolers.

I shook my head. "You have to knock this off, Kevin. I mean, I know I'm completely irresistible and everything—"

"See, Nikki would never say that. She never says anything funny. And she hasn't ever once laughed at a single thing I said."

It was my turn to shrug. "When we were married, I never laughed at anything you said either. You're just not that funny."

Kevin started to laugh. Then I started to laugh.

"See," he said.

That got us laughing even more.

Finally, we wound down. I sniffed, grabbed a tissue from a box tucked behind the stage curtains, handed one to my whatever he was.

"Thanks," he said. "Hey, did I ever tell you I'm sorry? For everything that, you know, happened."

"Nope," I said.

"Well—"

"Wait," I said as it hit me just how long I'd left Polly's replacement alone with my students while my ex baggage and I dangled our feet off the edge of the Arts Barn stage and strolled down memory lane.

I grabbed my phone, sent a quick text to Damien.

I glanced down at the text again to make sure my phone had actually sent it.

I'll be black in a minute.

"Noooo," I said. Seriously? What had I ever done to Auto-correct to deserve its wrath?

I jumped off the stage. Why, oh why, couldn't the Arts Barn stage have been a towering cliff?

"I have to go," I said. Kill myself, I didn't add.

"Wait," Kevin said. He reached into his pocket, handed me another conversation heart. I gave it a quick look: YOU'VE GOTTA SHOW UP.

"I'm sorry," my wasband said, "and I take full responsi-bility for the way it all went down. But I've been thinking about this a lot lately, and that's the one thing you didn't do. When we were together, you were never quite there, you never really showed up."

I was already walking away. If I could have kept walking past my classroom and out of the school and my life without my family tracking me down immediately, I might have done it. Just so I didn't have to face Damien.

I took a deep breath, cleared my throat. When I walked back into the classroom, the kids were curled up with indi-vidual work on a patchwork of yoga mats they'd rolled out on the floor. Nobody was roaming around aimlessly or fighting or vomiting. I could feel that beautiful hum that happens when kids are focused and learning on their own. It's every teacher's dream. It's why we do what we do.

Damien walked right over to me, his eyes aimed slightly above my head, his cheek muscles tense beneath his chiseled cheekbones.

I gestured for him to follow me, stepped just outside the door into the hallway so I could still see the kids.

"I got your text," he said. "I'll be filing a formal complaint this afternoon."

My heart stopped beating, then started up again in triple time.

"Please forgive me," I teacher-whispered. "It wasn't even a Freudian slip. It was that damn Autocorrect. Not that I don't take full responsibility for hitting Send."

Damien held his expression until his eyes started to water. "You'll be black in a minute," he teacher-whispered back. "And here I was worried that I'll be Irish in a minute."

After the kids had gone home for the day, Damien and I sat at opposite ends of the reading boat. I had the Three Good Things notebook clasped in my arms, and he had one of the nautical-striped reading boat pillows clasped in his. I'd just finished apologizing for either the thirteenth or the fourteenth time.

"So how did it go with the kids while I was gone?" I asked, mostly to break up the apologies.

"Let's see," Damien said. "Pandora asked me if I was married to Rosa who cleans her house, but other than that it went pretty well."

"Yikes," I said. "If it makes you feel any better, Pandora once asked me if I thought I'd be an old maid until I died. And we weren't even playing the card game."

"Thanks," Damien said. "That actually does make me feel better."

"Here's the thing," I said. "The environment children are exposed to in their first years of education has a profound effect on how they view the world for the rest of their lives. You're going to be a huge part of that."

Damien nodded.

"Holy crap," I said. "I really am sorry about that text. And I promise you this is the last time I'll apologize. At least for today."

"I can't even tell you," Damien said, "how much I needed a good belly laugh like that."

"Well," I said, "thanks for making me suffer for a moment before you caved. It really helped my lapsed Catholic sensibilities."

He shrugged. "I totally get the suffering thing."

"Once," I said, "someone I know sent me a text that said *You've been in my thighs*."

"Good one," Damien said.

I almost added that before John and I bought my family house, we once looked at a house for sale because of a typo that said it had a huge dick for entertaining. If Damien had been a woman, I probably would have said it. But with a guy, it seemed like you should wait until you know for sure he's not going to turn out to be a creep before you let down your guard like that. Come to think of it, I probably should have waited on the thigh thing, too.

"So, tell me the truth, Damien," I said. "What's a nice unicorn like you doing in a place like Bayberry? I mean, how did our b——, Kate Stone even find you?"

Damien flipped his pillow up in the air, caught it. "A teacher job fair in Boston. I'd been working on my early childhood education certification, so I figured I should check out the options. I was wandering around aimlessly, feeling the overwhelm, and we bumped right into each other."

"Ha," I said. "I've been working for her long enough to know that she totally orchestrated that."

Damien grinned. "Yeah, I got that. But it was still pretty smooth. We had a cup of coffee together. I handed her my resumé and told her my story, and she told me if we could work out the details and my background check and references cleared, I had a job."

"So you already lived in this neck of the woods?" I asked. "I mean, you're clearly within run home and shower off the puke distance."

"Yeah," he said. "We just found a place in Scituate. My sister already lives down here. She was a METCO student in high school."

METCO stands for Metropolitan Council for Educational Opportunity. It's the longest running voluntary school deseg-regation program in the country. Its purpose is to expand educational opportunities, increase diversity and reduce isola-tion by allowing students in Boston and Springfield to attend public schools in other communities that have agreed to participate. Most of the Irish Riviera participates in METCO and helps fund it within its public schools.

"So," I said. "Were you a METCO student, too?"

"No way," Damien said. "My sister's a couple years older than I am, so I saw all the pain she went through. Insanely early mornings with long bus rides, not being able to do lots of the afterschool activities because she'd miss the bus ride back home. And I think she felt pretty isolated. You want to feel your color, try going to high school on the Irish Riviera."

He pulled one hand away from the pillow, looked at it. Raised his eyebrows.

"Brave," I said. "Both of you." I took a moment to wish that I'd paid more attention to the METCO students I'd gone to high school with instead of being so caught up in my own feelings of isolation and angst and self-pity.

"Anyway," Damien said, "my sister got the high-level

advanced classes she was looking for, and my parents were able to keep her out of trouble with those long bus rides, which is what they were looking for. When it was my turn, I tested for the Boston public exam schools, lucked out and got into Boston Latin, so that was my out."

"Impressive," I said. "But your sister liked it enough here to come back and settle down?"

"Her first job after college, she ended up working with this guy she'd had a couple of classes with at Scituate High. They'd barely spoken back then, but it turned out they'd had big crushes on each other. And the rest is history."

"So they just jumped in the car and moved back?" I said.

"They moved back when they decided to have kids." He raised his eyebrows. "I have to admit that sometimes my sister almost looks Irish now. Scary."

"I wouldn't worry about it," I said. "The cultural influence is pretty inescapable. Like catching a cold when you teach in a preschool. So what does your wife do?"

"Nothing anymore." Damien hugged his pillow. "She died."

Chapter Twenty-One

"I'm so sorry for your loss," I said. My mother had taught us to say that back when we were young. Don't tell them about someone in your own life who has died. Don't tell them it'll get easier one day. Just tell them you're so sorry for their loss. And don't ask them to let you know if you can do anything to help. Just do something. When my mother died, I wanted to yell at all the people who said and did the wrong things. All these years later, I could still see their faces.

"Thank you," Damien said. It took me a moment to realize what he was thanking me for.

"What happened to her?" I asked, just in case he wanted to talk about it.

Damien tapped one toe of his gray suede wingtips up and down, the blue sole appearing and disappearing. "You sure you want to hear it?"

I nodded, even though I really wasn't.

"She was everything," Damien said. "Kind, smart, beautiful."

I smiled, hoped she could somehow hear him talking about her like that, wished that someone would talk about me like that someday. Not that I'd probably deserve it.

Damien took a deep breath in, let it out slowly. "We met at a mutual friend's wedding. I almost didn't go. She almost didn't go. But we both went. We hit it off right away, fell in love, built a great life together. Decided we wanted kids. Ace was born first."

"Cool name," I said.

"Thanks. It means unity. And it also felt like we'd gotten the lucky card finding each other against the odds, having this baby together. Anyway, she had the bigger career, made the serious money, which gave me the freedom to stay home to take care of Ace and hopefully find myself along the way. I had this vague idea that I'd take some classes, start a little home daycare, maybe turn it into a small preschool, do some homeschooling down the road. My wife thought it was just a phase. She wanted us to live this big, diverse, active urban life —you know, to make a difference, be a part of the solution."

I nodded. I'd always admired people like that. From afar, while I stayed in my charming little beach town finger-painting and playing with Play-Doh.

Damien was still tapping his toe. "She—we—got pregnant again almost right away."

I swallowed down a bolt of jealousy. Why did everyone else in the whole damn world and their goats get pregnant like it was no big deal at all?

"Everything was going fine," Damien was saying. "She was fit, healthy, no real issues with the pregnancy. And then one day she came home from work early. Ace was napping. One thing led to another and we ended up in bed. She had an ischemic stroke and intracerebral hemorrhage while we were having sex. And she was dead by the time the ambulance got her to the hospital. Not a coma. Not a persistent vegetative state. Totally and irreversibly brain dead."

I'd always thought people only gasped in books and not in real life, but I heard myself gasp.

Tears were rolling down Damien's face. "I know the sex part is an overshare. I don't talk about my wife's death often, but when I do I feel like I'm letting myself off the hook if I don't tell the whole thing. Maybe it wouldn't have happened at all if we'd waited until after the baby was born. Or maybe she would have at least lived another week, another day. I would have settled for another hour or two. I didn't get to say goodbye. She didn't get to say goodbye either. Or leave us a video we could watch over and over again. Or write letters for the boys to open every year on their birthdays."

"Shit," I said. "Shit, shit, shit." I wiped away the tears that were pooling on my chin with the back of my hand.

Damien stopped tapping his toe and went back to hugging the boat pillow. "She was 36 weeks pregnant. Miraculously, the baby was fine. Perfect in every way, no damage at all. But they kept my wife on life support for another two weeks to minimize the chances of complications for him. I guess they figured his life was going to be complicated enough."

Damien took another deep breath. "And then they delivered him by C-section. We'd made a playlist for the birth a few nights before it all went down, so the next day they left us alone while I held the baby and played it for my wife on my phone. Then they came in. And turned off her life support machine."

I opened my mouth, closed it. I had no words.

"Anne was an organ donor," he said. "I know she would have been happy that her organs were still good and could help some other people out. We hadn't settled on a name yet, so I named him, the baby, Anson, which means Anne's son. I think she would have been okay with that."

Damien cleared his throat, sat up straighter. "Sorry about the epic overshare. It won't happen again."

I swallowed hard. "Thank you for telling me," I said. My voice came out all scratchy.

"The boys and I are doing okay. I just have to figure out a way to stop feeling like I'm not wearing any skin, you know?"

I pushed myself out of the reading boat, wiped my eyes so I could see the way to our mini fridge, grabbed water bottles for both of us.

"Thanks," Damien said when I handed him one.

"So why take a job like this?" I said. "I know from personal experience that it doesn't really pay the bills. And I'm a lead teacher, not an assistant."

Damien took a long drink of water. "While we were at Anne's funeral, our house was robbed. They took all her jewelry, the wedding ring I was too out of it to put back on after I showered that morning, the electronics, even some of the toys and baby stuff."

I closed my eyes, opened them. "That could have happened in Marshbury. You'd probably just know the person who did it. Or their parents or cousins or something."

"I get that. And I feel guilty that I'm not giving the boys the big urban life Anne wanted for them. But I just want them to be safe and to be able to ride their bikes in the driveway and play in the sand at the beach. I want to stay close enough to keep an eye on them. I've got Anne's life insurance, some other stuff. I was a software designer at one point, so I can always moonlight if I have to."

I opened the Three Good Things notebook, wrote *I'm so glad you're here.* I flipped it and held it out for Damien to read.

I'm grateful that our students have a unicorn in their lives, I wrote. I held it out for him.

I will never whine about my own life again, I wrote, held it out. Damien smiled.

"Okay," I said. "We're officially done for the day."

"Great," Damien said. "My kids are with Polly in child-care, so I should probably get down there fast and spring her. I have to tell you that was the biggest draw of the job. Ace will be able to skip to the front of that long Bayberry admissions line and attend school here in the fall, and Anson and Ace will both get to go to childcare whenever I'm working or in a meeting."

"It's how we get all the good teachers," I said. "The pay sucks, and free tuition and childcare for staff kids are about the only perks. But if you have kids, your kids get to attend a school you could never afford to pay for on your salary, and you never have to worry about a babysitter while you're working." I'd turned this over and over in my head so many times through the years as I wondered if I'd ever get lucky enough to take advantage of it.

Damien pushed himself out of the reading boat, reached a hand to me.

"Thanks," I said, "but I grew up on boats." I grabbed onto the starboard side, swung my leg over the edge. Miscalculated, started falling headfirst.

Damien grabbed me before I went over. I leaned on his forearm, stepped semi-gracefully out of the boat. He smelled like cedarwood soap and sadness.

"Good thing I was wearing a life jacket," I said. "Hey, you don't want to help me throw a baby shower for Polly, do you?"

"Sure, just tell me what you want me to do." He tilted his head. "I'm actually glad to hear that. I thought there was some kind of drama going on between you two, and I was hoping not to get caught in the crossfire. I have to tell you I've had enough drama to last a lifetime."

When Damien left, I just stood there. Was there drama between Polly and me? I couldn't remember. I couldn't even really remember what was going on with John and me. I wasn't quite sure I remembered how many people in my family were driving me crazy at this particular moment in time.

All I knew was that, right now, this very hour, this very

minute, I was one lucky woman. But anything could happen, and my life could change in a nanosecond.

And before that happened, I had to shake off my February slump. Cupid's arrows were everywhere. I was surrounded by love. Now I just had to find my way back to it.

Chapter Twenty-Two

I found a parking spot right near the entrance to Marshbury Provisions. That almost never happened to me, so who knew, my luck might be changing already. I grabbed a shopping cart, decided to cruise the perimeter of the grocery store, where I was pretty sure all the healthy items hung out.

If John and Polly were both home when I got there, the three of us would enjoy a lovely dinner together. When Polly excused herself to head up to her room, I'd ask her if she had time to talk before school started tomorrow. I'd stop at Morning Glories on the way to school for coffee and muffins. I knew there were conflicting studies about whether or not it was okay for pregnant women to drink coffee, so I'd check in with Polly first to see if she'd prefer tea or milk or something else. Or I'd skip Morning Glories and just grab some chocolate from the teachers' room so we had more time to talk. If there was any drama between Polly and me, we'd put an end to it by the time our students arrived.

Once Polly went up to her room tonight, John and I would spend the rest of the evening getting things right between us. All thoughts of honeymoons and/or vasectomies would be talked through and dismissed. After that, John and I would curl up on the family room couch with the cats and the dogs. We'd check the weather channel together and find out that an extended February thaw was on the way, long enough that Joe and his crew could get the new garage foundation poured, no problem at all. My father would show up, of course, and we'd send him on his way with a plate of my very own home-cooked leftovers and a glass of the fancy pants wine we'd opened. And then John and I would go up the stairs with the animals to our tiny private living room. We'd cuddle up in the new loveseat in front of the new gas fireplace that was vented through the now-exposed old brick chimney. We'd finish sipping our own wine.

I realized I was still standing in the grocery store with an empty shopping cart. I threw in a box of organic mixed greens, green onions, lemons. A bottle of wine, in case my father had found all the stashes. I banged a left toward the fresh seafood counter.

Polly and I crashed our carts right into each other.

"Are you okay?" I said.

She nodded, cradled her baby bump with one hand. "Are you?"

"I must have conjured you up," I said. "I was just thinking about you. Hey, why don't you just throw anything you need in my cart and go home and put your feet up. I'll finish shopping and cook for all of us. Is wild salmon still on the list of pregnancy-safe foods?"

Polly's cheeks turned red, camouflaging her freckles. When I looked down at the contents of her cart, it looked like she was shopping for a family.

"I told Damien I'd pick up some things on the way over," she said. "We're cooking dinner together tonight."

I didn't say anything.

"Listen," Polly said. "I want you to know I've been looking for another place to live, but I'm just too afraid. You know, to live alone. Until after the baby is born."

I could hear her words. I just didn't know what to do with them.

When Polly grasped the handle of her cart, her knuckles went white and the freckles on her fingers jumped out. "Damien has a tiny in-law suite at his place. I'm thinking of asking him if I can move in. That way I wouldn't have to live alone. And I could help him out with his kids."

"You can't do that," I said. "You've only known him for like five minutes." I started to add that it was completely unprofessional, realized that probably wouldn't fly since Polly already lived with another co-worker, me.

"It's just," Polly said, "that I can't figure out what else to do. I know your sisters think I'm a gold digger. And one of the times your father asked me to marry him, you should know that I almost said yes. Not for money or anything, but for, I don't know. Sorry."

"Wait," I said, but Polly was already rolling away from me.

I stood in line to order my wild salmon, circled the grocery store aimlessly a few times, grabbed some cat and dog food, made it through the checkout line.

I was just climbing back into my car when a text popped in from John.

Heading out for a thing tonight. Animals fed.

No signature. Definitely no *Love, John*. Not even a *John*. Or a *-J*.

In my rearview mirror, Polly's car pulled past mine. At the street, she turned on her blinker. I'd been sure she was long gone by now, out of the grocery store, probably even out of my life. She'd start working in childcare from now on, every day, all day. Somehow, she'd manage to move all her stuff out of my parents' old bedroom when I wasn't home. When we ran into each other in the hallway at Bayberry, we'd be polite, professional. She'd send me a postcard with a generic beach

scene the next time she went on vacation—GREETINGS
FROM SANTA FE—and I'd be pretty sure she wasn't being
funny.

Without consciously deciding to follow Polly, I followed
her. I hung back a safe distance so she wouldn't spot me,
channeling my inner Nancy Drew, Pepper Anderson,
Cagney and Lacey, Miss Marple, Jessica Fletcher. I really
wished I could check in with one or all of them to see if I
was intentionally following Polly the way a good private
investigator should or just pathetically trying not to lose her
from my life.

If you blink, you could miss the WELCOME TO SCIT-
UATE sign and think you were still in Marshbury. The same
winding tree-lined, slush- and sand-splattered roads continued
as Polly headed in the direction of the ocean. She took a left
long before we got to the houses that realtors could claim were
a hop, skip and a jump to the beach.

The more blue you saw, the more green you paid on the
Irish Riviera, and in beach towns everywhere. This neighborhood might not have been as valuable as waterfront, or even
water view, but just like the neighborhood I'd grown up in and
moved back to, you wouldn't have to pack up and evacuate
when the next ocean storm hit either. You wouldn't have to be
rescued in a nor'easter, the way Ethan and my father and I
had rescued Polly from her beachfront winter rental that she
was too terrified to ever return to.

I followed Polly down a street filled with people who felt
they were lucky enough to live in a beach town. They were
grateful to be just a short drive to the beach. Most of the
houses were former summer cottages that had been renovated
to year-round over the years—central air and heat finally
added, choppy or sweeping additions tacked on, crushed
mussel-shell driveways like the one at my new old house, swing
sets, honeysuckle- or rose-covered trellises.

When Polly pulled into the driveway of a yellow Cape

with black shutters and a turquoise door, her headlights lit up two snow saucers perched in the front yard.

The door to the house swung open and Damien came out, jacketless. Polly popped the trunk, and Damien leaned in to scoop up the grocery bags. As I drove past the house in the dark, I looked straight ahead, like that might somehow keep Polly and Damien from spotting me.

I turned around at the end of the street, came back. They were gone now, so I pulled over across the street from Damien's new house, where I hoped I'd be shielded by a clump of bushes. I put my car into park, turned off my headlights, stared out my dark empty window at the brightly lit house across the street.

I flashed back to high school, to what my friends and I used to call a mission, when we'd scout out a guy one of us had a crush on. We'd drive through his neighborhood, cruise past the place he worked. It was crucial not to get caught. These were fact-finding expeditions only. Parents home after school? Basketball hoop in yard? Saturday job shift ends at eight-thirty? Planning the eventual approach could take months. In retrospect, it was the most fun part.

My heart was beating as it had more than a couple of decades ago. I felt again the combination of the fear of getting caught and the thrill of invading the personal space of the ordinary boys we pretended were something more. Now, as then, I was propelled by some kind of angsty loneliness and longing that apparently never quite goes away. That and the overpowering urge to risk messing up my life.

I turned off my car and then immediately wished I hadn't. My trusty Honda Civic was somewhere in the double digits age-wise, old enough that one of these cold winter days it just wasn't going to start. And with my luck it would be while I was spying on my current and future teaching assistants. Spying seemed like a better word than stalking—it was more like intense research.

I climbed out, even though I really, really knew better. I shut my door softly, pulled the hood of my black down coat down over my eyes, tried not to crunch in the frozen slush as I crossed the street. I fumbled for just-in-case excuses, came up empty.

The snow saucers were the blow-up kind that created a soft donut around the kids to cushion them from crashes. If I'd been through what Damien had, I'd probably want to cloak my kids in bubble wrap for added protection before I let them sled. Or do anything.

Two adorable snowmen, with fleece scarves and carrot noses and tiny snow shovels resting in hands made out of twigs, stood next to the snow saucers. I could already surmise that Damien was a good dad from seeing him with the kids at school, but this was all proof positive.

I walked around to the back of the house, stood furtively off to one side as I peeked into the kitchen window. Damien opened the refrigerator door. He reached down and picked up a cute little boy, held him while the little boy put a carton of eggs on a shelf.

It was such a tiny interaction, but it hit me hard. I wanted it. All of it. The sweet little Cape I hadn't grown up in. The nice guy I wasn't fighting with. The adorable kids I was probably never going to have.

I forced myself to walk away. I circled around to the front of the house, carefully pulled the carrot nose off one of the snowmen.

I drew a big fat Valentine's heart for all of them on a patch of untrampled snow. Then I returned the carrot nose to the snowman.

I climbed back in my car, turned the key in the ignition. My trusty old Honda coughed once then purred like a cat.

I sat there. And I sat and I sat and I sat there some more.

Until finally I had a plan.

Chapter Twenty-Three

The dogs and cats met me at the door, barking and meowing as if they hadn't been fed in centuries. I petted my way through them, gave them treats all around.

Even I knew that fish doesn't keep, so I unwrapped the wild salmon and flopped it onto a cookie sheet I'd covered with foil. I drizzled some olive oil over the fish, added some salt and pepper, popped it in the fridge where it would be safe from the animals while the oven preheated. Horatio was well-trained, and the kittens were still too small for counter-jumping. But Pebbles and Scruffy Dog had kept themselves alive by foraging for food, so they would both probably enjoy an impromptu indoor fishing expedition.

Once the salmon was safe, I rolled up my sleeves and got to work. I started with my dad because he was the closest. I opened the mudroom door, crossed to the door of his mancave in two steps. My father had never locked a door in his life, so of course it was unlocked.

"Dad," I yelled as I opened the door.

No answer, which probably meant he was out on a date tonight. Or two.

It could take you forever to text each person in my family

individually. Because of that, we had a running Hurlihy family group text chain. I pulled it up, got to work, made sure I checked for random typos before I pressed Send, so I didn't have to deal with being made fun of for the rest of my life.

Surprise Baby Shower for Polly
This Sunday, promptly at 2 PM
at the Hurlihy Family Residence
(now owned by Sarah and John)
Mandatory Attendance
Compulsory Good Behavior
Bring Thoughtful and Substantial Gifts
Say Kind Things and Give Hugs
No Excuses
Minimal Refreshments Provided
No Need to RSVP, Because You MUST Attend
Or I Will Come Find You
P.S. No Marriage Proposals and That Means YOU

Then I called Lorna.

"Hey," I said. "I'm planning a baby shower for Polly."

"Well, it's about flippin' time," Lorna said.

"Glad we're on the same page," I said. "So my question is whether to invite all the teachers and staff—"

"You mean all the teachers and staff *we like*."

"A baby present is a baby present," I said.

"Fine," Lorna said. "I can concede that."

"Thank you. So should I just invite everybody who works at Bayberry to the family baby shower I'm having for Polly at my house on Sunday—"

"Are you kidding me? And let Polly miss out on getting decadent presents from those disgustingly rich momzillas?"

"I take it that's a no."

"Of course, it's a no," Lorna said. "You'll throw a second shower in the Arts Barn right after the first one and invite every single damn Bayberrian, from the barely paid staff to the significantly overpaying families."

I thought for a moment. "Wouldn't it make sense to have that shower on a workday, so the teachers don't have to go all the way back to school on a weekend?"

"Absolutely not," Lorna said. "Because if we're not technically working, then as soon as Polly grabs her loot, we can just pack up and get the hell out of there."

Like that was going to happen, but I let it go. "So, tomorrow's Friday. I'm not exactly Martha Stewart, but I'm pretty sure that's not a lot of notice for a baby shower on Sunday."

"Not to worry. Remember back at the Halloween parade when I told all the mean moms that Polly's husband was really a CIA operative, so she had to pretend to be pregnant and single?"

"Vaguely," I said. Lorna said so many outrageous things to so many people that they had a tendency to blur after a while.

"I'll just call one of them," Lorna said, "and let it slip that the baby shower is top secret and we didn't want to risk word getting out with a longer lead time. That will immediately activate the rumor mill. Everybody will be refreshing their inboxes nonstop, so they don't miss the invitation. I guarantee you all the competitive gift-givers will show up at that baby shower, fully armed with expensive presents."

"We don't even have permission to use the Arts Barn on Sunday," I said.

"We?" Lorna said. "What have you got, a frog in your pocket? If you're too chicken shit to call Kate Stone, make Ethan do it. Even a godbitch won't say no to her godson."

"I'm pretty sure frogs and chicken shit in the same sentence constitutes a mixed metaphor," I said.

"For your information, grammar cop, it was two separate sentences."

"Fine," I said. "I'll ask Ethan to get permission. I'm sure

he'll help us with the shower, too. Oh, and Damien—the new unicorn—also said he'd help."

"Okay, then," Lorna said. "Allow me to make myself your right-hand woman for Polly's official Arts Barn baby shower. That way I can be within full drool-worthy distance of both of them."

"Wait," I said. "We still need an invitation." Under normal circumstances, Polly was the one I would have asked to help me make one. She'd do the drawing and I'd do the writing. But obviously I couldn't ask her since it was her surprise baby shower. I didn't even have time to call my sister Carol so she could take over and do all the work while she bossed me around. These invitations needed to go out yesterday, and Lorna was all I had to work with.

"Does she know whether it's a girl or a boy?" Lorna said.

"I don't think so," I said. "She told me the rest of her life is a complete unknown, so she figured she might as well stick with the theme."

"What about this?" Lorna said. "You have a picture of a massive pregnant belly at the top—Polly's if you can get your hands on one, but you can use clip art in a pinch. And then the invitation says, *Join us for some big belly laughs!*

"That would be a hard no," I said. "It sounds like they're being invited to come laugh at Polly's belly."

"Whatever gets the gifts," Lorna said.

I closed my eyes to try to picture the invitation. "I'll find a photo of a baby sleeping in a crib. And the invitation will say, *Shhh…. Please join us for a surprise baby shower honoring our much-loved Polly at 4 PM this Sunday in the Bayberry Preschool Arts Barn.*"

"Not bad," Lorna said, "but I think you need to punch it up a little."

"Fine," I said. I scribbled some words on the back of my grocery store receipt, crossed some out, wrote some more. "Okay, beneath that, it will say:

Roses are red
Showers are wet
Don't forget to bring
All the gifts you get!

"Couldn't have said it better myself," Lorna said. "Now if only we could keep them from bringing their kids and expecting us to watch them."

"Never happen," I said. "Plus, I think Polly would actually rather hang out with the kids than their parents." I decided to add something to the bottom of the invitation:

P.S. In addition to your baby gift
Please bring a copy of your child's favorite book
Signed by your child
To help start Polly's baby's library

"Good idea," Lorna said. "I can't wait to see how many copies of *War and Peace* we get from those bloodthirsty mombies."

Lorna and I hung up so we could both get to work. I had things so uncharacteristically under control that I even remembered to put the wild salmon in the oven.

I called Ethan. He called Kate Stone, called me right back to say it was a go, although in the future she'd appreciate more attention to time management as well as to the rules of etiquette. I rolled my eyes, put the email invitation together in a flash. I sent it to Ethan to forward to his godmother, who would send it out immediately via the Bayberry parent and staff group email list. Ethan volunteered to decorate the Arts Barn for Polly's baby shower, just like I knew he would.

Next I called Betty Ann, the ringleader of the Bark & Roll Forever Ladies, to invite them to the family shower. My father worked for them, and because they put up with my father, they were practically family. I also told Betty Ann about the

Bayberry shower in case they'd rather go to that one, so they could spread the word about Bark & Roll Forever.

Betty Ann said she'd let Doris and Marilyn know. She called right back and said not only were they all totally onboard, but they even had a surprise contribution that would add to the festivities.

I almost tried to get her to tell me what it was. But then I didn't. Because there's nothing like a good surprise. Especially in the dead of winter.

Chapter Twenty-Four

When the timer went off on the ancient oven I'd grown up with, I took a moment to congratulate myself on the amount of work I'd accomplished in a mere twenty minutes. I had to admit I was surprisingly productive when I focused.

I ate a few handfuls of salad, standing at the kitchen counter like I used to in my tiny ranchburger after Kevin left. The best part about living alone was that I didn't have to sit down to eat. When I burped, I didn't have to say excuse me to anyone. The rest of living alone pretty much sucked.

I cut up the salmon into tiny pieces and divided them into small bowls for the animals, plus a bigger one for me. Then I sat on the cracked linoleum kitchen floor with the cats and the dogs.

"So, this is where we are, kids," I said while we chowed down. "I've attended a lot of teacher inservices at school over the years, some good, some ridiculous. But there's one that keeps coming back to me given our current predicament. This brain and relationship expert came to speak to us. She started out talking about this thing called the Gottman Ratio."

Pebbles and a couple of the kittens looked up at me.

"Relax," I said. "There won't be a test."

The cats went back to eating. The dogs had been eating all along.

"Okay, so the Gottman Ratio was developed as a way of predicting whether couples would make it or not, but you can apply it to basically any relationship, two-legged or four-legged. The gist of it is that the bad things that happen to us are weighted more strongly than the good things. You have to have five good experiences to make up for every bad one. Essentially, the trick is that you should try to eliminate the bad things and then add lots of little good things. And before you know it, presto change-o, you have a happy life. With me so far?"

Nobody even meowed, so I continued. "The other thing the brain expert said that stayed with me is that the more contact you have with someone, the stronger the bad experiences become in contrast to the good. Essentially, being close to someone is like a multiplier for becoming enemies. Scary, huh?"

Sunshine finished eating. Then he sat on his bowl, maybe hoping to lay some more salmon.

"I know it's a lot to take in, you guys," I said. "I mean, wouldn't you think that the closer you are to someone, the better things would get? But no, you have to keep that damn good-to-bad ratio right or the whole relationship—any relationship—comes crumbling down."

Scruffy Dog licked the bottom of her bowl, then plopped down next to Squiggy and started grooming Squiggy's head. Horatio licked the bottom of his bowl, then plopped down next to Catsby and started grooming Catsby's head.

"Don't worry," I said. "Good can absolutely win in the end by virtue of numbers. So my plan is that I'm going to do good things all day long for everybody I care about."

I paused, spread my arms wide. "Hence, the salmon."

I gave them a moment to appreciate my generosity. "I've got plans for John, too. And as you probably heard, I've already planned not one but two baby showers for Polly. But that's just a start—I'm going to turn myself into the freakin' love bug of February. And before you know it, abracadabra please and thank you, everybody will be crazy about me again."

Oreo headbutted Pebbles, then he went right down the line, headbutting Squiggy and Scruffy Dog and Catsby and Horatio and Sunshine. Horatio took a break from grooming Catsby and went down the line in the opposite direction and headbutted everybody. Then all the animals stood up and everybody milled around and headbutted everybody else.

John pushed the kitchen door open. A gust of cold air blew in as he pulled it closed behind him.

"Hey," I said. "Have you noticed the dogs think they're cats now? They're headbutting like they were born to do it."

John took in the bowls on the floor.

"We're having a salmon party." I gave John my most dazzling smile. "Would you like to join us for dessert, handsome?"

John slid out of his parka. "I thought we'd agreed not to give them any people food."

"It's not people food. It's pure wild salmon with no additives." I got my focus back. "But have I told you how wonderful I think you are for caring so much about our pets' well-being?"

I pushed myself off the floor, held out my hand to take John's parka so I could actually hang it up in the coat closet for him. This good-experiences stuff was a workout.

John took a step back, held on to his parka. He squatted down to pet his way through the animals as they clumped around him.

I took a step forward, pulled John back up to a standing position. I put my arms around his neck, kissed him, gave him *the look*.

He didn't quite meet my eyes. "How 'bout a raincheck?"

He hung up his parka in the hallway coat closet. He came back and picked up the small dishes from the floor, loaded them systematically into the dishwasher. As if I wouldn't have gotten around to picking them up eventually.

I followed John to the bottom of the staircase, watched him climb the worn maple treads, thought of how many good experiences we'd have to add to make up for the bad one we were having right now, so we didn't end up enemies. Decided that sometimes you just have to forget about ratios, Gottman or otherwise, and go with the freakin' flow.

"Rainchecks for sex are not okay!" I yelled.

Sleep is a great escape when it works. I conked out before I even figured out whether John was asleep or only pretending to be asleep. I fell into a deep, heavy slumber, like I was covered by a weighted blanket topped by a mountain of snow.

Somewhere in the middle of the night I dreamed that I was late for Polly's baby shower because I couldn't find the part of my house where it was being held. I circled around my father's round bed in his mancave, over and over again, while the bed's LED lights flashed some kind of directions in Morse code that I couldn't understand. I walked up the center staircase to John's and my new space. When I pushed the new door open, I fell through a hole in the floor and landed on John's Addams Family pinball machine in the front parlor. As I peered down through the shattered glass, Gomez and Morticia looked up at me.

Gomez was getting a vasectomy. His eyes were opened wide. Morticia and Uncle Fester were dressed in matching white nurse outfits. I begged them to call their friend Jeannie from *I Dream of Jeannie* to fix the glass before John found out. Thing popped its disembodied hand up from its box and handed Uncle Fester a lightbulb. Uncle Fester put the lightbulb in his mouth to contact Jeannie. When he pulled the lightbulb out of his mouth again, dogs and cats were barking and meowing everywhere, like a Disney movie gone wild.

I startled awake, opened my eyes to check on the real cats and dogs. Horatio and Scruffy Dog had ditched their dog beds and were curled up between John and me. Pebbles and the kittens had ditched the big fluffy cat bed and were sound asleep in one of the dog beds on the floor.

For the rest of the night, I tossed and turned, kicked off the blankets because I was sweating, pulled them back over me because I was freezing.

It was a relief to finally get out of bed. I realized I'd never even heard Polly come in last night. By the time I finished showering and getting dressed for school, I could tell when I walked by her room that she was already gone.

John was feeding the animals when I tiptoed into the kitchen, so I made the coffee. We circled around each other carefully, as if we were seabirds who know the exact distance they'll let people get to them before they flap their wings and fly away.

I'd worked up an appetite tossing and turning all night, so I swallowed a few quick bites of cold leftover casserole that still smelled okay, washed it down with a cup of coffee. I slid into my puffy down coat, slung my teacher bag over my shoulder, put my hand on the kitchen doorknob.

"Wait," John said. "We need to talk."

It was beneath me, but I did it anyway.

I smiled sweetly. "How 'bout a raincheck?" I said.

Then I gave the kitchen door a satisfying slam on my way out.

I shivered as I waited in vain for my car to warm up. I gave up and started backing out of the driveway, slid sideways on a patch of ice, got stuck in a rut.

Crushed mussel shell driveways are lovely in spring, summer and fall. But you can't really plow them, or you lose half the mussel shells, and you even have to be careful when you shovel them. So in the winter in coastal New England, crushed mussel shell driveways are the pits.

I rocked my car forward and back, forward and back, switching gears quickly and trying to create enough of a rhythm to break free. Finally, the tires churned up a whirlwind of mussel shells and frosty mud. My car flew backwards. I smelled rubber.

The kitchen curtains parted. John's judgement-filled face peeked out.

"What are *you* looking at?" I said. I knew I was better than that, but I gave him my most expressive finger anyway.

When I'd made it safely out to the street, I turned on the radio.

The Kinks were singing, "Where Have All the Good Times Gone."

"Oh, shut up," I said as I turned off the radio.

Chapter Twenty-Five

My classroom door was heart-less. Even though the conversation heart cupid had turned out to be only my wasband, I still felt a tiny wave of sadness. The mystery had been something to look forward to, to wonder about. Maybe that was why Nancy Drew, Pepper Anderson, Cagney and Lacey, Miss Marple, Jessica Fletcher and all the rest kept taking on new cases. So they'd have something bigger to think about than their ordinary, humdrum lives.

Thinking about conversation hearts gave me an idea for a classroom activity. I was just grabbing stacks of pink construction paper when Polly arrived.

"Good morning," Polly said, her eyes not quite meeting mine.

"Good morning," I said, matching my eye drift to hers.

Once I told Polly the plan, she immediately folded one of the pieces of construction paper in half and cut a shape without even having to draw it first. When she opened it, we had the perfect heart template.

"You're so talented," I said. I was back on track with the Gottman Ratio again.

"Thanks," Polly said. She was already tracing and cutting,

tracing and cutting. I grabbed another pair of teacher scissors, jumped in. When Damien arrived, we had a second professional round of good mornings. Then I handed him my scissors and he went to work.

I wrote LET'S READ in big block letters with a chubby red crayon on a pink heart, tucked it into a picture book.

"Okay," I said. "Once the kids are all here, we'll gather for circle time and give everyone a heart and a crayon. The idea is that they'll make giant conversation hearts with their own sayings. We can help with the writing if they need it, and the older kids can help the younger ones, too. And then we'll go around the circle and everyone can take a turn reading their heart."

"You're so creative," Polly said. Apparently, she was Gottman Ratio-ing me, too. Maybe it was a little bit like Marie Kondo-ing, sparking joy, but without making your closets look any neater.

"Thanks," I said.

I stationed myself out in the hallway to greet our students, leaving Polly and Damien to get the kids settled in with individual activities while they waited for everyone else to arrive.

Damien came out to join me in the hallway. He looked over his shoulder to make sure Polly wasn't within lip-reading distance.

"I got the email invitation. How can I help with the baby shower?" I had to admit his teacher-whisper was coming along nicely.

"I'm meeting Ethan and Lorna here tomorrow morning at ten to start decorating the Arts Barn," I teacher-whispered back. "If you can stop by for a while, that would be great."

"I'll be there," Damien said.

Polly looked out at us. We both stopped talking and over-smiled at her.

"What else?" Damien said once Polly had looked away again.

I shook my head. "Secrets have a way of getting out around here, so if any of the kids let anything slip, just try to redirect them as best you can."

Damien nodded, walked casually back into the classroom as if he'd never left.

It didn't take long for parents and nannies to show up carrying extravagantly wrapped presents. I mean, what part of surprise baby shower did they not understand? It was anybody's guess how they'd managed to get their hot little hands on baby shower gifts already. I could only imagine that they'd ordered them online last night as soon as the email invitation popped in. And then the gifts had been delivered by drone this morning. Either that or maybe these were the kind of families that had entire closets or even wings filled with just-in-case gifts.

I wrestled the presents away as soon as I spotted them. I made a towering pile outside Ethan and June's classroom, hoped Polly wouldn't suspect anything.

Once the kids had all shown up, I did a headcount to double check. Then I caught Polly's and Damien's eyes and held up one finger. They both nodded. It was kind of nice having two assistants so I could take off guilt-free. Even if it was only temporary, and one of them didn't want to live at my house anymore. I'd peered in the windows of Polly's car on my way into school this morning. I didn't see any sign of moving boxes, but that didn't mean they weren't coming.

I loaded myself up with presents and staggered to the Arts Barn.

I'd barely managed to open the door and was trying to hold it with one foot so the presents and I could wiggle through, when a male hand grabbed the door from behind and held it open.

I knew that hand. I stepped through the door, dropped the presents to the floor, turned around.

"Seriously?" I said. "I mean, if you're going to keep

stalking me, you should at least leave more candy on my classroom door."

Kevin put a big wrapped present next to the pile. "Nikki asked me to deliver a gift for Polly when I dropped off the twins. Somebody gave it to Nikki at her baby shower, but she didn't want it." He pressed his lips together, opened his mouth again. "I'm not supposed to say that."

"Whatever," I said. "It's not like I had a high opinion of her before you said that. Here, help me open up one of those folding tables over there so I can start a gift table."

We got the table set up, arranged the lavishly wrapped presents as best we could. I decided I'd wait till my wasband wasn't around before I partially unwrapped the present Nikki was regifting, so I could take a quick peek at it.

"Teamwork is the dreamwork," Kevin said, as if he'd ever helped me with anything when we were married.

"If you don't love someone, set them free," I said over my shoulder as I walked away. The way I looked at it, one bad cliché deserved another. And at least I'd given mine an original twist.

"Wait. I didn't get to finish talking to you yesterday."

I stopped, turned all the way around. "Make it quick. And only because you helped me with the table."

Kevin rested both hands on top of his head as if he was trying to keep his brain from escaping. He closed his eyes, opened them again.

"Nikki," he said, "wants me to ask you and John to be the new baby's godparents."

"Is she insane?" I said.

"I don't think so," Kevin said. "At least I'm pretty sure she's not. She just has this idea that the two of you are almost like inlaws because, you know—"

"Because she screwed around with you while you were married to me? I think that's more like outlaws."

"I didn't think you'd go for it," Kevin said, "but I figured it was worth a shot. I guess I thought maybe that way we'd get to hang around once in a while. It's good having another adult to talk to."

I hadn't been accused of being another adult all that often in my life. And half the time I didn't even feel like a real adult, more like some kind of eternal angst-ridden adolescent. But grownup or still-has-a-lot-of-growing-left-to-do, I knew one thing for sure.

"This is the last time I'm going to say it," I said. "You blew it. I'm over it. I'm over you. I forgive you, not because you deserve it, but because I don't want to do that stupid thing where you keep drinking the poison and waiting for the other person to die."

Maybe with every ex there is that exact moment you know, beyond a shadow of a doubt, that nothing he can say to you will ever touch you again. I felt it now, some heady combination of growth and acceptance and release. I wished it for every woman out there who had a wasband, or any unreasonable facsimile, in her life.

I gulped down some air. "But you don't get to hang out with me anymore, Kevin. You lost that privilege. And in her wildest dreams, Nikki will never be my inlaw, outlaw or anything in between."

A text beeped into Kevin's phone. He pulled it out of his pocket, tapped the screen.

I was standing close enough to see a picture of Nikki pop up. She was wearing something lacy, obscenely tight, lowcut. Her enormous pregnant breasts looked like they'd been blown up with a bicycle pump.

"Ohmigod, is she sexting you?" I averted my eyes quickly, hoping the image wasn't burned into my eyeballs forever.

Kevin squinted at the text that came with the photo. "She just wants to know if the dress makes her look fat."

"That's a dress?" I said. "I thought it was a handkerchief."

My ass-HAAT gazed skyward for support. I pictured St.

Brigid and her white cow with the red ears giggling down at him.

"You're a woman," Kevin said. "What should I say?"

"Thanks for noticing," I said. "Obviously, there's only one answer to the does this make me look fat question: no."

I watched Kevin take as long as humanly possible to hunt and peck two letters.

"Type a couple extra Os at the end for emphasis," I said, mostly because I couldn't resist torturing him.

"Got it." My X hunted and pecked some more, apparently needing to re-find the letter O each time. Finally, he pushed Send.

He held out his phone to me. "Did I send it right?"

Autocorrect had changed his *Nooooooo* to *Mooooooo*.

"Ha," I said.

Kevin took his phone back, looked at the screen. "Nooo," he said.

"I think you mean mooo," I said.

We stood there for a moment. I actually felt kind of bad for Nikki. All this evolving I was doing was getting to be a drag.

"Any ideas?" my hasbeen finally said.

"Not really," I said. "I think your best bet is to turn in your iPhone and have it declared a lethal weapon."

Kevin's phone rang. I didn't even have to look at his screen to know it was Nikki.

"Have a nice life," I said. "You won't be in my thighs."

———

I carried a kiddie chair over to the circle for Polly, which I hoped counted toward our Gottman Ratio of good experiences. I called the kids over. Damien passed out paper hearts while I passed out chubby crayons.

Josiah looked up at me, held out his hand.

"Would you like to give out the crayons, Josiah?" I said.

"It's my ponsibility," Josiah said, the weight of the crayon world on his little shoulders.

Pandora gave Polly a knowing smile. "Do you like showers?"

"April showers bring May flowers," Damien said by way of distraction as I gave Pandora a warning look.

"My mommy," Max said, "likes to give presents that are bigger than the baby."

"My nanny," Ember said, "says some people have money to burn."

I cleared my throat. "Today we're all going to make conversation hearts."

"We're getting candy?" Max said.

"Actually," I said. "It's more like pretend candy."

"That's no fun," Jaden said.

"Yeah, that's no fun," some of the other kids said.

The holes in this activity were becoming apparent already.

I thought for a moment. "But," I said, "the words are real, and each of us is going to make up our own words and write them on our heart. Then we'll go around the circle and read them."

"I can't read," Griffin said.

"That's okay," Polly said. "I can help you read."

Gulliver crinkled his paper heart into a ball. "I hate pink," he said. "It's a girl color."

"Pink is one of my favorite colors," Damien said.

Gulliver picked up his heart again. He opened it up, tried to iron out the wrinkles with his fist. "I hate wrinkles," he said.

"Oh, well," I said. In my earlier teaching days, I would have given Gulliver a new paper heart. Which would have resulted in half the kids crinkling their own hearts to get new ones.

Pandora smiled at Polly. "Do you like show—"

"One, two, three, write," I said, cutting Pandora off in the nick of time.

The focused buzz of kids writing their sayings and decorating their paper hearts filled the room. Maybe this activity was a keeper after all.

Once everybody was finished, we went around the circle and shared. Clearly, these kids knew their conversation hearts. We had CALL ME and KISS ME and UR HOT and GIGGLE. But we'd also helped some of the kids upgrade to DREAM BIG and BE HAPPY and SHINE BRITE. Polly's heart said BABY MINE. Damien's said COOL KIDS.

I was about to pat myself on the back for my brilliance when I noticed that some of the younger kids were eating their paper hearts. This is the kind of thing that can spread like wildfire in a preschool classroom. And my entire evening would be taken up with phone calls from parents complaining that I was teaching their child to eat paper, and did I know that paper-eating causes a multitude of physical and psychological illnesses.

"Stop," I said. "Eating paper is not okay."

"It's candy, baby," Depp said.

"I want real candy," Harper said. Her lower lip started to quiver.

"Real candy is not for school," I said.

Before I knew it, we'd have so many dietary restrictions that the kids would only be able to drink triple-filtered natural artisan water from the Swiss Alps for snack. For a moment, I missed the root beer barrels and candy cigarettes from my own childhood. I wished I could run into the teachers' room, come back with a decadent box of chocolates, not worry if the candy had peanuts or sugar or milk or eggs or soy or shellfish or gluten or preservatives or latex in it. I'd pass the box around and we'd all chow down.

But this was the world we lived in.

I reached for my own conversation heart, turned it around to face the kids, held it up: LET'S READ.

"Let's read," the readers in the group yelled.

"Let's read," the other kids yelled like preschool parrots.

I reached behind my back and pulled out a book. "*Best Valentine's Jokes for Kids*," I read. I turned it around so the kids could see the cover, held it up. The kids cheered. Joke books were a big deal in preschool.

"What did the stamp say to the envelope?" I read.

"I don't know," Polly said. "What *did* the stamp say to the envelope?"

"I'm stuck on you," I yelled.

"What's a stamp?" Max said.

"What's an envelope?" Harper said.

Of course. My students lived in a world of thank-you texts and bills paid online. I checked my big analog teacher watch to see if it was too early to move on to snack. Or even an afterschool drink.

I flashed back to a few months after June started working as my assistant. I was knee-deep in finger painting with the kids, and my back was to our big wall clock, so I asked her what time it was because she was facing the clock.

"I think it's about eleven," June said.

Since school had just started, I thought it best to get a second opinion, so I pushed myself off the floor and looked. It was ten past ten. I realized that June, along with lots of other millennials, had no idea how to tell time unless it was a digital clock.

Most kids didn't reliably learn to tell time until they were somewhere between six and eight years old. But we still spent time on time-telling at Bayberry because like most of learning, it was a process. And we divided our time between analog and digital clocks.

But the writing was on the wall. Analog time-telling was on its way to becoming obsolete, soon to share museum space with floppy disks and corded phones and encyclopedias and irons and ironing boards and stamps and envelopes. More and more, when babies were presented with a picture book, instead of turning the pages, they'd pinch and poke and swipe the paper like an iPad. If against all odds, I ever actually had a baby of my own, the first thing I'd do would be to teach it to turn pages.

I closed the book. "Anybody know any good jokes?"

"Knock-knock," Damien said.

"Who's there?" I said.

"Wooden shoe," Damien said.

"Wooden shoe who?" Polly said.

"Wooden shoe like to hear another joke?" Damien said.

Damien and Polly and I cracked up.

"What's a wooden shoe?" Morgan said.

Chapter Twenty-Six

I didn't think it was necessarily all my *ponsibility*, but the sooner things got back on track for John and me and turned our February from flawsome to awesome, the better. So my plan was to Gottman Ratio John within an inch of his life to fast forward us through this winter rough patch.

I loaded up my car with confiscated candy from the teachers' room. The decadent piles were still multiplying daily, so I figured I could grab some for John and the baby shower at my house, and still have plenty for the Bayberry shower without completely bankrupting the teachers' stash.

"Sweets to the sweet," I said over the din of the cats and the dogs greeting me. I placed a box of chocolate truffles in front of John on the kitchen table. Belatedly, I remembered that was a line from Shakespeare. The sweets Hamlet's mother the queen delivers aren't make-up sweets or even a hostess gift, but funereal bouquets to be scattered on Ophelia's grave. Maybe not the most optimistic image to invoke. I could only hope John wasn't up on his Shakespeare quotes.

John looked up from his laptop. "If you're planning to host a baby shower here, don't you think you should at least run it by me first?"

"You were on the family group text invitation," I said.

"At that point, it's hardly a conversation," he said.

"I'm more in love with you than I was yesterday," I said. "My heart still races when I see you. You look better today than on the day we met. I can't imagine anything more magnificent than growing old together."

I counted them on my fingers, added one more. "I love everything there is to love about you."

Then I grabbed the chocolate truffles back and stomped off to the family room to pout my Friday night away.

———

Carol texted me that she was on the way over. It was ridiculously early, especially for a Saturday morning. But as we used to say when we were kids, beggars can't be choosers. And I needed her.

By the time I finished chugging my coffee, her minivan had pulled up to the side of my new old house, close to the entrance to the mudroom and my father's mancave, the motor running.

I grabbed a jacket and met her outside. Even through the minivan's slush-stained windows, I could see a huge orange net bag filled with about five gazillion yellow rubber duckies.

I looked up at the second-floor windows of the main house to make sure Polly wasn't peering out at us. Then I put my hands on either side of my face and leaned into the minivan to get a better look. A second net bag, this one yellow, was filled with naked plastic baby dolls. Next to the two bags, clear plastic umbrellas with yellow handles were tied in bunches.

Carol flung her door open and jumped out. "I've got exactly one hour, so let's get cracking."

"Couldn't you have wrapped some blankets or something around that stuff?" I said. "What if Polly sees it?"

Carol rolled her eyes. "She won't. She has total pregnancy

brain by now. Which essentially means that the baby has hijacked her head, and she has momnesia about everything that isn't directly related to napping or eating. My minivan is so outside the jurisdiction of said pregnancy brain that it's a total nonissue. And even if Polly did happen to notice we were planning a baby shower, she'd forget all about it while she was taking her next nap."

"Okay, then," I said as I started unloading the minivan. Carol was so convincing that even when she had no idea what she was talking about, it was easier to just go along with her.

Carol grabbed a handful of umbrellas and walked ahead of me. Instead of taking a right into the main house, she banged a left into my father's mancave.

"We're having the baby shower *here*?" I said. My father's big round bed took up most of the available real estate. His mancave had a second floor, but his new round bed was his pride and joy, so he'd wanted it positioned where no one could miss it.

"Of course, we're having the baby shower here," Carol said. "We can't set it up in the house—it's supposed to be a surprise shower. I brought eye hooks and picture-hanging wire so we can hang the umbrellas over Dad's bed. Then we'll cover the edges of the bed with the rubber duckies and the baby dolls. Just you wait, once we turn on the LED lights around the bed, it'll be totally amazing."

"People actually *pay* you to come up with this stuff?" I said. Spending time with my sisters could be frustrating enough to make me talk in italics.

Carol ignored me.

Our dad didn't appear to be home. Maybe he had an early day at work. Maybe he'd had an overnight with a date.

"Da-ad," I yelled, just to be sure. Nobody answered.

I followed Carol back out to her minivan. She grabbed a ladder. I loaded up the bag of baby dolls, some more umbrellas.

"One question," I said once we were back inside. "Where is Dad going to sleep tonight?"

"On his *bed*. It's not like a few ducks and baby dolls are going to *bother* him." Apparently, I brought out the italic-speak in at least one of my sisters, too.

Carol set up the ladder on one side of the room, climbed up, screwed in an eye hook, twisted one end of a long length of picture-hanging wire around the eye hook.

I was a quick study when I concentrated, so I stretched the wire to the other side of the room and waited for Carol and the ladder to arrive.

Carol plopped the ladder down beside me, opened her eyes wide. "Unless you think we need to leave space in his bed for *Polly* to fit, too."

"Knock it off." I glared at her. "I mean it. What do you have against Polly anyway?"

"Besides the fact that she's a gold digger?" Carol said.

I fought off the urge to regress to my childhood self and pull Carol's hair.

"She's absolutely *not* a gold digger," I said. "Not that it's any of your business, but her parents even left her a trust fund. And anything Dad doesn't manage to spend before he dies isn't going to amount to all that much anyway by the time it's divided between the six of us. So I just don't get it."

"Dad wants to marry her," Carol said softly. "She's our age. We'll all end up on a Dr. Phil show. Mom would be mortified." The way that she said it, I could almost picture our mother flying down from heaven and sitting with us for the taping of *Dr. Phil*.

I swallowed down the sadness of missing my mother that would never go away no matter how long I lived.

"I don't think Dad really wants to marry Polly," I said, although I wasn't one hundred percent sure this was true. "He thinks it's the chivalrous thing to do. He wants Polly and her baby to be safe. And I think Polly just wants to feel safe, too."

"Well, Polly's certainly not going to marry Johnny either," Carol said. "He and Kim are practically almost back together."

"Why does Polly have to marry anyone?" I said. "Why can't we just make her feel safe by accepting her as a part of our family? Let her know that she's one of us, that she and the baby can stay forever if they want to. And that she doesn't need to marry Dad or anyone else to make that happen."

"I hate to say it," Carol said, "but you're right."

"Can I have that in writing?" I said. "Like maybe a big honkin' tattoo on the inside of your forearm?"

"Funny," Carol said. "So funny I forgot to laugh. Oh, that reminds me. What if we both get another hole pierced in our ears for Valentine's Day? That's really all the rebellion I have time for. Lobe piercing only. I don't think I can handle the pain of piercing cartilage."

"The pain of piercing cartilage would make a great song title," I said.

"Good thing you're a preschool teacher and not a song-writer," Carol said.

Carol climbed up the ladder again, screwed in another eye hook. I handed her the free end of the picture hanging wire. She stretched it tight, twisted it around the eye hook.

When we opened up the umbrellas, there were little yellow ducks stamped on the clear plastic. We kicked off our boots and climbed up on my father's bed and trampoline-jumped to hang the umbrellas on the wire. They all slid to the center of the wire. Carol pushed and prodded them until they clumped adorably.

"Wow," I said. "It looks pretty damn good. Almost as if you know what you're doing."

Carol checked the time on my father's alarm clock. Even that was digital. Maybe I'd buy him an analog alarm clock for Father's Day. If I could find one that didn't have eighty USB ports or wake you with the sound of birds chirping with ever-increasing volume until you had no choice but to throw something at the clock or get out of bed. Maybe I'd buy everyone I knew analog alarm clocks, too, so we could fight the good fight.

"Okay," Carol was saying. "I have exactly twelve minutes left. Let's see, I picked up some frozen mini quiches. I've got some tinier rubber duckies I can stick on the top of the quiches to keep our theme cohesive."

I thought about asking Carol what she used to get the rubber duckies to stick to the mini quiches, so I could try making rubber duckie sandwiches for snack at school. Decided my kids would probably try to eat the duckies, so I didn't really need to know.

"I'll buy, I mean make, veggies and dip," I said. "And I'll pick up some decadent chocolates for balance. I've got a case of bottled water. And I thought I could make that punch, you know, the kind they have at showers."

I waited for Carol to offer to make the punch. She didn't.

"How do you make that punch again?" I asked, as if I'd ever made a punch in my life.

Carol shook her head. "Orange sherbet and something fizzy like seltzer. I'll save some of the smaller rubber duckies so we can float them on top. Make sure you use the punch bowl."

"Right," I said. "Which one is the punch bowl?"

"Google it," my bossy big sister said.

Carol ran out to her minivan and came back in rolling a helium tank. She had a pile of mylar balloons tucked under one arm.

"Wonder Woman lives," I said.

"Shut up and get to work," Carol said.

"Wait," I said. "If we blow them up now, are you sure they won't be deflated by tomorrow? We'll never live it down if we have another Deflategate on our hands."

"I'm a professional," Carol said. "Mylar balloons will

continue to float for up to two weeks, and they remain full and taut for three to five days—"

"What's the secret?" I said. "Viagra?"

Carol shook her head. "Air conditioning can cause them to shrivel, but if you crank up the heat, they'll return to their previous state."

"I'm not even going to touch that," I said.

We fired up the tank and blew up orange balloons that said JUST DUCKY and yellow balloons that said BABY LOVE. We blew up orange polka dot balloons and yellow polka dot balloons. We tied long orange and yellow strands of curly ribbon to them all.

"Where are the people going to fit?" I said.

"We'll have plenty of room," Carol said. She pulled all the balloons into one big bouquet and started trying to stuff them into our father's bathroom.

"What are you *doing*?" I said.

"I don't want the *balloons* to get tangled up with the *umbrellas*," Carol said.

I put my hands on my hips. "But it's fine for Dad to have a *heart attack* when he opens the door to use the facilities?"

Carol put the hand not holding the balloons on her hip. "Fine, then you figure it out, *Sherlock*."

I grabbed the balloons away from Carol and bumped them up the stairs since it appeared that my father was living a one-story life in a two-story mancave. As far as I knew, he never even went up to the second floor.

"You're in charge of the music," Carol was saying as I came back down. "It's the least you can do."

"Got it," I said. "I'll plan some shower games, too."

"What in tarnation is going on in here?" my father said as he opened the door. "I have the extinct impression that my very own daughters have broken into my man cavern."

He circled the round bed, checking out the rubber duckies and baby dolls.

He looked up at the umbrellas hanging over the bed. "Are we expecting rain?"

"It's for Polly's surprise baby shower tomorrow, Dad," I said. "Remember, I texted everybody the invitation?"

"Wouldn't miss it," he said. "Where is it?"

"Here," Carol said.

"You didn't *ask him* first?" I said to Carol, so my father would know it was all her fault. What are sisters for if not to occasionally throw each other under the bus.

"Guess I'll be on time then, won't I now," our dad said. "And will the libations include some nice Irish brewskis?"

"Of course, Dad," Carol said. "Sarah's in charge of the beer."

I pulled my phone out of my pocket, texted my backyard trailer-dwelling brother Johnny to bring the beer.

Our dad was eyeing the helium tank. "Am I on oxygen now?"

"It's for the balloons," I said. "Which are upstairs, by the way."

"Good to know," our dad said. "When he takes a lady friend out to watch the submarine races, I hear those oxygen tanks can slow a fellow down."

Christine walked in, slammed the door behind her.

"I can't believe you *decorated* without me," she said, jumping right into sister italics.

"We were just going to text you," I said. "We put you in charge of making sure the rubber duckies don't jump off Dad's bed tonight."

"Funny," Christine said. "So funny I forgot to laugh. Okay, I'll bring fruit kabobs and some cheese and crackers."

"Thanks," I said. "But the most important thing you can do is to be nice to Polly."

"Yeah," Carol said. "Otherwise, she might end up married to you-know-who." Carol held up one hand to block her finger, pointed to our dad.

"The only insignificant other our Polly is going to tie the knot with is yours truly," our dad said. "You can bet your sweet bippy on that one."

For extra emphasis, he leaned over and thumped one hand on his bed, scattering rubber duckies and baby dolls everywhere.

Chapter Twenty-Seven

By the time I got to the Arts Barn, it looked like Ethan had already been working for days.

"Wow," I said. "Just wow."

Ethan had rolled the postcard-covered bulletin boards out to the front of the stage. He'd added a big sparkly sign to each bulletin board that said OH, THE PLACES YOU'LL GO, BABY.

Blow-up globes dangled from the wooden beams on the ceiling. Multiple signs hung from the beams, too: WELCOME TO THE WORLD, LITTLE ONE.

My eyes teared up.

Ethan looked down from his ladder. "I figured we might as well use those postcards as a jumping off point since they were already here."

"Who knew," I said. "It's almost like they had a purpose all along." I took it all in again, grateful for possibly the first time in my career for our feared leader's busywork. "Polly's going to love this so much."

Ethan smiled. "Maybe we could hang up some of this stuff in Polly's room at your house after the shower?"

"Great idea." I only hoped Polly's room would still be in my house.

I squinted at the pile of yellow construction paper I was holding. "Tell me if this is stupid, but I thought I could cut out a whole bunch of yellow stars, and the parents and students could write wishes for Polly's baby on them."

"Sounds great to me," Ethan said.

"I wish you early acceptance into Harvard by the time you're twelve, and your own brand spankin' new Lamborghini before you're sixteen," Lorna said as she and Damien walked in.

"Tell me it's not that bad," Damien said.

I shook my head. "Your first rule of surviving Bayberry is not to listen to anything Lorna says."

Lorna and Damien checked out Ethan's handiwork. "Amazing," they both said at once.

"Owe me a drink," Lorna said.

"Done," Damien said.

"Glad you like it," Ethan said as he climbed down from the ladder. He grabbed the last remaining empty bulletin board and rolled it over. Then he started arranging the rows of unused tacks at the top into star shapes. The rest of us joined in, teacher see, teacher do.

"How about if we pile the stars and markers on a small table next to this?" Ethan said.

"I'll grab one from my classroom," I said. "We can also write a few sample stars so everybody will get the idea."

I ran to get the table while Ethan made a star template.

We all began tracing and cutting, tracing and cutting.

"This is feeling too freakin' much like a school day," Lorna said. She grabbed a star and a marker, wrote: THIS WILL BE ONE OF THE LAST SHOWERS YOU ENJOY IN PEACE.

"Cute," I said. I grabbed a star and wrote: LOVE IS ALL AROUND YOU.

Lorna grabbed another star, wrote: LORNA IS A GREAT NAME FOR A BABY. JUST SAYING.

"Jump in, you guys," I said.

Ethan picked up a star, did a quick cartoon of Edvard Munch's "The Scream." Below it, he wrote: THIS JUST GOT REAL.

Damien looked at his star for a while before he wrote: CHERISH IT ALL.

———

I swung by Marshbury Provisions on my way home. As soon as I carried the groceries into my kitchen, I relocated the pre-cut veggies to a round platter I found in the cupboard and the premade dip to a matching bowl that sat in the middle of the round platter. It looked pretty homemade without the grocery store packaging, if I did say so myself.

I put the orange sherbet in the freezer, the seltzer in the fridge. I Googled *punch bowl* on my phone. A picture came right up. I carried my phone to my parents' old china cabinet in the dining room and found the actual item, like the Suzy Homemaker version of a preschool matching game.

Pebbles and the kittens looked up at me.

"Don't get all judge-y," I said. "I still remember what an ironing board is."

I put the found punch bowl on the kitchen counter so it would be ready for action. Since I already had my phone out, I started pulling up songs to make a playlist that would work for both baby showers.

The kitchen door swung open. John and the dogs made their entrance. The cats and dogs started head-butting immediately. John was a bit more restrained.

"The shower is at my father's mancave," I said. I glanced down at my song list for inspiration. "Love is all there is. Love will keep us together. I will always love you."

I needed one more, according to the Gottman Ratio, so I rummaged in my teacher bag for my wasband's last conversation heart.

I found it at the bottom of the bag, brushed some unidentifiable crumbs from it so the letters were legible.

"YOU'VE GOTTA SHOW UP," I read.

"Bingo," John said. "That's exactly it. The minute things get tough, you stop showing up."

There is nothing worse than finding out that your former husband and your fingers-crossed-someday-husband are in complete agreement about you.

I kept my mouth shut, which seemed like my best option given the circumstances.

John hung the leashes on the hook next to the door, took off his parka. "Let me know when you're ready to have an adult conversation."

"How adult?" I said.

"Never mind." John bit his lower lip. It seemed to have gone from adorably chapped to seriously stressed since the month of February had begun.

"Okay, fine," I said. "But can we wait till after—"

"You always do that," John said. "It's always after this or after that. There's always going to be another after."

"It's not going to be February forever," I said.

"It's not about February," he said.

"It's not?" I said. So much for that theory. For all I knew, the Gottman Ratio didn't hold up either.

The kitchen door opened again. Polly came in, took one look at us, kept walking in the direction of her room.

I met John's eyes.

"I'm ready," I said.

———

John's car was behind mine, so he drove. We wove our way

through the backroads, then jumped on the highway heading north.

Neither of us said a word. When I couldn't take it anymore, I finally took my chances and turned on the radio. The Cars were playing "All Mixed Up." I turned the radio off again, fast, but not before I heard them sing that line about how I wait for her forever, but she never does arrive.

About halfway to Boston, John put on his blinker and we pulled off the highway. We drove around until we found a restaurant that neither of us had ever been to. It was too late for lunch and too early for dinner, but we hadn't eaten either one of them, so we were mostly looking for open.

We rolled into a parking lot. John pulled up the restaurant on his phone.

"The reviews are good," John said. "And it looks like it's open."

"More importantly," I said, "it has no history for either of us and the likelihood of running into someone we know here is slim to none."

John got out of the car, came around and opened my door. In my mind, there is no more chivalrous gesture a man can make than opening a car door. I took it in, along with John's long camel-colored wool coat, which exactly matched the inner circle of his Heath Bar eyes. I liked the way he put one hand on the small of my back as we walked into the restaurant, not like I couldn't manage to walk on my own, but like I was some kind of sexy woman he had to touch, at least a little, even when we weren't exactly getting along.

I realized I was Gottman Ratio-ing John to myself, instead of to him, which possibly defeated the whole purpose.

We both ordered big salads topped with shrimp because there's nothing like a salad you don't have to make yourself. Or shrimp you don't have to clean.

We sipped our lemon water. I waited him out. Because

there's also nothing like a heavy-duty conversation you don't have to start.

"So," he said. "When your brother Michael saw me, I was not in the process of getting a vasectomy consultation."

"Good to hear," I said.

John took a long drink of water, put his glass down. "I was getting a sperm count."

"Wow," I said. "I didn't see that coming."

"Pun intended," I added.

"Sorry," I said when John didn't say anything. "Bad joke. It's that damn kneejerk Hurlihy glib gene."

John still didn't say anything.

"Not that I don't take full responsibility for saying it," I said. I grabbed my water to give me something to do besides continuing to say stupid things.

John raised his eyebrows, asking me if I was finished. I nodded.

"Or more accurately," he said, "a semen analysis. I figured that since you were dragging your feet on getting things checked out at your end, I might as well jump in, in case the reason we weren't getting pregnant was in my court."

"Hmm," I said. I'd never even considered this possibility. It seemed to me that if anyone was screwing things up in the pregnancy department, it would automatically have to be me.

Beyond that, the whole baby thing seemed mysterious, out of reach, something that happened to other people. "How did you even know where to go?" I asked.

John raised his eyebrows. "There were brochures all over the place when we were at Seaside with Siobhan."

I'd never even noticed the brochures. John took another drink of water while we both remembered the awful day when we found out that Siobhan had a tubal pregnancy, and the baby that could have been ours wasn't going to be anybody's.

"It's like one-stop shopping over there," John said. "Seaside."

"So, you're fine, right?" I said.

John shrugged. "They analyzed two different samples, two weeks apart."

I knew it was my own fault, but I still felt left out. We could have been sitting in the waiting room together. I'd make a crack about the magazines in the room they were about to send him to. He'd tell me to keep it down, everybody could hear me. As if they weren't all making the same stupid crack, I'd say.

The waiter put our salads in front of us. Too late, I realized I should have ordered something else since the shrimp looked like giant sperm swimming around in the dressing. At least even I knew this was the kind of observation best kept to oneself.

When the waiter was out of earshot, John said, "I'm not producing good quality sperm. Some were okay, but a little slow. Some of them were swimming in circles instead of straight ahead. Some were deformed. Only some had tails. Of the two to three hundred million sperm in the average ejaculate, as few as four percent will be functional. I wasn't even close."

"I'm so sorry," I said.

"Thank you," John said. "So there's a chance that lifestyle changes can have an impact. Optimal temperatures for sperm are lower than standard body temperature. No tight jeans, boxers instead of tighty whities, keeping my laptop off my lap. Exercise. Sleep. Reducing stress and alcohol. Eating a better diet."

"It's all my fault," I said. "It's the damn casseroles."

"Don't think I haven't considered that," John said. To his credit, he smiled when he said it.

"I'm banishing the entire casserole collection to my father's mancave the second we get home." I took a bite of salad greens for emphasis, washed it down with a gulp of lemon water. "What else?"

"Leafy greens, walnuts, citrus fruits, seafood, dark chocolate, bananas, garlic, asparagus. They gave me a list. It's worth
a try, and if it doesn't work, we'll go right to the next step."

We both took a break so John could get a jump on eating
some leafy greens and seafood.

"What's the next step?" I said.

"The other option," he said, "is that I'm producing some
good quality sperm, but it can't get out because the vas defer-
ens, the tubing, is blocked. So the next step would be that they
go in and unwind the testes and find the good sperm and
harvest it."

"Ouch," I said.

John looked a little green around the gills when he
nodded. "But going through that procedure doesn't make
sense unless it's coordinated with whatever is or isn't going on
at your end. And we have no idea what that is—"

"Because I haven't even made an appointment," I said.

"We're not getting any younger," John said.

"Even though one of us occasionally acts like a child," I
said.

"Whether we're able to have a baby or not," John said, "I
want to spend the rest of my life with you. And if a baby is
not going to happen for us, I want to know so we can
move on."

"Do you have the number?" I asked.

John pulled up Seaside OB/GYN/Infertility Group on his
contacts list, handed me his phone.

I hit Call. And a real person answered, even on a Saturday. So I made an appointment. For which I was actually
going to show up.

Chapter Twenty-Eight

"So," Carol said when she called me Sunday morning. "How are you planning to get Polly to the shower?"

"At Bayberry?" I said.

Carol, I mouthed to John. We were sitting at the kitchen table, eating walnuts and drinking green smoothies. And talking about everything and nothing. It was nice to talk again. Whatever did or didn't happen babywise, it was good to be in it together.

Carol sighed. "No, Einstein, the *family* shower."

"How much planning do I need?" I said. "Polly lives here, so I'll just grab her and drag her to Dad's mancave. I brought her a green smoothie a few minutes ago, so I know she's in her room."

"You are so lucky to have me," Carol said. "I invited Polly out for Sunday brunch at High Tide. That'll get her out of the house, and I can deliver her at the perfect time."

"Really?" I said as John poured the rest of the smoothie from the blender, dividing it exactly between us. "Polly actually said yes? The way you treat her? Are you sure you didn't bully her into brunch?"

Thanks, I mouthed to John. It barely aggravated me when

I watched him wash the blender before he put it into the dish-washer. I mean, if you've already washed it, why put it in the dishwasher? Why not leave room for all the other things that someone else might not want to wash first?

"Of course, I didn't bully Polly into it," Carol said. "I was my usual sweet and charming self."

I rolled my eyes. "Why do I have such a hard time picturing that?"

I could practically see Carol rolling her own eyes back at me. "So get your butt over to Dad's mancave and finish setting up that baby shower. I'll bring Polly over at exactly 2:05. Make sure you send everyone a reminder text and tell them if they screw up the surprise, you'll. Whatever. Make up your own threat. I've got enough on my plate as it is."

"You're so bossy," I said.

Carol hung up on me before I could hang up on her.

"Hey," I said to John. "You don't want to help me arrange some rubber duckies, do you?"

He grinned. "I thought you'd never ask."

My father was long gone by the time we opened the door to his mancave. We'd spent a little quality time in bed first, then showered and dressed for the baby shower. And walked the dogs and played with the cats.

Rubber duckies and baby dolls were scattered everywhere.

"Interesting placement of baby shower décor," John said.

"I told Carol they'd never stay on the bed," I said.

John and I made my father's round bed, which scattered the rest of the ducks and dolls. I kicked off my shoes and started trampoline-jumping on the bed so I could reach up to tidy the umbrellas, which seemed to have lost some of their artful arrangement overnight. John took off his shoes and joined me.

We gave the umbrellas a nudge with each jump. Art is in the eye of the beholder, so it was hard to say whether we were making things better or worse. But I knew for sure we were having fun.

"See," I said between jumps. "I knew deep down inside you were a wild man."

"You haven't seen the half of it." John jumped up high, spun around in the air, landed on his sock-covered feet.

"Impressive," I said. I jumped as high as I could, attempted a seat drop. Instead of bouncing from my seat back to my feet again, I flopped backwards, my arms and legs spread wide like I was making an angel in the snow.

John dove on top of me, pinned my arms back, nuzzled my neck.

"Wouldn't it be bizarre," I said, "if we actually got pregnant on our own, in the nick of time, on a round bed under an explosion of umbrellas?"

"Surrounded by an abundance of rubber duckies?" John said.

"And a plethora of baby dolls," I said. "It would make a great story someday, except for the yuck factor of this being my father's bed."

At the thought, John rolled off me.

I rolled on top of him. "Maybe we could rent another round bed, borrow some of the duckies." We kissed, long and luxuriously, the clear plastic umbrellas stamped with rubber duckies rippling overhead.

"My eyes, my eyes," Carol said from the doorway.

John and I rolled in opposite directions as quickly as we could, like we were trying to put out a fire. Which we kind of were.

"Hey," I said. "We were just—"

"Don't even," Carol said.

John was already squatting on the floor, intent on lining up the rubber duckies around the perimeter of the bed while his blush went away. I sat on the edge of the bed, casually tried to juggle three rubber duckies, lost them all.

Carol walked by us, all made up and dressed for Sunday brunch. She dropped a massive sheet cake on the little dining table. Tiny rubber duckies swam on top of thick yellow frosting. Curly orange letters spelled out LOVE YOU BOTH.

"A cake," I said. "I didn't even think about a cake."

"What would you do without me?" Carol said. She disappeared and came back carrying two big cookie sheets loaded with a multitude of mini quiches.

"Okay," she said. "Preheat the oven at exactly 1:50. I'll pop them in when Polly and I get here. I don't want to take any chances on you burning them. And then I'll add the tiny rubber duckies once the quiches cool a bit, so the duckies don't melt."

"Got it," I said. "Add the rubber duckies and put the quiches in the oven at exactly 1:50, and you'll take them out when the ducks are melted and you and Polly get here."

"Funny," Carol said. "So funny I forgot to laugh."

"Speaking of Polly," I said, "aren't you worried she might have noticed you bringing party food in here?"

Carol went into full Wonder Woman power mode—wide stance, hands on hips. "I told you, Polly has pregnancy brain so it's not an issue. But just to be on the safe side, I'm going to drive around the block once before I pick her up. I'll park over by the kitchen door. In Polly's fuzzy head, the second minivan sighting will completely erase the first one."

"Just don't forget," I said. "You promised you'd be nice to her."

⸺

The entire family managed to pack into my father's mancave. The adults circled his round bed, talking amongst themselves. The younger kids sat on the stairs, not happy that they had to wait until Polly *oohed* and *aahed* over the decorations before they were allowed to jump on the bed. The older kids sat on the floor, interacting with their phones. The dogs and cats were safely locked in John's and my new master suite with treats and water and their favorite toys, so nobody could accidentally let them outside.

My brother Johnny had stocked the fridge with beer and was on lookout duty now, peeking out between the crack in the blinds so we'd know the minute Carol and Polly pulled into the driveway. Johnny's wife Kim was standing next to him, a little bit awkwardly. That she had dared to make an appearance was a brave move, since she had to know that we all knew the story about her having left Johnny for her work husband. It was hard to tell whether Johnny and Kim were completely back together or if the baby shower was just an extension of one of their trailer dates. I caught Kim's eye and smiled. She smiled back.

Michael's wife Phoebe had showed up, too. When Michael and I made eye contact, I raised my eyebrows. He shook his head no, then gave me a thumbs up. He raised his eyebrows. I shook my head no, gave him a thumbs up. Sometimes we took our sibling-speak for granted, but right now it felt pretty magical. Without saying a word, we both knew that no one would have their privates packed in ice watching March Madness. And we were both in a good patch again with our significant others.

Even Billy Jr. and his wife Moira, the two least likely to show up at family events, had put in an appearance. I was proud of us all for being there for Polly. In the scheme of our lives, family was the most important thing, and we certainly had more than enough of it to share.

The baby shower presents were piled on and around my father's old and new recliners. John and I had bumped the balloons down from the second floor and tied all the ribbons to the stair railing to make a big balloon bouquet. I wondered if Carol and Polly would get here before the younger kids untied the balloons, and they ended up on the ceiling. I gave my nieces and nephews my best preschool teacher glare. They gave me their best wide-eyed innocent looks.

Veggies and dip were perched on the small round dining table, next to the fruit kabobs and the cheese and crackers. The oven was preheating for the mini quiches per Carol's actual instructions.

The punch bowl was sitting on the counter next to the refrigerator, waiting for the punch. I'd even memorized how to make it, but I was waiting to throw it all together because I didn't want the orange sherbet to melt before Polly got any.

The playlist was all set up on my phone, and John had connected it to a little Bluetooth speaker he'd brought in for the occasion.

"Don't touch anything until they get here," I said to everybody for the fourth or fifth time. "We want to get full credit for this baby shower."

As if summoned by the newly restocked beer, my father made his entrance. He'd ditched his winter outerwear in the mudroom on the way in, and he was wearing a long-sleeved pink Bark & Roll Forever T-shirt. When he ran his fingers through his thick white hair, flyaways danced above his head, propelled by static electricity. He crossed his arms over his chest, glared at us all.

"Who invited you?" he roared.

"You did, Grandpa," one of the kids yelled.

"Well, that's a fine how-do-you-do," he said.

"Sorry about all those rubber duckies and baby dolls on the bed last night," I said.

He opened the fridge to verify the beer for future reference, shut it again. "Best night's sleep I've had in a dog's age."

Our dad grabbed an empty punch glass, held it up high. "May your day be touched by a bit of Irish luck, brightened by a song in your heart, and warmed by the smiles of the people you love."

Christine looked up from maneuvering her fruit kabobs into a slightly better location than my veggies and dip. "Save it for the shower, Dad."

"It was merely a run-through," our dad said, "to make sure my vocal oars are in working order."

"Grandpa just said vocal whores," Trevor said. Or maybe it was Ian.

"Swear jar!" the younger kids yelled.

"Heads up," Johnny said from his lookout spot. "They're here."

"Copy that, good buddy," I said. I switched off the lights in the mancave.

"Can we jump on the bed now?" Maeve whispered.

"Shhh," all the other kids said. It sounded like a gust of winter wind.

Carol came in first. Polly was right behind her.

I flicked on the lights.

"Surprise," we all yelled, including Carol.

Polly looked behind her. I couldn't tell if she was trying to see who the surprise was for or if she was getting ready to run.

I ran over, gave her a big hug, held on to her wrist just in case. "It's a baby shower," I whispered. "For you."

"Really?" she said. Her entire face turned red, completely engulfing her freckles.

Chapter Twenty-Nine

I pushed Play on my phone. John's Bluetooth speakers blasted out "We Are Family."

It was a Hurlihy family tradition that whenever this song came on, we all started dancing around like idiots. Michael and Johnny and Billy Jr. put their arms around one another and attempted some chorus kicks. My father grabbed Polly and tango-ed her across the room. Polly's baby bump was so pronounced at this point that it almost looked like three people were dancing. John and I held hands and did some kind of lame dance that was all our own. The younger kids danced on the round bed, baby dolls and rubber duckies flying every which way.

The rest of the playlist kicked in. "Sweet Child Of Mine," "I Don't Want to Miss a Thing," "Somewhere Over the Rainbow," "What a Wonderful World," "Sunshine of My Life," "Can't Get Enough of You Babe."

We mingled around, nibbling on the food, taking turns hugging Polly. My youngest nieces and nephews helped Polly open her presents. She got some good loot—an audio and video baby monitor that was also a nightlight and played lullabies, a stylish waterproof backpack that was also a diaper bag, swaddle blankets that were simply swaddle blankets, a fluffy fleece bathrobe for Polly, a huge DO NOT DISTURB sign for Polly's and the baby's room, a baby-sized Red Sox jacket, a gift certificate from Siobhan for a night of babysitting, which was pretty bighearted for a teenager. My family could be aggravating, but they were definitely generous.

Carol sidled up to me. "You were supposed to put diapers on the dolls," she hissed. "Why do you think I left you those boxes of diapers?"

"I thought they were presents," I hissed back. "How was I supposed to know?"

"Because they weren't wrapped?" Carol said. "For future reference, the presents are the ones covered in wrapping paper. And just so you know, extra small toy baby doll-sized diapers rarely fit human babies."

"Let's turn that frown upside down," I said in my best preschool teacher's voice. I knew I owed Carol for this shower, so I pretty much had to be nice to her, at least for a while.

I thought fast. "Relay races," I yelled as I scooped up the diaper boxes. "Everybody grab a baby doll and line up in the hallway."

They all stampeded behind me to the wide center hallway of the main house. I got everyone divided into two teams consisting of equal numbers of adults and kids, as well as roughly the same number of cutthroat competitors, which basically meant anyone with Hurlihy blood coursing through their veins.

I opened two boxes of baby doll diapers and placed them at the opposite end of the hallway.

"Okay," I said. "When Dad lets out the official Hurlihy whistle, the first person in each line runs the length of the hall-way, grabs a diaper, fully diapers their doll, runs back to their line with their diapered doll, and has to high five the next person in line before that person can go. When the final person gets back with their diapered baby doll, the winning team yells *Oh, Baby*."

I gulped down some air. "Any false starts or cheating of any kind results in an automatic win for the other team. Questions?"

I waited for someone to ask what the winning prize was, but nobody did. In our family, it was prize enough to kick the other team's butts.

"Ready, Dad?" I said. I stepped to the front of my line, so I could model appropriate race behavior.

Polly was at the front of the other line. We grinned at each other. "You're going down," Polly said.

My father put his thumb and forefinger in his mouth. Even the youngest kids knew enough to cover their ears.

"One . . . two . . . three," I said.

My father let out his ear-piercing version of the Hurlihy family whistle.

I ran by Polly and her pregnancy waddle, no problem at all. I grabbed a tiny diaper, flicked it open, managed to tape one of the sticky tabs to my wrist.

"Damn," I yelled.

"Damn, damn, damn," Maeve and Sydney yelled.

"Thanks for that," one of my sisters said.

By the time I detached the diaper from my wrist and managed to actually diaper the doll, Polly was way ahead of me. I made up as much time as I could. At the front of our line, I high-fived Siobhan, who exploded like a seventeen-year-old firecracker.

We ran. We screamed. We diapered expertly and ineptly. We cheered. We high-fived. We screamed some more. Above us, the dogs barked, dying to get in on the fun.

"*Oh, Baby*," the other team yelled first. It was probably only fitting that Polly's team won, but our team wasn't happy about it. Some serious trash talking broke out, along with accusations of false starts and incomplete diapering.

I tucked my baby doll under my arm, reached out to shake Polly's hand. "Congratulations," I said, modeling good behavior for my family of savages.

My father stepped up beside me. I stepped back so he could shake Polly's hand.

Instead, he held one hand to his heart. "May your day be touched by a bit of Irish luck," he said to Polly in a brogue that belonged to his father, or maybe even his father's father, "brightened by a song in your heart, and warmed by the smiles of the people you love."

Our dad got down on one knee. "Marry me, sweet Polly, so you can give that baby a good Irish name. And be buried with my people."

"How romantic," Christine said. "Don't you just love a good burial proposal?"

"But," Carol said, "the good news is that Dad finally learned how to diaper."

"Knock it off, you old coot," Johnny said. "If Poppy's going to marry anyone, it's going to be—" He stopped, glanced over at Kim. Then he dove on top of my father.

My father and Johnny rolled around on the hard maple floor. When Billy Jr. jumped in, too, it was hard to tell whether he was trying to separate our dad and Johnny or to get in on the action.

"This is why we can't have nice things," Michael said. Somebody grabbed Michael's leg and pulled him into the fray. Annie and Lainie pig-piled on top of their dad. The younger kids pig-piled on top of Annie and Lainie.

Carol and Christine corralled Dennis and Joe, just in case they were getting any big ideas.

I crossed over to John, put my arm around him.

"Don't worry," John said. "Not my thing. But feel free."

"Here," I said. "Hold my earrings. I'm going in."

When I saw his face, I burst out laughing.

"Just kidding," I said. "I'm all for equal gender rights until there's a high probability of a concussion."

"Your family is so much more interesting than mine," John said. "If my parents were here, they'd be sitting behind his and her TV tables and asking each other what just happened."

My brother Billy Jr.'s argyle cardigan sweater was hanging off his arms, and the button-down shirt under it was actually untucked. "He's so hot when he wrestles," his wife Moira said. My oldest brother was born shy and awkward and thinking about his stock portfolio. Nothing gave me more pleasure than knowing he'd found someone who thought he was hot.

Billy Jr. blew a kiss at Moira. Johnny grabbed him by the cardigan and pulled him back into the fray.

"Every single damn time we come here, something like this happens," Kim said.

"I'll be in the car reading, Michael," Phoebe said. "And if you need to go to the emergency room again, get an Uber."

I checked my big analog teacher's watch, gave John a kiss. "Meet me at Bayberry?" I whispered.

I found my phone, fake-checked for messages. Everybody was still rolling around on the floor, though all but the youngest kids were losing momentum now. When I disconnected my phone from the Bluetooth speaker, nobody appeared to notice the music was no longer playing.

I waved across the mob at Polly, who was smart enough to have tucked herself into a corner to stay safe.

"You're not going to believe this," I said once I'd worked my way over to her. I flashed my phone quickly. "Boss Bitch wants us to show up at some kind of emergency meeting in the Arts Barn. Now. Something about the Bayberry Valentine's Day rules being too strict, or not strict enough. Or whatever."

The pig pile was just starting to unpile. I grabbed Polly's arm, steered her toward the coat closet.

For a quick getaway, I'd left my car down at the end of the driveway, pointed toward the street. My trusty Civic started up right away. I side-eyed Polly to see how we were doing. Apparently, pregnancy brain was a real thing, since she didn't look the least bit suspicious.

"Thank you for that amazing, amazing baby shower," Polly said. "I feel like I should have at least helped with the clean-up,"

"Christine said she'd take care of it," I said. I grabbed my phone, sent Christine a text:

You're in charge of clean-up.

A moment later an emoji of a middle finger came back from Christine.

"All set," I said as I rolled out of the driveway. "Sorry things got a little bit crazy at the end. You get used to it after a while."

"I've never had anyone fight over me before I met your family," Polly said.

"It must be kind of awesome in a weird way," I said. Not that I'd ever know, because I wasn't the kind of person anyone ever fought over.

"Maybe a little bit awesome," Polly said. "Mostly I've just felt so alone lately. And scared. That's why I told you that thing about almost considering marrying your dad. You know, that way I'd know I could stay."

"Knock it off," I said. "You don't have to marry anyone to stay. You and the baby can stay forever if you want. You're an honorary member of the Hurlihy family, and you've just seen up close and personal how messy that can be."

"Thank you." Polly sighed. "I guess I didn't think the rest

of your family liked me. But Carol made me feel so much better at brunch."

"She comes in handy once in a while," I said.

Polly cradled her baby bump through her winter coat. "Carol's going to be my labor coach."

"What?" A lightning bolt of envy hit me dead center. Why did Carol get everything? What was wrong with me? Why did everybody else get a baby?

"I can't tell you how grateful I am," Polly said. "And relieved."

My whole life, Carol had bossed me around. She'd barged in and taken anything of mine she wanted without asking. Sweaters. Earrings. Clearasil. Lipstick. Tampons. Boyfriends. Friends. I fought with everything I had not to try to poison this for Polly just to get back at Carol.

"You know," I said carefully, "Carol will probably have the baby for you."

Polly grinned. "That's what I'm counting on."

"Diabolical," I said.

"I know, right?" Polly said. "I thought of asking you, but you've already done so much for me. And I wanted it to be all fresh for you when you have your own baby."

I could almost picture it, just for a split second.

"But," Polly said, "I was thinking I'd ask you and John to be the baby's godparents. That way I'll know you'll always be in our lives. Obviously, you have to talk to John first—"

"Does that mean you're moving in with Damien?" I said. I tried not to sound as pathetic as I felt.

Polly burst out laughing. "Wowser, you were so right about that. I've only known him for like five minutes. And I'm so glad I didn't ask. I think it would have scared the crap out of him. He's so protective of Ace and Anson—I think he only lets me near them because he knows they'll be in childcare with me."

I breathed a huge sigh of relief. "I'm glad you're staying.

And I'll ask John, of course, but I'm sure he'll want to be the godfather. And Carol is going to be so insanely jealous that I'm the godmother and not her—I can't wait."

"Most of the time," Polly said, "I really wish I had brothers and sisters. But I have to tell you, sometimes I feel like I dodged a bullet."

Chapter Thirty

Instead of risking the radio, I grabbed my phone again at a stop sign and cranked up the baby playlist. Before we got to Bayberry, Polly and I had just enough time to belt out "Rubber Duckie, You're the One," at the top of our lungs with Ernie from *Sesame Street*.

I hung a right off the main road, peered up at a sky sparkling with stars. I didn't even bother to wish on the first one I saw. I just thanked them all silently—for love and luck and the fact that it looked like I might even survive February.

A perfectly positioned floodlight lit up the totem pole made out of brightly colored clay fish that still looked like they were dotted with huge fluffy white cotton balls. The row of painted plywood cutouts of teddy bears, each with their own uplight, still had their snow helmets on.

"Whoa," Polly said as we cruised around looking for a parking place. "Full house. This must be some big emergency."

"The biggest," I said.

I jammed my car in between two new gargantuan SUVs. I figured I'd get the last laugh when they opened their doors since I'd certainly never notice another dent on my ancient Honda.

Polly and I both quacked as we passed the snow-covered boxwood sheared into the shape of ducks that edged the walkway to the Cape Cod shingled building. Some clueless parents had changed out the camel and red plaid Burberry scarves tied around their topiary necks to fluffy pink and blue feather boas. I mean, what part of surprise baby shower did they not understand? Fortunately, Polly's pregnancy brain was fully operational. She didn't seem to notice the scarf change.

I caught a quick peek of Ethan peering out of a window in the front entrance, and then he was gone.

As Polly and I walked down the empty hallway to the Arts Barn, the rumble of the crowd stopped.

"Uh-oh," Polly whispered. "I hope we're not late."

"They'll wait," I whispered back.

When I opened the door for Polly, the Arts Barn was pitch black. Polly froze. I stepped up beside her, looped my arm through hers, took a giant step forward.

The lights came on. An Arts Barn full of Bayberrians yelled, "Surprise!"

Polly looked over her shoulder. I looped my arm tighter so she couldn't get away.

"Seriously?" she said over the cheering.

"Yup," I said. "All for you."

I handed off my phone to Ethan so he could connect my baby shower playlist to the massive Arts Barn speakers. Lorna grabbed Polly's other arm. We squeezed in close like celebrity bodyguards and escorted Polly over to read the signs that said, OH, THE PLACES YOU'LL GO, BABY.

Polly started to cry. "It's all too beautiful."

Lorna and I broke into an impromptu chorus of "Itchycoo Park." Polly sniffled for a moment, then joined in.

"Who knew those stupid postcards would come in handy," Lorna teacher-whispered when we finished singing. "We got all fifty states though, plus Canada, Poland, Australia, New Zealand, Spain, Germany, Hungary, England, India, Ireland, Denmark, South Korea, South Africa, France, Italy, Mexico. And a helluva lot of beach towns, with and without beaches. Those Bayberrians are competitive, I'll give them that."

We stopped at the bulletin board covered with yellow stars and good wishes. "I think I need to read those later," Polly whispered. "I'm too overwhelmed to take them in right now."

I followed Lorna's gaze. Two bulletin boards down, Damien was surrounded by a cluster of mean moms. They appeared to be flirting with him, but it was hard to tell for sure from here.

"Do you think we should jump in and rescue him?" I said.

"No way," Lorna said. "The sooner Damien finds out it's sink or swim in this hellhole, the more likely he'll be to survive."

"I don't think you can use sink or swim and hellhole in the same sentence," I said. "It's a mixed metaphor."

"Life," Polly said, "is a mixed metaphor." I was pretty sure it was just her pregnancy brain talking, but I still wanted to write it down.

The parents and kids were starting to mob us, so we kept walking. Polly waved and smiled and cried and said thank you to everyone we passed. We came to another table piled with the Bayberry students' favorite baby books. About a gazillion copies of *Pat the Bunny* and *Goodnight Moon*. A copy of *War and Peace* and two of *Anna Karenina*. I could only hope they were supposed to be funny, even though I knew it was highly doubtful.

I pointed up to the dangling blow-up globes and the signs that said WELCOME TO THE WORLD, LITTLE ONE.

"Aww," Polly said as she rested one hand over her heart.

Lorna handed her another tissue.

I might have smelled the hay before I saw it. In the back corner of the Arts Barn, the Bark & Roll Forever ladies had set up a portable corral. It was filled with baby Nigerian goats dressed in colorful baby onesies that said NEW TO THE HERD.

Our bitch of a boss was looking our way. I pretended I didn't see her.

"I just hope I don't get fired for this," I teacher-whispered. "I was pretty sure goats were a no-go after that goat yoga inservice."

"Not to worry," Lorna said. "You should have heard those flowy silver-haired chicks razzle-dazzle Kate Stone. They convinced her that this was a thoughtful reboot of their original plan to bring goats into the classroom. We could learn a lot from those women. We need to have drinks with them. And possibly even a goddess party."

I waved at The Great Mighty Poo Poo. She actually smiled and waved back.

The baby goats bounced hither and yon, as my father would say, inside the corral, each one an effervescent, four-legged bundle of joy. A crowd of kids and adults circled the corral, waiting for a goat to bounce close enough to get a selfie with it. Lorna and I walked Polly over so we could take goat pictures of her with her cellphone. A bunch of kids photobombed Polly, but we still managed to get some goats and her baby bump in there.

My father's white hair and pink shirt jumped out from the sea of people. He looked like a walking billboard for Bark & Roll Forever, which was essentially his job. He worked the crowd, flirting and handing out Bark & Roll Forever cards. He had a tiny rip in the back of his shirt, and a small Band-Aid covered with hearts on his cheek. But all things considered, he didn't look half bad. When our eyes met, he raised his bushy white eyebrows, then gave me a big wink. I knew he was probably really winking at Polly, but I blew him a kiss anyway.

"The sooner you open those ridiculously ostentatious presents, the sooner we can all get home before we have to turn right around and come back again," Lorna said as we steered Polly toward the massive table of gifts.

"Got it," Polly said. "I'll get the kids to help speed things up."

Gloria was waiting for us. "Here you go, honey," she said. Gloria had set up a chair decorated like a paper- and balloon-covered throne next to the gift table.

Polly sat down and began opening presents. Ethan stood beside Polly's throne like a sentry. Polly tilted her head up at Ethan. The look they exchanged was wistful and happy and sad and made me wonder if someday they'd find their way to each other in real life after all.

Damien stepped up to the other side of Polly. He and Ethan locked eyes. They both looked like they wanted to pee a circle around Polly and her throne to mark Polly as their territory. I thought, not for the first time, that underneath their innocent exterior, preschools are really petri dishes of intrigue and impending drama.

The kids squished around to help Polly rip the wrapping paper off. Gloria and Lorna and June stuffed the used wrapping paper and ribbons into tall white trash bags. Tomorrow, we'd divide it all up and upcycle it to make collages with the kids.

Since this was my second baby shower of the day, I stood back and took a well-deserved break.

My wasband sidled up beside me. "You're never going to believe this."

"Did you hear about the female shark in an aquarium in Seoul, Korea, that ate a male shark because it kept bumping into her?" I said. "She started with the head and slowly consumed the rest of his body. I'm pretty sure they were exes."

"Huh?" Kevin said.

"Don't you have a wife you can irritate?" I said.

Kevin shook his head. "Nikki made us come without her. She wanted to stay home so she could nap. And eat. I think she can do both at once now. While watching some dipshit, bottom-feeding reality show."

"And you thought you had it tough with me," I said. "At least my family only behaves like a reality show instead of watching them."

My former problem put his hands over his ears and made a face not unlike the sketch of "The Scream" Ethan had drawn on one of the yellow stars. "One of the twins locked me out of my iPad. The message says it's disabled for 25,536,442 minutes. That's almost 49 years."

"Your kids don't have their own iPads yet?" I said. "What kind of parent *are* you?"

"Of course, they do. They just want mine, too."

"You've got two choices," I said. "Hide your iPad or share the password so they can't get you locked out."

"That's all you've got?" Kevin said, as if his problems were still my problems. If they'd ever been.

"Try N-O spells no. Consistently." I smiled. "It's only going to get worse once you have a baby in the house."

"Thanks," my wasband said. "I needed that right now."

In front of us, Polly was just opening the re-gifted present from Nikki. I elbowed Kevin, harder than was technically necessary. He scrunched his eyes closed.

When Polly peeled off the wrapping paper with the help of a couple of kids, Lorna cracked up and grabbed the box away from her. Lorna ripped open the box and pulled out what looked like some kind of infant carrier. When Lorna put it on, there was a peekaboo hole in the front. Gloria got down on her knees and Lorna pulled the contraption over Gloria's head, too. As Gloria's face peered out, it was almost like watching a C-section in real time. Or a clip from the movie *Alien.*

Lorna put one hand on her hip and made a spout with the other. She rocked Gloria's face back and forth with the dance to "I'm a Little Teapot."

The Bayberrians roared.

"Wow," I said. "No wonder Nikki regifted that. It's even worse than one of those kiddie leashes that look like a twisted umbilical cord."

John came out of nowhere and put his arm around me. I turned, kissed him in a rare public display of affection. A couple of the kids pointed at us and giggled. I ignored them.

Kevin and John shook hands across me.

"Can't get this one to marry you yet, huh?" my X said, like the idiot he was.

I watched a cloud pass across John's face, braced myself for tragedy. John would assume I told Kevin I didn't want to marry John. John would stomp off and we'd go back to our February freeze. Eventually, we'd make up, time would pass, and something else would set one of us off again. We'd circle around and around, up and down, an endless loop of never quite getting it right.

John pressed his hand into my lower back. Just a slight pressure, enough to tell me we were on the same side. I leaned into him.

John looked over one shoulder, then the other. "So," he said to Kevin. "Lose another wife already?"

I started to say something witty like *he wishes*. But then I stopped myself to give John his moment.

Kevin squinted at the crowd, either looking for his twins or trying to figure out an escape route.

"Way to go," I said once my wasband had walked away. "That might have been your best line ever."

"Thanks, Babe," John said. "I think your family might be rubbing off on me. I have to warn you, next time I might just jump in on one of those family brawls."

I opened my eyes wide. "Did you just call me Babe?"

John put his arm around me again. "To babe or not to babe, that is the question."

"That's a tough one," I said. "As a term of endearment,

babe is kind of next generation. But hon feels more than a little dinosaur-y. Hmm. What about sweetie?"

"Nah," John said. "It makes me feel too much like a boy toy."

"Ha," I said.

"We could go with Boo," John said. "But I have to warn you that I'm not sure I could pull it off with a straight face."

"Yeah," I said. "Me either." I almost said *me neither*, like we used to when I was a kid, but I caught myself just in time. Maybe I was finally growing up after all. I was just a late-bloomer.

"We could both work on our British accents and try love," John said. "You know, like 'ello, love."

"'Ello, love," I said.

It was hard to tell whose fake accent was worse. But I liked the concept.

Chapter Thirty-One

"Happy Valentine's Day," John said.

"Happy Valentine's Day," I said.

John reached his arm around my shoulders. "Wow. You didn't say *ditto*. I'd say that's some serious progress."

"Why thank you." I tilted my head against his. "It almost feels like we're growing into a deeper stage of our relationship. Either that or we're both coming down with the flu."

I was already wearing the present John had given me. It was a satin baby doll negligee set. The top looked like something Nancy Kerrigan might have skated in a long time ago, except for the extreme peekaboo lace panels. The bottom was about the size of one of her headbands, but more thonglike.

The worst thing about it was that it was yellow. Yellow was not my color. Negligees were not my thing. But I was pretending to love it because I loved John. He'd paired my lingerie with a bouquet of matching yellow roses, and he said he'd chosen the color because yellow means forever. It was a lovely sentiment, but I only hoped it didn't mean I had to wear this monstrosity forever.

John held my hand and turned it palm up so he could see the tattoo on the inside of my forearm.

"Is this new?" John asked diplomatically, as if a purple animal-print heart might have been something he'd over-looked before.

"Don't worry," I said. "It's a temporary stick-on from Carol. Sister solidarity or midlife rebellion or something like that. I gave her a troll-headed pencil."

John nodded. He was wearing the gift I'd given him, too, a pair of organic cotton cooling underwear for men that came with ice wedges I'd pre-chilled for him in the freezer. Adding extra ice cubes to a drink and resting it in the appropriate vicinity probably would have worked just as well, but I had to admit that it was the name that sold me: Snow Balls. That and the book that came with it: *A Gentleman's Guide to Cooling*. Everything was better with a book. The pitch was that testicular cooling had been shown to increase sperm count. For backup, I'd draped my St. Brigid's Day handkerchief strategically over John once he was wearing the underwear. St. Brigid was the patron saint of parents who weren't married, so I figured it couldn't hurt.

John shivered gamely. I held out the tray of stuffed figs I'd actually made myself as part of his present.

He popped one in his mouth. "What's the backstory on these again?"

I held up one finger while I finished chewing mine. "The theory is that because figs are full of seeds and hang in twos while they grow, eating them might increase both the mobility and the numbers of male sperm."

"Or propagate an old wives' tale," John said. "They're delicious though. My compliments to the chef."

"Thanks," I said. "Although I'm not sure I'll ever look at a pair of figs quite the same way again."

The two dogs and five cats finished headbutting on the floor. Horatio and Scruffy Dog and Pebbles jumped up on the bed to join us. John and I leaned over to help the kittens up.

"Hearts or barks," I said. I held out two closed fists in John's direction.

John tapped a fist.

I reached over and grabbed a strawberry I'd sliced into a perfect heart and dipped in a tiny bit of dark chocolate. I fed it to John.

The dogs barked anyway.

"Come on, you two," I said. "You know the rules."

John held out two fists to them. "Hearts or barks."

Horatio and Scruffy Dog started barking like crazy. John opened his fists to reveal a treat in each hand. The dogs lapped them up.

Cats are above meowing on command, so I just passed out kitty treats to all of them.

John and I leaned back against the sleek modern headboard again.

John held up his wineglass filled with seltzer. "'You were made perfectly to be loved—and surely I have loved you, or the idea of you, my whole life long.'"

"Ditto," I said.

"Cute," John said.

"Kanye West?" I guessed.

"Elizabeth Barrett Browning."

I leaned over and gave him a kiss, then held up my glass. "'Love is space and time measured by the heart.'"

"Vanna White?" John tried.

"Marcel Proust," I said.

We clinked our wine glasses together, took a sip of seltzer. It wasn't wine, but it had a nice fizz to it.

We sat for a moment, taking in the warmth of the room, the howl of the wind, the rattle of the windows. John shivered some more.

Pebbles climbed right up on my lap.

"Ohmigod, she's never done that before."

"She loves her Proust," John said.

I tried not to move so I wouldn't scare her away. Pebbles circled around on my lap, once, twice, then hunkered down. I patted her tricolored fur, massaged the back of her tiny neck.

The kittens crawled over to Pebbles, tried to worm their way in close enough to nurse. Pebbles batted them away with her paw.

"I think she's done, you guys," I said.

"They'll work it out," John said.

"Easy for you to say," I said. "All those claws aren't on your lap."

"Good point," John said. "Pun intended."

The kittens gave up and wandered over to roll around on the bed with the dogs. My father and the Bark & Roll Forever ladies and Polly were downstairs celebrating. Every few minutes, a blast of laughter traveled up to us. I knew my father would head off to the cemetery soon to celebrate Valentine's Day with my mother, but I was glad he was surrounded with live women now.

I put my glass down on the bedside table, careful not to spook Pebbles.

I reached for John's hand. "Are you disappointed we're not in Tulum getting married at the beach on turquoise beach cruisers?"

John considered this. "With your family wrestling like maniacs on the sand beside us?"

I considered that. "Well, we certainly would never have gotten away with eloping without them. Maybe we could have set up your family's TV trays on the sand next to my family, so they didn't feel left out?"

"I think," John said, "the part that's hard for me to accept is that you don't want to get married. Marrying each other doesn't have to remind us of our first marriages."

"Our first *failed* marriages," I said. "And let's not forget the fact that sixty percent of second marriages end in divorce."

John sighed. "One hundred percent of couples who aren't fully committed break up."

I turned to look at him. Pebbles hung on. "Did you just make that up?"

John smiled. "It's good, right?"

I shook my head. "I *am* fully committed. But I don't think marriage is the issue or the answer. We have everything we need right here, without leaving this room. Without going to Tulum. Without going anywhere. Now we just have to figure out how not to screw it up."

"There's a February thaw coming," John said. "Joe and I have been texting back and forth, and he thinks it might last just long enough to pour the foundation for the new garage."

"A private entrance," I said. "That might solve everything. And I'm almost not kidding."

"It'll certainly help," John said.

We wove our fingers together. At the foot of the bed, Scruffy Dog started to snore.

"Also," I said softly, "I think I might be afraid that if we get married, you'll figure out that I'm not good enough."

John kissed me on top of my head. "How about this. Let's decide right here and now that we're both good enough—for each other, for a great life, for furbabies or baby-babies—and we'll take that one right off the table."

I considered it. "Can we do that? I mean, I've spent my entire life thinking I'll never be good enough. If all these big mental barriers I built for myself aren't actually there, that would mean the only thing standing between me and a happy life—is me."

"There you go," John said.

"But, what if—"

"Don't question it. Just believe it and enjoy the magic."

John and I kissed. The wind whistled outside our bedroom. Pebbles purred in my lap. Laughter roared downstairs.

"Done," I said.

———

Sarah's Valentine's Day Stuffed Figs

8 figs, cut in half
    8 oz. goat cheese (preferably sourced from local yoga goats)
    16 walnut halves
    8 slices bacon, slightly cooked and cut in half
    16 toothpicks

Preheat oven to 400 degrees.
    Stuff each fig half liberally with goat cheese. Press walnut half into the cheese. Wrap with half a slice of bacon and secure with a toothpick. Arrange on baking sheet.
    Cook approximately 10 minutes, until bacon is evenly crisp and goat cheese is bubbly.
    Remove from oven before smoke alarm goes off.

———

Thank you so much for reading *Must Love Dogs: Hearts & Barks*, Book 7 of my novel-turned-movie-turned-series. If you enjoyed it, I'll hope you'll tell your friends and take a moment to leave a short review. I really appreciate your help getting the word out!
    Sign up for my newsletter (http://ClaireCook.com/newsletter) to be the first to find out when the next book in the *Must Love Dogs* series is released. Stay in the loop for give-aways and insider extras, too!

If you'd like to know more about how the **Must Love Dogs** movie really happened, you might want to read my nonfiction book, **Never Too Late: Your Roadmap to Reinvention (without getting lost along the way)**, which is also a #1 Amazon bestseller in Women's Personal Growth!

Keep turning the virtual pages for an excerpt of **The Wildwater Walking Club: Back on Track**.

Read an Excerpt

Day 1

198 steps

On the one-year anniversary of the day I became redundant, I woke up between crisp white sheets I'd sprayed with a new batch of homemade lavender water before hanging them out to dry on my backyard clothesline. I took a moment to inhale the invigorating fragrance of fresh summer air mixed with the soothing caress of lavender.

"It's okay," I whispered to the dark blur of my ceiling. "I still have six months of base pay and benefits left. I don't need to panic. Yet."

As a positive affirmation designed to get my morning off on the right foot, even I knew it could use some work.

"Every day in every way I'm getting better all the time," I

whispered.

I gave the sheets another reassuring sniff. "Amazing opportunities exist for me in every avenue of my life," I tried.

"Every little thing is going to be all right," I whisper-sang in my best Bob Marley imitation.

My best Bob Marley imitation wasn't much, so I lip-synched to an imaginary version of Bobby McFerrin's "Don't Worry, Be Happy" playing in my head.

I'd completely forgotten I wasn't alone until Rick rolled over in my bed. I chose to see this not as proof of my lack of focus on our relationship, but as evidence that I was getting comfortable in said relationship. I wiped an index finger across the corners of my lips in case I was getting so comfortable that I'd inadvertently drooled in my sleep. I cupped the palm of one hand and blew into it to assess my level of morning breath.

"Hey," I whispered.

A small screen glowed softly as he held his phone above us.

I got ready to pull the sheets over my head in case just-woke-up selfies were a new thing.

Rick swung both legs over the side of the bed and reached for his clothes. He put his phone down on the bedside table and pulled on his boxer briefs and jeans.

Rick and I had met at a series of small group outplacement counseling classes offered by a company called Fresh Horizons that had been a part of our buyout packages. The classes had seemed helpful at the time, but I also had to admit that almost a year later, we were both still unemployed, or at least underemployed.

Before we'd taken our respective buyouts, I'd been a Senior Manager of Brand Identity at Balancing Act Shoes. Rick had been some kind of IT ethical hacking wizard at a company that helped financial institutions, as well as the occasional political party, identify their website vulnerabilities. Because the word *wizard* had actually been in his official job title, I always pictured him sitting at his computer behind a red velvet curtain, shirtless and wearing a pointy white wizard hat with Senior Overlord of Ethical Hacking emblazoned across the brim in gold letters. It was sexy, in a geeky kind of way.

You could say that Rick's and my former companies had unwittingly played cupid and brought us together. Or because we'd both taken buyouts, you could say that maybe like really did attract like. But then again, you could also say that two people as messed up as we were right now had absolutely no business attempting a relationship until they got their rebound career paths figured out.

A shadowy Rick slid into his flip-flops and yanked his T-shirt over his head.

"Hey," I said again. I was romantic like that. "What's up?"

He didn't seem to hear me. Maybe he was sleepwalking. Or at least sleepdressing.

Rick picked up his phone again and held it arm's distance away. He gazed at it as if it were some kind of magic orb. Or as if someone really important was on the other end, and he didn't want to chance losing his phone before he could take the call privately.

Then he flip-flopped out of the bedroom without even glancing in my direction. A long moment later, my front door clicked shut.

"This can't be good," I whispered.

◁▭▷

I stood on my front steps and watched puffy white clouds and soft blue sky jostle for territory above picture perfect green trees. I swatted a mosquito.

I did a time check: 8:05. The deal was that if my walking partners hadn't joined me by now, I'd head out on our regular route without them. I'd start off slowly to give them a chance to catch up, in case one or both was running late instead of simply blowing me off.

I sat down on the top step and retied one of my laces. I was wearing a pair of the sneakers I'd bought just in the nick of time before my employee discount expired. This particular model was called the Walk On By. It was strictly a women's model, and I'd been part of the team that had positioned it as the shoe every woman needed to walk away from the things that were holding her back and toward the next exciting phase of her life. *Shed the Outgrown. Embrace Your Next Horizon. Walk On By*.

I'd logged lots of miles in these sneakers, but I wasn't sure I'd gotten much closer to that next exciting phase of my life.

After I'd been tricked into taking a buyout from Balancing Act Shoes and dumped by the guy who'd tricked me in one fell swoop, I'd wallowed for a while. But even rock bottom doesn't last forever, and eventually I was all wallowed out. At that point I'd somehow managed to get back up on my feet and start walking. Before long two of my neighbors, Tess and Rosie, joined me.

My house was the smallest of five houses built on the grounds of a working lavender farm when the owners decided to sell off some of their property. As my realtor had explained it to me, if you imagined a pie, the original house still owned half, and the five newer houses each had a pie-shaped slice of the other half.

Rosie lived directly behind me on the original lavender farm. I lived on the middle pie slice. Tess lived on a slightly larger slice next to me. The street Tess and I lived on was called Wildwater Way, although there was neither any noticeable wildness nor water in the immediate vicinity. The three of us called ourselves The Wildwater Walking Club, which was a little goofy, but so what.

I took a moment to retie my other shoelace, even though it didn't actually need it.

Walking solo today would make me feel virtuous. Perhaps even a tad superior. I'd head for the beach and fill my lungs with great big gulps of life-affirming salt air. I thought about how good I'd feel once I found my rhythm and the endorphins started to kick in. How I'd be strengthening my bones and muscles. Preventing heart disease, high blood pressure, type 2 diabetes. Improving my balance, my coordination, even my mood.

I extended my non-dominant wrist, the one wearing my Fitbit. I twisted my arm back and forth, and back and forth some more, for as long as I could take it.

My faux walk complete, I swore softly and went back to bed.

⸻

Day 2

231 steps

I'm not going to think about Rick. I'm not going to think, period.

Apparently I'm not going to walk either.

Just when I thought I was doing so well.

⸻

Day 3

54 steps

Why is it that my life is always two steps forward and one long pathetic slide back?

Day 4

132 steps

I know what I'll do. I'll create a lavender ice cream flavor for Ben & Jerry. I'll call it Lavender Fields Forever. They'll love it. They'll love me. The three of us will live happily ever after.

But first I have to try all their other ice cream flavors. Research.

Day 5

1179 steps

I contemplated the weeds in my garden as I circled my spoon around and around in a pint of Ben & Jerry's Hazed & Confused. Then I took a massive bite and let the hazelnut and chocolate iciness melt in my mouth while I checked my Fitbit. 38 steps without moving a foot. Not bad.

I contemplated the weeds some more. They appeared to be coexisting happily with all three varieties of my lavender— Grosso, Hidcote and Munstead. When Rosie had started my lavender garden for me, she'd told me that the trick to taking care of lavender is not to overlove it. Not much danger of that happening.

I stroked Grosso's foliage to release its feisty fragrance, which was laced with a hint of camphor. I loved its tall, brave, pointy stems and the way the whole plant stretched gracefully and unapologetically, not afraid to take its full space in the world. I widened my own stance and tried to access my inner Grosso.

I racked up 23 additional steps of ice cream-stirring mileage. I sighed a time or two, checked to see if sighing registered on my Fitbit. No such luck.

As soon as I heard Tess's car pulling into her driveway, I bent over and yanked a weed just so she wouldn't think I'd noticed her. I stayed low until the whirring sound of her garage door closing stopped.

Tess and I had been doing a lot of this kind of ignoring lately. Waiting until the other one brought in her mail before checking our own mailbox. Making sure the coast was clear before we headed out to our adjacent backyards. Rosie was easier to avoid since a buffer of woods separated us, but I was pretty sure Rosie and I had both pretended not to see each other at the grocery store late one afternoon.

Dodging one another had turned into almost as much of a workout as walking together every day had been.

When I was vertical again, I juggled the ice cream I was holding and spoon-fed myself some Chocolate Therapy. I tried to separate the taste of the chocolate ice cream from the tastes of the other ingredients, chocolate cookies and chocolate pudding. As if somehow this level of discernment might lead me to a deeper understanding of my life, or lack thereof.

One arm was freezing from hugging three pints of ice cream and the other was getting tired from all that twisting. I put the Ben & Jerry's down on a grassy spot while I switched my Fitbit to my other wrist.

I racked up some more mileage by twisting my fresh arm back and forth.

"Why, Noreen Kelly," Tess's voice said behind me.

I jumped.

"Are you actually cheating your Fitbit *and* eating ice cream for breakfast at the same time?"

I ignored her and pulled another weed.

Tess put on her reading glasses so she could get a closer look at the Ben & Jerry's on the ground. "Ooh, Empower Mint—I don't think I've tried that one yet."

Three chickens emerged from the wooded path that connected Rosie's and my properties. They cut across my backyard in a well-choreographed row. I was pretty sure they were making a beeline for my ice cream.

"Yikes," I yelled. "The Supremes."

"Rod Stewart's right behind them," Tess yelled.

I scooped up the Ben & Jerry's containers from the ground and held them over my head.

The hens surrounded us. Rod, their rooster, stood off to one side for reinforcement.

"Come on, you guys," Tess said. "Cluck off."

The chickens kept circling.

Even chicken decisions were beyond me right now. "What do you think?" I asked Tess. "Should I let them split one pint, and then you and I can have the other two? Although I'm pretty sure I've read that dairy is bad for chickens."

Tess shrugged. "And then there's always the issue of ice cream headaches."

"Good point. Although maybe we could just warn them to eat slowly."

"There you are," Rosie yelled as she jogged our way shaking a box of Kashi Good Friends. As soon as they heard the sound of their favorite cereal, The Supremes ditched Tess and me and Ben & Jerry and headed for their owner.

"I'll be right back," Rosie yelled, still shaking the cereal box. The Supremes followed her in a single file, Rod Stewart hot on their heels. "And thank you for not giving them any of that. Poultry diarrhea is not a pretty sight."

Tess and I looked at each other. "Eww," Tess said. "Thank you for that lovely image."

I nodded. "Yeah, I know. It's almost enough to make me throw away the rest of this ice cream."

And then I dug back into the Hazed and Confused.

"Hey," Tess said. "You're not going to hog all that to yourself, are you?"

"Oh, cluck off," I said.

———

Rosie, Tess and I sat around my kitchen table, each with a pint of Ben & Jerry's and a big spoon. Tess had pulled her blond-streaked hair back in a ponytail so it wouldn't end up in the ice cream. Rosie must have just finished taking a shower right before The Supremes and Rod Stewart escaped, because her red hair was getting shorter and curlier as it dried. My dark brown hair was pretty much doing what it always did—just hanging around looking as ordinary as the rest of me.

We were all wearing the perfect ice cream binge outfits: yoga pants and baggy T-shirts.

"Okay, switch," Rosie said.

We rotated the ice cream counterclockwise.

"You both better be germ-free," Tess said. "I like to keep my summers healthy so I can build up my strength for another school year." Tess was a third grade teacher. Even though I'd never seen her in action, I knew she was awesome at her job. And if I ever doubted it, I was pretty sure she'd tell me. I wondered if it was possible to catch self-confidence instead of a virus from an ice cream spoon.

Rosie sampled her new flavor. Rosie was a landscape designer. She had her own clients and also drew plans for her contractor husband's clients. Her designs were gorgeous. Maybe I could catch some of Rosie's talent while I was catching Tess's self-confidence.

Rosie closed her eyes. "Hmm. I'd have to say Empower Mint, Chocolate Therapy, Hazed and Confused. In that order."

I closed my eyes. "Hazed and Confused, Empower Mint, Chocolate Therapy."

"No way," Tess said. "Empower Mint, Hazed and Confused, Chocolate Therapy. But maybe we should do one more round just to be sure."

We passed our pints again.

"Listen," I said. "I'm really sorry you caught me cheating my Fitbit, Tess." The truth was I was probably more sorry about the getting caught part than the cheating part. "And I'm sorry I haven't been walking lately. I just can't seem to get my act together."

"Shit," Tess said. "You can't seem to get your *shit* together. It's stronger that way."

"Act is classier," Rosie said.

"Shit is more real," Tess said.

"No shit," I said.

Even though it wasn't that funny, we all laughed anyway, in that laid-back way of friends who have passed the trying-to-impress stage and genuinely like one another.

"Well, it's not like Tess and I have been showing up to walk either," Rosie said.

"Speak for yourself," Tess said. "You have no idea if I've been showing up if you're not showing up. I could be walking every single morning without you."

"Sure you could," Rosie said.

We all sighed, one sigh overlapping the next, kind of like a wave at a ballgame.

"Okay," Rosie said. "So I tied my Fitbit to the ceiling fan in my office the other day. Just long enough to get caught up on some landscape plans."

"Genius," I said.

Rosie dug into the Empower Mint. "Not if you have two tweens in the house. Connor and Nick saw it spinning around and totally fitness-shamed me."

"One of the teachers at school," Tess said, "lets the kids

take turns wearing her Fitbit at recess. But personally I prefer the dryer."

"Seriously?" I said. "You put your Fitbit in the dryer? You're not afraid it'll melt?"

Tess shrugged. "You just use the air fluff setting and add some clothes to cushion it."

"Excuse me," Rosie said. "But I thought we were all supposed to be practically dryer-free now. You certainly made us work hard enough to get the town of Marshbury clothesline ban lifted."

"It's called upcycling," Tess said. "I mean, if we're not going to use our dryers for towels—"

"Or sheets," I said.

"Then we might as well find a good use for them," Tess said. "Plus the energy savings are tremendous on air fluff."

"Just FYI," Rosie said, "Dogs wearing a fitness tracker can rack up 7,000 to 35,000 steps per day."

"But," Tess said, "dogs really hate it when you put them in the dryer."

I looked from Tess to Rosie and then back to Tess again. "Not to get all mushy, but I really missed you two."

"Right," Tess said. "When you weren't dodging me out by the mailboxes."

"I loved it when the three of us were walking together every day," Rosie said. "But you miss one day, and then it's so much easier to miss the next one, and before you know it, the entire walking ritual falls apart. Just like family dinner at the dining room table."

"Maybe it's because things are so much easier to start than they are to maintain," I said. I took a quick bite of ice cream so I didn't have to think about how this might apply to the rest of my life.

"I hate, hate, hate maintenance," Tess said. She ran one hand through her freshly highlighted hair. "I mean, look at hair color. You should be able to dye your hair once and be done with it until you decide you want another color. Nails, too."

"Gardens, too," Rosie said. "People always want me to design and install these elaborate gardens for them, but they're totally unrealistic about how much work they'll have to put in to keep them up, even though I warn them."

"Don't look at me," I said. "I pulled three weeds today."

"So we just have to get back on track with walking then," Tess said. "Easy peasy lemon squeezy."

"I think it's easy peasy chocolate freezy," Rosie said.

"Potato-potahto," Tess said.

"I can start Monday morning," I said. "I've got that health coach certificate thing all weekend."

Tess eyed the empty ice cream containers. "Now I get the extreme ice cream binge. You needed to get it out of your system before you turn all healthy on us and become one of those obnoxious nutritionally superior people."

"It's research." I reached for her ice cream container. "I was thinking I might pitch a flavor to Ben & Jerry's. It could set me on a new career path."

"Good luck with that," Tess said. "Hannah pitched them a flavor for a school project one year, and she had to sign a waiver saying that if they used her idea, she understood that she might only get compensated in ice cream and/or promotional items."

"They must get inundated with flavor ideas," Rosie said. "Their lawyer probably makes them do that to protect themselves."

Getting paid in ice cream was probably not the kind of growth I was looking for. Disappointment rose in my chest as one more career door closed in my face.

I cleared my throat. "So how is Hannah anyway?"

"Hannah?" Tess said. "Hannah? Oh, right, you mean my daughter who finished her freshman year at college and then found a paid internship and a place to stay so she didn't have to come home for the summer. It took us years to get her brother completely out of the house, so I have to say I didn't see that one coming. And once again I didn't schedule any tutoring jobs over the summer because I wanted to have time to spend with her, so I can blame my reduced income on her, too. I think our best bet is to sell the house and buy one of those tiny houses we can hitch to the back of the car and hit the road before the next major holiday. Let our darling daughter see what it's like to try to track *us* down for a change the next time she needs mon—"

"I'd love to start walking again," Rosie said, interrupting Tess mid-rant. "But I keep thinking I'll never get all the work I have piled up finished before we go away. I mean, this trip sounded like such a good idea at the time. Plus, with the lavender angle, I can totally write it off."

Tess dug into the Empower Mint. "And I thought I was beyond brilliant getting a cultural enrichment grant. I just have to document the trip and bring back a bunch of cultural crap to share at school."

I shrugged. "And I figured I was going to be broke soon anyway, so I might as well go for it while I still could."

"I've been wondering when to bring this up," Rosie said. "And I know there's not much time left, but the truth is I'm not sure I should go after all—"

"Don't you dare back out," I said. "If anyone backs out, it should be me. No way should I be spending that kind of money right now."

"I'm kind of over the whole trip idea, too," Tess said. "I kept meaning and meaning to look into the refund policy. Maybe I can find a way to use the cultural enrichment grant for something closer to home. Or even online—I mean, it's not like the Internet isn't a boundless source of culture."

"You don't want to go with us?" Rosie opened her eyes wide. "Gee, thanks a lot, Tess."

Tess put her spoon back in the Chocolate Therapy and

slid the container to the center of the table. "It's not so much that I don't want to go. But at least you two get to be room-mates. It's really hitting me that I'm about to spend eight nights sharing a stateroom with someone I haven't seen since high school."

"Oh, you know those old friendships," Rosie said. "Five minutes in and the years will melt away and the two of you will be just as immature as you used to be. Plus Noreen and I will be there."

"What's her name again?" I said.

Tess rolled her eyes. "Joy."

"See," Rosie said. "How can we possibly have a bad time with someone named Joy?"

I grabbed three water bottles from the fridge to balance out the ice cream. "What's she like anyway? Will she want to walk with us?"

Tess took a long slug of her water before she answered.

"So the weird thing is," she finally said, "the more I think about it, the more I'm pretty sure we never even hung out together in high school."

"Not at all?" I said.

Tess shook her head. "I'm not sure we had a single conver-sation in all four years."

"Really?" Rosie said.

"Really," Tess said.

Rosie and I looked at Tess.

"Damn Facebook," Tess said.

———

Keep Reading—Buy *The Wildwater Walking Club: Back on Track!* Go to ClaireCook.com/read to find out more.

Have you read?

Seven Year Switch

Seven Year Switch is the story of a single mother whose husband ran off to join the Peace Corps, leaving her with a three-year-old. Seven years later, just when they've figured out how to make it on their own, he's *ba*-ack, proving he can't even run away reliably. Now Jill has to face the fact that there's simply no way she can be a good mom without letting her ex back into her daughter's life. They say that every seven years you become a completely new person, and it takes a Costa Rican getaway to help Jill make her choice—between the woman she is and the woman she wants to be.

Buy Seven Year Switch. Go to ClaireCook.com/read to find out more.

Never Too Late: Your Roadmap to Reinvention (without getting lost along the way)

Wondering how to get to that life you really thought you'd be living by now? Claire Cook shares everything she's learned on her own journey— from writing her first book in her minivan at 45, to walking the red carpet at the Hollywood premiere of *Must Love Dogs* at 50, to becoming an international bestselling author and a sought after reinvention speaker.

You'll hop on a plane with Claire as you figure out the road to your own reinvention: getting a plan, staying on track, pulling together a support system, building your platform in the age of social networking, dealing with the inevitable ups and downs, overcoming perfectionism, and tuning in to your authentic self to propel you toward your goals.

Buy Never Too Late. Go to ClaireCook.com/read to find out more.

Shine On: How To Grow Awesome Instead of Old

If you're a forty-to-forever woman who's interested in aging well, don't miss this motivating and inspiring book.

Join *New York Times* bestselling author Claire Cook on a transformative journey that will help you shake off all those worries about getting older and embrace what can be the most vibrant, creative and empowering chapter of your life.

Shine On: How To Grow Awesome Instead of Old speaks to midlife women everywhere and is filled with Claire's trademark humor, heart, honesty and encouragement.

Buy Shine On. Go to ClaireCook.com/read to find out more.

Life's a Beach

Life's a bit of a beach these days for Ginger Walsh, who finds herself single at 41 and back home living in the family FROG (finished room over the garage) in the fictional town of Marshbury. She's spent a few too many years in sales, and is hoping for a more fulfilling life as a sea glass artist, but instead is babysitting her sister's kids and sharing overnights with Noah, her sexy glassblower boyfriend with commitment issues and a dog Ginger's cat isn't too crazy about.

Buy *Life's a Beach*. Go to ClaireCook.com/read to find out more.

Multiple Choice

March Monroe and her daughter Olivia are going to college. Not together at the same school, of course, just at the same time. March knows Olivia is going, naturally, since she and her husband have just made their first exorbitant tuition payment. But Olivia doesn't exactly know the arrangement...yet. It's not as if March plans never to tell her; she just figures she'll wait a bit — until they've had a little time to miss each other. So imagine Olivia's surprise when one day she shows up for training at a local radio station and finds out that one of the other interns is . . . her mother.

Buy *Multiple Choice*. Go to ClaireCook.com/read to find out more.

About Claire

I wrote my first novel in my minivan at 45. At 50, I walked the red carpet at the Hollywood premiere of the adaptation of my second novel, *Must Love Dogs*, starring Diane Lane and John Cusack. I'm now the *New York Times*, *USA Today*, and #1 Amazon bestselling author of 19 books. I also teach workshops and speak about reinvention to groups around the world.

If you have a buried dream, take it from me, it is NEVER too late!

I was born in Virginia and lived for many years in Scituate, Massachusetts, an awesome beach town between Boston and Cape Cod. My husband and I now live on St. Simons Island, Georgia, a magical snowless place to walk the beach, ride our bikes, and make new friends.

I have the world's most fabulous readers and I'm forever grateful to all of you for giving me the gift of my late-blooming career.

Shine On!

HANG OUT WITH ME:

ClaireCook.com
Facebook.com/ClaireCookauthorpage
Twitter.com/ClaireCookwrite
Instagram.com/ClaireCookwrite
Pinterest.com/ClaireCookwrite
BookBub.com/authors/claire-cook
Goodreads.com/ClaireCook
Linkedin.com/in/ClaireCookwrite

Be the first to find out when my next book comes out and stay in the loop for giveaways and insider extras:
ClaireCook.com/newsletter/